JONATHAN STRANGE

&

Mr NORRELL

Volume I

JONATHAN STRANGE

Mr NORRELL

Volume I

Susanna Clarke

Illustrations by Portia Rosenberg

BLOOMSBURY

Published by Bloomsbury Publishing, New York and London
Distributed to the trade by Holtzbrinck Publishers

All papers used by Bloomsbury Publishing are natural, recyclable products
made from wood grown in well-managed forests. The manufacturing
processes conform to the environmental regulations of the country of origin.

The Library of Congress has cataloged the hardcover edition as follows:

Clarke, Susanna.
Jonathan Strange & Mr Norrell / Susanna Clarke.—1st U.S. ed.
p. cm.
ISBN 1-58234-416-7
1. Teacher-student relationships—Fiction. 2. London (England)—Fiction.
3. York (England)—Fiction. 4. Magicians—Fiction. 5. Fairies—Fiction.
I. Title: Jonathan Strange and Mr Norrell. II Title.

PR6103.L375J65 2004
823′.92—dc22
2004002402

First published in the United States by Bloomsbury Publishing in 2004
This paperback three-volume edition published in 2005

Paperback ISBN 1-59691-153-0
ISBN-13 978-1-59691-153-6

1 3 5 7 9 10 8 6 4 2

Typeset by Hewer Text Ltd, Edinburgh
Printed in the United Kingdom by Clays Ltd.

This volume is not for sale individually
but only as part of a three-volume set

In memory of my brother,
Paul Frederick Gunn Clarke, 1961–2000

CONTENTS

Volume I
Mr NORRELL

He hardly ever spoke of magic, and when he
did it was like a history lesson and no one
could bear to listen to him.

1

The library at Hurtfew

Autumn 1806–January 1807

SOME YEARS AGO there was in the city of York a society of magicians. They met upon the third Wednesday of every month and read each other long, dull papers upon the history of English magic.

They were gentleman-magicians, which is to say they had never harmed any one by magic – nor ever done any one the slightest good. In fact, to own the truth, not one of these magicians had ever cast the smallest spell, nor by magic caused one leaf to tremble upon a tree, made one mote of dust to alter its course or changed a single hair upon any one's head. But, with this one minor reservation, they enjoyed a reputation as some of the wisest and most magical gentlemen in Yorkshire.

A great magician has said of his profession that its practitioners ". . . must pound and rack their brains to make the least learning go in, but quarrelling always comes very naturally to them,"[1] and the York magicians had proved the truth of this for a number of years.

In the autumn of 1806 they received an addition in a gentleman called John Segundus. At the first meeting that he attended Mr Segundus rose and addressed the society. He began by compli-

---

[1] *The History and Practice of English Magic*, by Jonathan Strange, vol. I, chap. 2, pub. John Murray, London, 1816.

menting the gentlemen upon their distinguished history; he listed the many celebrated magicians and historians that had at one time or another belonged to the York society. He hinted that it had been no small inducement to him in coming to York to know of the existence of such a society. Northern magicians, he reminded his audience, had always been better respected than southern ones. Mr Segundus said that he had studied magic for many years and knew the histories of all the great magicians of long ago. He read the new publications upon the subject and had even made a modest contribution to their number, but recently he had begun to wonder why the great feats of magic that he read about remained on the pages of his book and were no longer seen in the street or written about in the newspapers. Mr Segundus wished to know, he said, why modern magicians were unable to work the magic they wrote about. In short, he wished to know why there was no more magic done in England.

It was the most commonplace question in the world. It was the question which, sooner or later, every child in the kingdom asks his governess or his schoolmaster or his parent. Yet the learned members of the York society did not at all like hearing it asked and the reason was this: they were no more able to answer it than any one else.

The President of the York society (whose name was Dr Fox-castle) turned to John Segundus and explained that the question was a wrong one. "It presupposes that magicians have some sort of duty to do magic – which is clearly nonsense. You would not, I imagine, suggest that it is the task of botanists to devise more flowers? Or that astronomers should labour to rearrange the stars? Magicians, Mr Segundus, study magic which was done long ago. Why should any one expect more?"

An elderly gentleman with faint blue eyes and faintly-coloured clothes (called either Hart or Hunt – Mr Segundus could never quite catch the name) faintly said that it did not matter in the least whether any body expected it or not. A gentleman could not do

4

magic. Magic was what street sorcerers pretended to do in order to rob children of their pennies. Magic (in the practical sense) was much fallen off. It had low connexions. It was the bosom companion of unshaven faces, gypsies, house-breakers; the frequenter of dingy rooms with dirty yellow curtains. Oh no! A gentleman could not do magic. A gentleman might study the history of magic (nothing could be nobler) but he could not do any. The elderly gentleman looked with faint, fatherly eyes at Mr Segundus and said that he hoped Mr Segundus had not been trying to cast spells.

Mr Segundus blushed.

But the famous magician's maxim held true: two magicians – in this case Dr Foxcastle and Mr Hunt or Hart – could not agree without two more thinking the exact opposite. Several of the gentlemen began to discover that they were entirely of Mr Segundus's opinion and that no question in all of magical scholarship could be so important as this one. Chief among Mr Segundus's supporters was a gentleman called Honeyfoot, a pleasant, friendly sort of man of fifty-five, with a red face and grey hair. As the exchanges became more bitter and Dr Foxcastle grew in sarcasm towards Mr Segundus, Mr Honeyfoot turned to him several times and whispered such comfort as, "Do not mind them, sir. I am entirely of your opinion;" and "You are quite right, sir, do not let them sway you;" and "You have hit upon it! Indeed you have, sir! It was the want of the right question which held us back before. Now that you are come we shall do great things."

Such kind words as these did not fail to find a grateful listener in John Segundus, whose shock shewed clearly in his face. "I fear that I have made myself disagreeable," he whispered to Mr Honeyfoot. "That was not my intention. I had hoped for these gentlemen's good opinion."

At first Mr Segundus was inclined to be downcast but a particularly spiteful outburst from Dr Foxcastle roused him to a little indignation. "That gentleman," said Dr Foxcastle, fixing Mr Segundus with a cold stare, "seems determined that we should share in the unhappy fate of the Society of Manchester Magicians!"

Mr Segundus inclined his head towards Mr Honeyfoot and said, "I had not expected to find the magicians of Yorkshire quite so obstinate. If magic does not have friends in Yorkshire where may we find them?"

Mr Honeyfoot's kindness to Mr Segundus did not end with that evening. He invited Mr Segundus to his house in High-Petergate to eat a good dinner in company with Mrs Honeyfoot and her three pretty daughters, which Mr Segundus, who was a single gentleman and not rich, was glad to do. After dinner Miss Honeyfoot played the pianoforte and Miss Jane sang in Italian. The next day Mrs Honeyfoot told her husband that John Segundus was exactly what a gentleman should be, but she feared he would never profit by it for it was not the fashion to be modest and quiet and kind-hearted.

The intimacy between the two gentlemen advanced very rapidly. Soon Mr Segundus was spending two or three evenings out of every seven at the house in High-Petergate. Once there was quite a crowd of young people present which naturally led to dancing. It was all very delightful but often Mr Honeyfoot and Mr Segundus would slip away to discuss the one thing which really interested both of them – why was there no more magic done in England? But talk as they would (often till two or three in the morning) they came no nearer to an answer; and perhaps this was not so very remarkable, for all sorts of magicians and antiquarians and scholars had been asking the same question for rather more than two hundred years.

Mr Honeyfoot was a tall, cheerful, smiling gentleman with a great deal of energy, who always liked to be doing or planning something, rarely thinking to inquire whether that something were to the purpose. The present task put him very much in mind of the great mediaeval magicians,[2] who, whenever they had some seemingly

---

[2] More properly called *Aureate* or Golden Age magicians.

impossible problem to solve, would ride away for a year and a day with only a fairy-servant or two to guide them and at the end of this time never failed to find the answer. Mr Honeyfoot told Mr Segundus that in his opinion they could not do better than emulate these great men, some of whom had gone to the most retired parts of England and Scotland and Ireland (where magic was strongest) while others had ridden out of this world entirely and no one nowadays was quite clear about where they had gone or what they had done when they got there. Mr Honeyfoot did not propose going quite so far – indeed he did not wish to go far at all because it was winter and the roads were very shocking. Nevertheless he was strongly persuaded that they should go *somewhere* and consult *someone*. He told Mr Segundus that he thought they were both growing stale; the advantage of a fresh opinion would be immense. But no destination, no object presented itself. Mr Honeyfoot was in despair: and then he thought of the other magician.

Some years before, the York society had heard rumours that there was another magician in Yorkshire. This gentleman lived in a very retired part of the country where (it was said) he passed his days and nights studying rare magical texts in his wonderful library. Dr Foxcastle had found out the other magician's name and where he might be found, and had written a polite letter inviting the other magician to become a member of the York society. The other magician had written back, expressing his sense of the honour done him and his deep regret: he was quite unable – the long distance between York and Hurtfew Abbey – the indifferent roads – the work that he could on no account neglect – etc., etc.

The York magicians had all looked over the letter and expressed their doubts that any body with such small handwriting could ever make a tolerable magician. Then – with some slight regret for the wonderful library they would never see – they had dismissed the other magician from their thoughts. But Mr Honeyfoot said to Mr

Segundus that the importance of the question, "Why was there no more magic done in England?" was such that it would be very wrong of them to neglect any opening. Who could say? – the other magician's opinion might be worth having. And so he wrote a letter proposing that he and Mr Segundus give themselves the satisfaction of waiting on the other magician on the third Tuesday after Christmas at half past two. A reply came very promptly; Mr Honeyfoot with his customary good nature and good fellowship immediately sent for Mr Segundus and shewed him the letter. The other magician wrote in his small handwriting that he would be very happy in the acquaintance. This was enough. Mr Honeyfoot was very well pleased and instantly strode off to tell Waters, the coachman, when he would be needed.

Mr Segundus was left alone in the room with the letter in his hand. He read: ". . . I am, I confess, somewhat at a loss to account for the sudden honour done to me. It is scarcely conceivable that the magicians of York with all the happiness of each other's society and the incalculable benefit of each other's wisdom should feel any necessity to consult a solitary scholar such as myself . . ."

There was an air of subtle sarcasm about the letter; the writer seemed to mock Mr Honeyfoot with every word. Mr Segundus was glad to reflect that Mr Honeyfoot could scarcely have noticed or he would not have gone with such elated spirits to speak to Waters. It was such a *very* unfriendly letter that Mr Segundus found that all his desire to look upon the other magician had quite evaporated. Well, no matter, he thought, I must go because Mr Honeyfoot wishes it – and what, after all, is the worst that can happen? We will see him and be disappointed and that will be an end of it.

The day of the visit was preceded by stormy weather; rain had made long ragged pools in the bare, brown fields; wet roofs were like cold stone mirrors; and Mr Honeyfoot's post-chaise travelled through a world that seemed to contain a much higher proportion of chill grey sky and a much smaller one of solid comfortable earth than was usually the case.

Ever since the first evening Mr Segundus had been intending to ask Mr Honeyfoot about the Learned Society of Magicians of Manchester which Dr Foxcastle had mentioned. He did so now.

"It was a society of quite recent foundation," said Mr Honeyfoot, "and its members were clergymen of the poorer sort, respectable ex-tradesmen, apothecaries, lawyers, retired mill owners who had got up a little Latin and so forth, such people as might be termed half-gentlemen. I believe Dr Foxcastle was glad when they disbanded – he does not think that people of that sort have any business becoming magicians. And yet, you know, there were several clever men among them. They began, as you did, with the aim of bringing back practical magic to the world. They were practical men and wished to apply the principles of reason and science to magic as they had done to the manufacturing arts. They called it 'Rational Thaumaturgy'. When it did not work they became discouraged. Well, they cannot be blamed for that. But they let their disillusionment lead them into all sorts of difficulties. They began to think that there was not now nor ever had been magic in the world. They said that the *Aureate* magicians were all deceivers or were themselves deceived. And that the Raven King was an invention of the northern English to keep themselves from the tyranny of the south (being north-country men themselves they had some sympathy with that). Oh, their arguments were very ingenious – I forget how they explained fairies. They disbanded, as I told you, and one of them, whose name was Aubrey I think, meant to write it all down and publish it. But when it came to the point he found that a sort of fixed melancholy had settled on him and he was not able to rouse himself enough to begin."

"Poor gentleman," said Mr Segundus. "Perhaps it is the age. It is not an age for magic or scholarship, is it sir? Tradesmen prosper, sailors, politicians, but not magicians. Our time is past." He thought for a moment. "Three years ago," he said, "I was in London and I met with a street magician, a vagabonding, yellow-curtain sort of fellow with a strange disfiguration. This man

9

persuaded me to part with quite a high sum of money – in return for which he promised to tell me a great secret. When I had paid him the money he told me that one day magic would be restored to England by two magicians. Now I do not at all believe in prophecies, yet it is thinking on what he said that has determined me to discover the truth of our fallen state – is not that strange?"

"You were entirely right – prophecies are great nonsense," said Mr Honeyfoot, laughing. And then, as if struck by a thought, he said, "We are two magicians. Honeyfoot and Segundus," he said trying it out, as if thinking how it would look in the newspapers and history books, "Honeyfoot and Segundus – it sounds very well."

Mr Segundus shook his head. "The fellow knew my profession and it was only to be expected that he should pretend to me that I was one of the two men. But in the end he told me quite plainly that I was not. At first it seemed as if he was not sure of it. There was something about me . . . He made me write down my name and looked at it a good long while."

"I expect he could see there was no more money to be got out of you," said Mr Honeyfoot.

Hurtfew Abbey was some fourteen miles north-west of York. The antiquity was all in the name. There had been an abbey but that was long ago; the present house had been built in the reign of Anne. It was very handsome and square and solid-looking in a fine park full of ghostly-looking wet trees (for the day was becoming rather misty). A river (called the Hurt) ran through the park and a fine classical-looking bridge led across it.

The other magician (whose name was Norrell) was in the hall to receive his guests. He was small, like his handwriting, and his voice when he welcomed them to Hurtfew was rather quiet as if he were not used to speaking his thoughts out loud. Mr Honeyfoot who was a little deaf did not catch what he said; "I get old, sir – a common failing. I hope you will bear with me."

Mr Norrell led his guests to a handsome drawing-room with a

good fire burning in the hearth. No candles had been lit; two fine windows gave plenty of light to see by – although it was a grey sort of light and not at all cheerful. Yet the idea of a second fire, or candles, burning somewhere in the room kept occurring to Mr Segundus, so that he continually turned in his chair and looked about him to discover where they might be. But there never was any thing – only perhaps a mirror or an antique clock.

Mr Norrell said that he had read Mr Segundus's account of the careers of Martin Pale's fairy-servants.[3] "A creditable piece of work, sir, but you left out Master Fallowthought. A very minor spirit certainly, whose usefulness to the great Dr Pale was questionable.[4] Nevertheless your little history was incomplete without him."

There was a pause. "A fairy-spirit called Fallowthought, sir?" said Mr Segundus, "I . . . that is . . . that is to say I never heard of any such creature – in this world or any other."

Mr Norrell smiled for the first time – but it was an inward sort of smile. "Of course," he said, "I am forgetting. It is all in Holgarth and Pickle's history of their own dealings with Master Fallowthought, which you could scarcely have read. I congratulate you – they were an unsavoury pair – more criminal than magical: the less one knows of them the better."

"Ah, sir!" cried Mr Honeyfoot, suspecting that Mr Norrell was speaking of one of his books. "We hear marvellous things of your library. All the magicians in Yorkshire fell into fits of jealousy when they heard of the great number of books you had got!"

"Indeed?" said Mr Norrell coldly. "You surprize me. I had no idea my affairs were so commonly known . . . I expect it is

---

[3] *A Complete Description of Dr Pale's fairy-servants, their Names, Histories, Characters and the Services they performed for Him* by John Segundus, pub. by Thomas Burnham, Bookseller, Northampton, 1799.

[4] Dr Martin Pale (1485–1567) was the son of a Warwick leather-tanner. He was the last of the *Aureate* or Golden Age magicians. Other magicians followed him (c.f. Gregory Absalom) but their reputations are debatable. Pale was certainly the last English magician to venture into Faerie.

Thoroughgood," he said thoughtfully, naming a man who sold books and curiosities in Coffee-yard in York. "Childermass has warned me several times that Thoroughgood is a chatterer."

Mr Honeyfoot did not quite understand this. If *he* had had such quantities of magical books he would have loved to talk of them, be complimented on them, and have them admired; and he could not believe that Mr Norrell was not the same. Meaning therefore to be kind and to set Mr Norrell at his ease (for he had taken it into his head that the gentleman was shy) he persisted: "Might I be permitted to express a wish, sir, that we might see your wonderful library?"

Mr Segundus was certain that Norrell would refuse, but instead Mr Norrell regarded them steadily for some moments (he had small blue eyes and seemed to peep out at them from some secret place inside himself) and then, almost graciously, he granted Mr Honeyfoot's request. Mr Honeyfoot was all gratitude, happy in the belief that he had pleased Mr Norrell as much as himself.

Mr Norrell led the other two gentlemen along a passage – a very ordinary passage, thought Mr Segundus, panelled and floored with well-polished oak, and smelling of beeswax; then there was a staircase, or perhaps only three or four steps; and then another passage where the air was somewhat colder and the floor was good York stone: all entirely unremarkable. (Unless the second passage had come before the staircase or steps? Or had there in truth been a staircase at all?) Mr Segundus was one of those happy gentlemen who can always say whether they face north or south, east or west. It was not a talent he took any particular pride in – it was as natural to him as knowing that his head still stood upon his shoulders – but in Mr Norrell's house his gift deserted him. He could never afterwards picture the sequence of passageways and rooms through which they had passed, nor quite decide how long they had taken to reach the library. And he could not tell the direction; it seemed to him as if Mr Norrell had discovered some fifth point of the compass – not east, nor south, nor west, nor north, but somewhere quite different and this was the direction in which he led them. Mr Honeyfoot, on the other hand, did not appear to notice any thing odd.

The library was perhaps a little smaller than the drawing-room they had just quitted. There was a noble fire in the hearth and all was comfort and quiet. Yet once again the light within the room did not seem to accord with the three tall twelve-paned windows, so that once again Mr Segundus was made uncomfortable by a persistent feeling that there ought to have been other candles in the room, other windows or another fire to account for the light. What windows there were looked out upon a wide expanse of dusky English rain so that Mr Segundus could not make out the view nor guess where in the house they stood.

The room was not empty; there was a man sitting at a table who rose as they entered, and whom Mr Norrell briefly declared to be Childermass, his man of business.

Mr Honeyfoot and Mr Segundus, being magicians themselves, had not needed to be told that the library of Hurtfew Abbey was dearer to its possessor than all his other riches; and they were not surprized to discover that Mr Norrell had constructed a beautiful jewel box to house his heart's treasure. The bookcases which lined the walls of the room were built of English woods and resembled Gothic arches laden with carvings. There were carvings of leaves (dried and twisted leaves, as if the season the artist had intended to represent were autumn), carvings of intertwining roots and branches, carvings of berries and ivy – all wonderfully done. But the wonder of the bookcases was nothing to the wonder of the books.

The first thing a student of magic learns is that there are books *about* magic and books *of* magic. And the second thing he learns is that a perfectly respectable example of the former may be had for two or three guineas at a good bookseller, and that the value of the latter is above rubies.[5] The collection of the York society was reckoned very fine – almost remarkable; among its many volumes were five works written between 1550 and 1700 and which might reasonably be claimed as books of magic (though one was no more than a couple of ragged pages). Books of magic are rare and neither Mr Segundus nor Mr Honeyfoot had ever seen more than two or three in a private library. At Hurtfew all the walls were lined with bookshelves and all the shelves were filled with books. And the books were all, or almost all, old books; books of magic. Oh! to be sure many had clean modern bindings, but clearly these were volumes which Mr Norrell had had rebound (he favoured, it seemed, plain calf with the titles stamped in neat silver capitals). But many had bindings that were old, old, old, with crumbling spines and corners.

Mr Segundus glanced at the spines of the books on a nearby shelf; the first title he read was *How to putte Questiones to the Dark and understand its Answeres.*

---

[5] Magicians, as we know from Jonathan Strange's maxim, will quarrel about any thing and many years and much learning has been applied to the vexed question of whether such and such a volume qualifies as a book of magic. But most laymen find they are served well enough by this simple rule: books written before magic ended in England are books of magic, books written later are books about magic. The principle, from which the layman's rule of thumb derives, is that a book of magic should be written by a practising magician, rather than a theoretical magician or a historian of magic. What could be more reasonable? And yet already we are in difficulties. The great masters of magic, those we term the Golden Age or *Aureate* magicians (Thomas Godbless, Ralph Stokesey, Catherine of Winchester, the Raven King) wrote little, or little has survived. It is probable that Thomas Godbless could not write. Stokesey learnt Latin at a little grammar school in his native Devonshire, but all that we know of him comes from other writers.

Magicians only applied themselves to writing books when magic was already in decline. Darkness was already approaching to quench the glory of English magic; those men we call the Silver Age or *Argentine* magicians (Thomas Lanchester, 1518–90; Jacques Belasis, 1526–1604; Nicholas Goubert, 1535–78; Gregory Absalom, 1507–99) were flickering candles in the twilight; they were scholars first and magicians second. Certainly they claimed to do magic, some even had a fairy-servant or two, but they seem to have accomplished very little in this way and some modern scholars have doubted whether they could do magic at all.

"A foolish work," said Mr Norrell. Mr Segundus started – he had not known his host was so close by. Mr Norrell continued, "I would advise you not to waste a moment's thought upon it."

So Mr Segundus looked at the next book which was Belasis's *Instructions*.

"You know Belasis, I dare say?" asked Mr Norrell.

"Only by reputation, sir," said Mr Segundus, "I have often heard that he held the key to a good many things, but I have also heard – indeed all the authorities agree – that every copy of *The Instructions* was destroyed long ago. Yet now here it is! Why, sir, it is extraordinary! It is wonderful!"

"You expect a great deal of Belasis," remarked Norrell, "and once upon a time I was entirely of your mind. I remember that for many months I devoted eight hours out of every twenty-four to studying his work; a compliment, I may say, that I have never paid any other author. But ultimately he is disappointing. He is mystical where he ought to be intelligible – and intelligible where he ought to be obscure. There are some things which have no business being put into books for all the world to read. For myself I no longer have any very great opinion of Belasis."

"Here is a book I never even heard of, sir," said Mr Segundus, "*The Excellences of Christo-Judaic Magick*. What can you tell me of this?"

"Ha!" cried Mr Norrell. "It dates from the seventeenth century, but I have no great opinion of it. Its author was a liar, a drunkard, an adulterer and a rogue. I am glad he has been so completely forgot."

It seemed that it was not only live magicians which Mr Norrell despised. He had taken the measure of all the dead ones too and found them wanting.

Mr Honeyfoot meanwhile, his hands in the air like a Methodist praising God, was walking rapidly from bookcase to bookcase; he could scarcely stop long enough to read the title of one book before his eye was caught by another on the other side of the room. "Oh, Mr Norrell!" he cried. "Such a quantity of books! Surely we shall find the answers to all our questions here!"

"I doubt it, sir," was Mr Norrell's dry reply.

The man of business gave a short laugh – laughter which was clearly directed at Mr Honeyfoot, yet Mr Norrell did not reprimand him either by look or word, and Mr Segundus wondered what sort of business it could be that Mr Norrell entrusted to this person. With his long hair as ragged as rain and as black as thunder, he would have looked quite at home upon a windswept moor, or lurking in some pitch-black alleyway, or perhaps in a novel by Mrs Radcliffe.

Mr Segundus took down *The Instructions* of Jacques Belasis and, despite Mr Norrell's poor opinion of it, instantly hit upon two extraordinary passages.[6] Then, conscious of time passing and of

---

[6] The first passage which Mr Segundus read concerned England, Faerie (which magicians sometimes call "the Other Lands") and a strange country that is reputed to lie on the far side of Hell. Mr Segundus had heard something of the symbolic and magical bond which links these three lands, yet never had he read so clear an explanation of it as was put forward here.

The second extract concerned one of England's greatest magicians, Martin Pale. In Gregory Absalom's *The Tree of Learning* there is a famous passage which relates how, while journeying through Faerie, the last of the great *Aureate* magicians, Martin Pale, paid a visit to a fairy-prince. Like most of his race the fairy had a great multitude of names, honorifics, titles and pseudonyms; but usually he was known as Cold Henry. Cold Henry made a long and deferential speech to his guest. The speech was full of metaphors and obscure allusions, but what Cold Henry seemed to be saying was that fairies were naturally wicked creatures who did not always know when they were going wrong. To this Martin Pale briefly and somewhat enigmatically replied that not all Englishmen have the same size feet.

For several centuries no one had the faintest idea what any of this might mean, though several theories were advanced – and John Segundus was familiar with all of them. The most popular was that developed by William Pantler in the early eighteenth century. Pantler said that Cold Henry and Pale were speaking of theology. Fairies (as everybody knows) are beyond the reach of the Church; no Christ has come to them, nor ever will – and what is to become of them on Judgement Day no one knows. According to Pantler Cold Henry meant to enquire of Pale if there was any hope that fairies, like men, might receive Eternal Salvation. Pale's reply – that Englishmen's feet are different sizes – was his way of saying that not all Englishmen will be saved. Based on this Pantler goes on to attribute to Pale a rather odd belief that Heaven is large enough to hold only a finite number of the Blessed; for every Englishmen who is damned, a place opens up in Heaven for a fairy.

the queer, dark eye of the man of business upon him, he opened *The Excellences of Christo-Judaic Magick*. This was not (as he had supposed) a printed book, but a manuscript scribbled down very hurriedly upon the backs of all kinds of bits of paper, most of them old ale-house bills. Here Mr Segundus read of wonderful adventures. The seventeenth-century magician had used his scanty magic to battle against great and powerful enemies: battles which no human magician ought to have attempted. He had scribbled down the history of his patchwork victories just as those enemies were closing around him. The author had known very well that, as he wrote, time was running out for him and death was the best that he could hope for.

The room was becoming darker; the antique scrawl was growing dim on the page. Two footmen came into the room and, watched by the unbusinesslike man of business, lit candles, drew window curtains and heaped fresh coals upon the fire. Mr Segundus thought it best to remind Mr Honeyfoot that they had not yet explained to Mr Norrell the reason for their visit.

As they were leaving the library Mr Segundus noticed something he thought odd. A chair was drawn up to the fire and by the chair stood a little table. Upon the table lay the boards and leather bindings of a very old book, a pair of scissors and a strong, cruel-looking knife, such as a gardener might use for pruning. But the pages of the book were nowhere to be seen. Perhaps, thought Mr

---

[6] *cont'd* Pantler's reputation as a theoretical magician rests entirely on the book he wrote on the subject

In Jacques Belasis's *Instructions* Mr Segundus read a very different explanation. Three centuries before Martin Pale set foot in Cold Henry's castle Cold Henry had had another human visitor, an English magician even greater than Pale – Ralph Stokesey – who had left behind him a pair of boots. The boots, said Belasis, were old, which is probably why Stokesey did not take them with him, but their presence in the castle caused great consternation to all its fairy-inhabitants who held English magicians in great veneration. In particular Cold Henry was in a pickle because he feared that in some devious, incomprehensible way, Christian morality might hold him responsible for the loss of the boots. So he was trying to rid himself of the terrible objects by passing them on to Pale who did not want them.

Segundus, he has sent it away to be bound anew. Yet the old binding still looked strong and why should Mr Norrell trouble himself to remove the pages and risk damaging them? A skilled bookbinder was the proper person to do such work.

When they were seated in the drawing-room again, Mr Honeyfoot addressed Mr Norrell. "What I have seen here today, sir, convinces me that you are the best person to help us. Mr Segundus and I are of the opinion that modern magicians are on the wrong path; they waste their energies upon trifles. Do not you agree, sir?"

"Oh! certainly," said Mr Norrell.

"Our question," continued Mr Honeyfoot, "is why magic has fallen from its once-great state in our great nation. Our question is, sir, why is no more magic done in England?"

Mr Norrell's small blue eyes grew harder and brighter and his lips tightened as if he were seeking to suppress a great and secret delight within him. It was as if, thought Mr Segundus, he had waited a long time for someone to ask him this question and had had his answer ready for years. Mr Norrell said, "I cannot help you with your question, sir, for I do not understand it. It is a wrong question, sir. Magic is not ended in England. I myself am quite a tolerable practical magician."

2

The Old Starre Inn

January–February 1807

A
S THE CARRIAGE passed out of Mr Norrell's sweep-gate Mr Honeyfoot exclaimed; "A practical magician in England! And in Yorkshire too! We have had the most extraordinary good luck! Ah, Mr Segundus, we have you to thank for this. You were awake, when the rest of us had fallen asleep. Had it not been for your encouragement, we might never have discovered Mr Norrell. And I am quite certain that he would never have sought us out; he is a little reserved. He gave us no particulars of his achievements in practical magic, nothing beyond the simple fact of his success. That, I fancy, is the sign of a modest nature. Mr Segundus, I think you will agree that our task is clear. It falls to us, sir, to overcome Norrell's natural timidity and aversion to praise, and lead him triumphantly before a wider public!"

"Perhaps," said Mr Segundus doubtfully.

"I do not say it will be easy," said Mr Honeyfoot. "He is a little reticent and not fond of company. But he must see that such knowledge as he possesses must be shared with others for the Nation's good. He is a gentleman: he knows his duty and will do it, I am sure. Ah, Mr Segundus! You deserve the grateful thanks of every magician in the country for this."

But whatever Mr Segundus deserved, the sad fact is that

magicians in England are a peculiarly ungrateful set of men. Mr Honeyfoot and Mr Segundus might well have made the most significant discovery in magical scholarship for three centuries – what of it? There was scarcely a member of the York society who, when he learnt of it, was not entirely confident that he could have done it much better – and, upon the following Tuesday when an extraordinary meeting of the Learned Society of York Magicians was held, there were very few members who were not prepared to say so.

At seven o'clock upon the Tuesday evening the upper room of the Old Starre Inn in Stonegate was crowded. The news which Mr Honeyfoot and Mr Segundus had brought seemed to have drawn out all the gentlemen in the city who had ever peeped into a book of magic – and York was still, after its own fashion, one of the most magical cities in England; perhaps only the King's city of New-castle could boast more magicians.

There was such a crush of magicians in the room that, for the present, a great many were obliged to stand, though the waiters were continually bringing more chairs up the stairs. Dr Foxcastle had got himself an excellent chair, tall and black and curiously carved – and this chair (which rather resembled a throne), and the sweep of the red velvet curtains behind him and the way in which he sat with his hands clasped over his large round stomach, all combined to give him a deeply magisterial air.

The servants at the Old Starre Inn had prepared an excellent fire to keep off the chills of a January evening and around it were seated some ancient magicians – apparently from the reign of George II or thereabouts – all wrapped in plaid shawls, with yellowing spider's-web faces, and accompanied by equally ancient footmen with bottles of medicine in their pockets. Mr Honeyfoot greeted them with: "How do you do, Mr Aptree? How do you do, Mr Greyshippe? I hope you are in good health, Mr Tunstall? I am very glad to see you here, gentlemen! I hope you have all come to rejoice with us? All our years in the dusty wilderness are at an end. Ah! no one knows better than you, Mr Aptree and you, Mr Greyshippe what years they have been, for you have lived through a great many of them. But now we shall see magic once more Britain's counsellor and protector! And the French, Mr Tunstall! What will be the feelings of the French when they hear about it? Why! I should not be surprized if it were to bring on an immediate surrender."

Mr Honeyfoot had a great deal more to say of the same sort; he had prepared a speech in which he intended to lay before them all the wonderful advantages that were to accrue to Britain from this discovery. But he was never allowed to deliver more than a few sentences of it, for it seemed that each and every gentleman in the room was bursting with opinions of his own on the subject, all of which required to be communicated urgently to every other gentleman. Dr Foxcastle was the first to interrupt Mr Honeyfoot. From his large, black throne he addressed Mr Honeyfoot thus: "I am very sorry to see you, sir, bringing magic – for which I know you have a genuine regard – into disrepute with impossible tales and wild inventions. Mr Segundus," he said, turning to the gentleman whom he regarded as the source of all the trouble, "I do not know what is customary where you come from, but in Yorkshire we do not care for men who build their reputations at the expence of other men's peace of mind."

This was as far as Dr Foxcastle got before he was drowned by the loud, angry exclamations of Mr Honeyfoot and Mr Segundus's supporters. The next gentleman to make himself heard wondered that Mr Segundus and Mr Honeyfoot should have been so taken in. Clearly Norrell was mad – no different from any stark-eyed madman who stood upon the street corner screaming out that he was the Raven King.

A sandy-haired gentleman in a state of great excitement thought that Mr Honeyfoot and Mr Segundus should have insisted on Mr Norrell leaving his house upon the instant and coming straightway in an open carriage (though it was January) in triumph to York, so that the sandy-haired gentleman might strew ivy leaves in his path;[1] and one of the very old men by the fire was in a great passion about something or other, but being so old his voice was rather weak and no one had leisure just then to discover what he was saying.

There was a tall, sensible man in the room called Thorpe, a gentleman with very little magical learning, but a degree of common sense rare in a magician. He had always thought that Mr Segundus deserved encouragement in his quest to find where practical English magic had disappeared to – though like everyone else Mr Thorpe had not expected Mr Segundus to discover the answer quite so soon. But now that they had an answer Mr Thorpe was of the opinion that they should not simply dismiss it: "Gentlemen, Mr Norrell has said he can do magic. Very well. We know a little of Norrell – we have all heard of the rare texts he is supposed to have and for this reason alone we would be wrong to dismiss his claims without careful consideration. But the stronger arguments in Norrell's favour are these: that two of our own number – sober scholars both – have seen Norrell and come away convinced." He turned to Mr Honeyfoot. "You believe in this man – any one may see by your face that you do. You have seen something that convinced you – will you not tell us what it was?"

Now Mr Honeyfoot's reaction to this question was perhaps a little strange. At first he smiled gratefully at Mr Thorpe as if this was exactly what he could have wished for: a chance to broadcast the excellent reasons he had for believing that Mr Norrell could do magic; and he opened his mouth to begin. Then he stopped; he paused; he looked about him, as if those excellent reasons which had seemed so substantial a moment ago were all turning to mist and nothingness in his mouth, and his tongue and teeth could not catch hold of even one of them to frame it into a rational English sentence. He muttered something of Mr Norrell's honest countenance.

---

[1] The conquerors of Imperial Rome may have been honoured with wreaths of laurel leaves; lovers and fortune's favourites have, we are told, roses strewn in their paths; but English magicians were always only ever given common ivy.

The York society did not think this very satisfactory (and had they actually been privileged to see Mr Norrell's countenance they might have thought it even less so). So Thorpe turned to Mr Segundus and said, "Mr Segundus, you have seen Norrell too. What is your opinion?"

For the first time the York society noticed how pale Mr Segundus was and it occurred to some of the gentlemen that he had not answered them when they had greeted him, as if he could not quite collect his thoughts to reply. "Are you unwell, sir?" asked Mr Thorpe gently. "No, no," murmured Mr Segundus, "it is nothing. I thank you." But he looked so lost that one gentleman offered him his chair and another went off to fetch a glass of Canary-wine, and the excitable sandy-haired gentleman who had wished to strew ivy leaves in Mr Norrell's path nurtured a secret hope that Mr Segundus might be enchanted and that they might see something extraordinary!

Mr Segundus sighed and said, "I thank you. I am not ill, but this last week I have felt very heavy and stupid. Mrs Pleasance has given me arrowroot and hot concoctions of liquorice root, but they have not helped – which does not surprize me for I think the confusion is in my head. I am not so bad as I was. If you were to ask me now, gentlemen, why it is that I believe that magic has come back to England, I should say it is because I have seen magic done. The impression of having seen magic done is most vivid here and here . . ." (Mr Segundus touched his brow and his heart.) "And yet I know that I have seen none. Norrell did none while we were with him. And so I suppose that I have dreamt it."

Fresh outbreak of the gentlemen of the York society. The faint gentleman smiled faintly and inquired if any one could make any thing of this. Then Mr Thorpe cried, "Good God! It is very nonsensical for us all to sit here and assert that Norrell can or cannot do this or can or cannot do that. We are all rational beings I think, and the answer, surely, is quite simple – we will ask him to do some magic for us in proof of his claims."

This was such good sense that for a moment the magicians were silent – though this is not to say that the proposal was universally popular – not at all. Several of the magicians (Dr Foxcastle was one) did not care for it. If they asked Norrell to do magic, there was always the danger that he might indeed do some. They did not want to see magic done; they only wished to read about it in books. Others were of the opinion that the York society was making itself very ridiculous by doing even so little as this. But in the end most of the magicians agreed with Mr Thorpe that: "As scholars, gentlemen, the least we can do is to offer Mr Norrell the opportunity to convince us." And so it was decided that someone should write another letter to Mr Norrell.

It was quite clear to all the magicians that Mr Honeyfoot and Mr Segundus had handled the thing very ill and upon one subject at least – that of Mr Norrell's wonderful library – they did seem remarkably stupid, for they were not able to give any intelligible report of it. What had they seen? Oh, books, many books. A remarkable number of books? Yes, they believed they had thought it remarkable at the time. Rare books? Ah, probably. Had they been permitted to take them down and look inside them? Oh no! Mr Norrell had not gone so far as to invite them to do that. But they had read the titles? Yes, indeed. Well then, what were the titles of the books they had seen? They did not know; they could not remember. Mr Segundus said that one of the books had a title that began with a 'B', but that was the beginning and end of his information. It was very odd.

Mr Thorpe had always intended to write the letter to Mr Norrell himself, but there were a great many magicians in the room whose chief idea was to give offence to Mr Norrell in return for his impudence and these gentlemen thought quite rightly that their best means of insulting Norrell was to allow Dr Foxcastle to write the letter. And so this was carried. In due time it brought forth an angry letter of reply.

Hurtfew Abbey, Yorkshire,
Feb. 1st, 1807

Sir—

Twice in recent years I have been honoured by a letter from the
gentlemen of the Learned Society of York Magicians soliciting
my acquaintance. Now comes a third letter informing me of the
society's displeasure. The good opinion of the York society seems
as easily lost as it is gained and a man may never know how he
came to do either. In answer to the particular charge contained in
your letter that I have exaggerated my abilities and laid claim to
powers I cannot possibly possess I have only this to say: other men
may fondly attribute their lack of success to a fault in the world
rather than to their own poor scholarship, but the truth is that
magic is as achievable in this Age as in any other; as I have proved
to my own complete satisfaction any number of times within the
last twenty years. But what is my reward for loving my art better
than other men have done? – for studying harder to perfect it? – it
is now circulated abroad that I am a fabulist; my professional
abilities are slighted and my word doubted. You will not, I dare
say, be much surprized to learn that under such circumstances as
these I do not feel much inclined to oblige the York society in any
thing – least of all a request for a display of magic. The Learned
Society of York Magicians meets upon Wednesday next and
upon that day I shall inform you of my intentions.

Your servant
Gilbert Norrell

This was all rather disagreeably mysterious. The theoretical
magicians waited somewhat nervously to see what the practical
magician would send them next. What Mr Norrell sent them next
was nothing more alarming than an attorney, a smiling, bobbing,
bowing attorney, a quite commonplace attorney called Robinson,
with neat black clothes and neat kid gloves, with a document, the

like of which the gentlemen of the York society had never seen before; a draft of an agreement, drawn up in accordance with England's long-forgotten codes of magical law.

Mr Robinson arrived in the upper room at the Old Starre promptly at eight and seemed to suppose himself expected. He had a place of business and two clerks in Coney-street. His face was well known to many of the gentlemen.

"I will confess to you, sirs," smiled Mr Robinson, "that this paper is largely the work of my principal, Mr Norrell. I am no expert upon thaumaturgic law. Who is nowadays? Still, I dare say that if I go wrong, you will be so kind as to put me right again."

Several of the York magicians nodded wisely.

Mr Robinson was a polished sort of person. He was so clean and healthy and pleased about everything that he positively shone – which is only to be expected in a fairy or an angel, but is somewhat disconcerting in an attorney. He was most deferential to the gentlemen of the York society for he knew nothing of magic, but he thought it must be difficult and require great concentration of mind. But to professional humility and a genuine admiration of the York society Mr Robinson added a happy vanity that these monumental brains must now cease their pondering on esoteric matters for a time and listen to him. He put golden spectacles upon his nose, adding another small glitter to his shining person.

Mr Robinson said that Mr Norrell undertook to do a piece of magic in a certain place at a certain time. "You have no objection I hope, gentlemen, to my principal settling the time and place?"

The gentlemen had none.

"Then it shall be the Cathedral, Friday fortnight."[2]

---

[2] The great church at York is both a *cathedral* (meaning the church where the throne of the bishop or archbishop is housed) and a *minster* (meaning a church founded by a missionary in ancient times). It has borne both these names at different periods. In earlier centuries it was more usually called the *Minster*, but nowadays the people of York prefer the term *Cathedral* as one which elevates their church above those of the nearby towns of Ripon and Beverley. Ripon and Beverley have minsters, but no cathedrals.

Mr Robinson said that if Mr Norrell failed to do the magic then he would publicly withdraw his claims to be a practical magician – indeed to be any sort of magician at all, and he would give his oath never to make any such claims again.

"He need not go so far," said Mr Thorpe. "We have no desire to punish him; we merely wished to put his claims to the test."

Mr Robinson's shining smile dimmed a little, as if he had something rather disagreeable to communicate and was not quite sure how to begin.

"Wait," said Mr Segundus, "we have not heard the other side of the bargain yet. We have not heard what he expects of us."

Mr Robinson nodded. Mr Norrell intended it seemed to exact the same promise from each and every magician of the York society as he made himself. In other words if he succeeded, then they must without further ado disband the Society of York Magicians and none of them claim the title "magician" ever again. And after all, said Mr Robinson, this would be only fair, since Mr Norrell would then have proved himself the only true magician in Yorkshire.

"And shall we have some third person, some independent party to decide if the magic has been accomplished?" asked Mr Thorpe.

This question seemed to puzzle Mr Robinson. He hoped they would excuse him if he had taken up a wrong idea he said, he would not offend for the world, but he had thought that all the gentlemen present were magicians.

Oh, yes, nodded the York society, they were all magicians.

Then surely, said Mr Robinson, they would recognize magic when they saw it? Surely there were none better qualified to do so?

Another gentleman asked what magic Norrell intended to do? Mr Robinson was full of polite apologies and elaborate explanations; he could not enlighten them, he did not know.

It would tire my reader's patience to rehearse the many winding arguments by which the gentlemen of the York society came to sign Mr Norrell's agreement. Many did so out of vanity; they had publicly declared that they did not believe Norrell could do magic, they had publicly challenged Norrell to perform some – under such circumstances as these it would have looked peculiarly foolish to change their minds – or so they thought.

Mr Honeyfoot, on the other hand, signed precisely *because* he believed in Norrell's magic. Mr Honeyfoot hoped that Mr Norrell would gain public recognition by this demonstration of his powers and go on to employ his magic for the good of the nation.

Some of the gentlemen were provoked to sign by the suggestion (originating with Norrell and somehow conveyed by Robinson) that they would not shew themselves true magicians unless they did so.

So one by one and there and then, the magicians of York signed the document that Mr Robinson had brought. The last magician was Mr Segundus.

"I will not sign," he said. "For magic is my life and though Mr Norrell is quite right to say I am a poor scholar, what shall I do when it is taken from me?"

A silence.

"Oh!" said Mr Robinson. "Well, that is . . . Are you quite sure, sir, that you should not like to sign the document? You see how all your friends have done it? You will be quite alone."

"I am quite sure," said Mr Segundus, "thank you."

"Oh!" said Mr Robinson. "Well, in that case I must confess that I do not know quite how to proceed. My principal gave me no instruction what to do if only *some* of the gentlemen signed. I shall consult with my principal in the morning."

Dr Foxcastle was heard to remark to Mr Hart or Hunt that once again it was the newcomer who brought a world of trouble upon everyone's heads.

But two days later Mr Robinson waited upon Dr Foxcastle with a message to say that on this particular occasion Mr Norrell would be happy to overlook Mr Segundus's refusal to sign; he would consider that his contract was with all the members of the York society *except* for Mr Segundus.

The night before Mr Norrell was due to perform the magic, snow fell on York and in the morning the dirt and mud of the city had disappeared, all replaced by flawless white. The sounds of hooves and footsteps were muffled, and the very voices of York's citizens were altered by a white silence that swallowed up every sound. Mr Norrell had named a very early hour in the day. In their separate homes the York magicians breakfasted alone. They watched in silence as a servant poured their coffee, broke their warm white-bread rolls, fetched the butter. The wife, the sister, the daughter, the daughter-in-law, or the niece who usually performed these little offices was still in bed; and the pleasant female domestic chat, which the gentlemen of the York society affected to despise so much, and which was in truth the sweet and mild refrain in the music of their ordinary lives, was absent. And the breakfast rooms where these gentlemen sat were changed from what they had been yesterday. The winter gloom was quite gone and in its place was a fearful light – the winter sun reflected many times over by the snowy earth. There was a dazzle of light upon the white linen tablecloth. The rosebuds that patterned the daughter's pretty coffee-cups seemed almost to dance in it. Sunbeams were struck from the niece's silver coffee-pot, and the daughter-in-law's smiling china shepherdesses were all become shining angels. It was as if the table were laid with fairy silver and crystal.

Mr Segundus, putting his head out of a third-storey window in Lady-Peckitt's-yard, thought that perhaps Norrell had already done the magic and this was it. There was an ominous rumble above him and he drew in his head quickly to avoid a sudden fall of snow from the roof. Mr Segundus had no servant any more than he had a wife, sister, daughter, daughter-in-law, or niece, but Mrs Pleasance, his landlady, was an early riser. Many times in the last fortnight she had heard him sigh over his books and she hoped to cheer him up with a breakfast of two freshly grilled herrings, tea and fresh milk, and white bread and butter on a blue-and-white china plate. With the same generous aim she had sat down to talk to him. On seeing how despondent he looked she cried, "Oh! I have no patience with this old man!"

Mr Segundus had not told Mrs Pleasance that Mr Norrell was old and yet she fancied that he must be. From what Mr Segundus had told her she thought of him as a sort of miser who hoarded magic instead of gold, and as our narrative progresses, I will allow the reader to judge the justice of this portrait of Mr Norrell's character. Like Mrs Pleasance I always fancy that misers are old. I cannot tell why this should be since I am sure that there are as many young misers as old. As to whether or not Mr Norrell was in fact old, he was the sort of man who had been old at seventeen.

Mrs Pleasance continued, "When Mr Pleasance was alive, he used to say that no one in York, man or woman, could bake a loaf to rival mine, and other people as well have been kind enough to say that they never in their lives tasted bread so good. But I have always kept a good table for love of doing a thing well and if one of those queer spirits from the Arabian fables came out of this very teapot now and gave me three wishes I hope I would not be so ill-natured as to try to stop other folk from baking bread – and should their bread be as good as mine then I do not see that it hurts me, but rather is so much the better for them. Come, sir, try a bit," she said, pushing a plateful of the celebrated bread towards her lodger. "I do not like to see you get so thin. People will say that Hettie Pleasance has lost all her skill at housekeeping. I wish you would not be so downcast, sir. You have not signed this perfidious document and when the other gentlemen are forced to give up, you will still continue and I very much hope, Mr Segundus, that you may make great discoveries and perhaps then this Mr Norrell who thinks himself so clever will be glad to take you into partnership and so be brought to regret his foolish pride."

Mr Segundus smiled and thanked her. "But I do not think that will happen. My chief difficulty will be lack of materials. I have very little of my own, and when the society is disbanded, – well I cannot tell what will happen to its books, but I doubt that they will come to me."

Mr Segundus ate his bread (which was just as good as the late Mr Pleasance and his friends had said it was) and his herrings and drank some tea. Their power to soothe a troubled heart must have been greater than he had supposed for he found that he felt a little better and, fortified in this manner, he put on his greatcoat and his hat and his muffler and his gloves and stamped off through the snowy streets to the place that Mr Norrell had appointed for this day's wonders – the Cathedral of York.

And I hope that all my readers are acquainted with an old English Cathedral town or I fear that the significance of Mr Norrell's chusing that particular place will be lost upon them. They must understand that in an old Cathedral town the great old church is not one building among many; it is *the* building – different from all others in scale, beauty and solemnity. Even in modern times when an old Cathedral town may have provided itself with all the elegant appurtenances of civic buildings, assembly and meeting rooms (and York was well-stocked with these) the Cathedral rises above them – a witness to the devotion of our forefathers. It is as if the town contains within itself something larger than itself. When going about one's business in the muddle of narrow streets one is sure to lose sight of the Cathedral, but then the town will open out and suddenly it is there, many times taller and many times larger than any other building, and one realizes that one has reached the heart of the town and that all streets and lanes have in some way led here, to a place of mysteries much deeper than any Mr Norrell knew of. Such were Mr Segundus's thoughts as he entered the Close and stood before the great brooding blue shadow of the Cathedral's west face. Now came Dr Foxcastle, sailing magisterially around the corner like a fat, black ship. Spying Mr Segundus there he steered himself towards that gentleman and bid him good morning.

"Perhaps, sir," said Dr Foxcastle, "you would be so kind as to introduce me to Mr Norrell? He is a gentleman I very much wish to know."

"I shall be only too happy, sir." said Mr Segundus and looked about him. The weather had kept most people within doors and there were only a few dark figures scuttling over the white field that lay before the great grey Church. When scrutinized these were discovered to be gentlemen of the York society, or clergymen and Cathedral attendants – vergers and beadles, sub-choirmasters, provosts, transept-sweepers and such-like persons – who had been sent by their superiors out into the snow to see to the Church's business.

"I should like nothing better, sir," said Mr Segundus, "than to oblige you, but I do not see Mr Norrell."

Yet there was someone.

Someone was standing in the snow alone directly in front of the Minster. He was a dark sort of someone, a not-quite-respectable someone who was regarding Mr Segundus and Dr Foxcastle with an air of great interest. His ragged hair hung about his shoulders like a fall of black water; he had a strong, thin face with something twisted in it, like a tree root; and a long, thin nose; and, though his skin was very pale, something made it seem a dark face – perhaps it was the darkness of his eyes, or the proximity of that long, black greasy hair. After a moment this person walked up to the two magicians, gave them a sketchy bow and said that he hoped they would forgive his intruding upon them but they had been pointed out to him as gentlemen who were there upon the same business as himself. He said that his name was John Childermass, and that he was Mr Norrell's steward in certain matters (though he did not say what these were).

"It seems to me," said Mr Segundus thoughtfully, "that I know your face. I have seen you before, I think?"

Something shifted in Childermass's dark face, but it was gone in a moment and whether it had been a frown or laughter it was impossible to say. "I am often in York upon business for Mr Norrell, sir. Perhaps you have seen me in one of the city book-selling establishments?"

"No," said Mr Segundus, "I have seen you . . . I can picture you . . . Where? . . . Oh! I shall have it in a moment!"

Childermass raised an eyebrow as if to say he very much doubted it.

"But surely Mr Norrell is coming himself?" said Dr Foxcastle.

Childermass begged Dr Foxcastle's pardon, but he did not think Mr Norrell would come; he did not think Mr Norrell saw any reason to come.

"Ah!" cried Dr Foxcastle. "then he concedes, does he? Well, well, well. Poor gentleman. He feels very foolish, I dare say. Well indeed. It was a noble attempt at any rate. We bear him no ill-will for having made the attempt." Dr Foxcastle was much relieved that he would see no magic and it made him generous.

Childermass begged Dr Foxcastle's pardon once more; he feared that Dr Foxcastle had mistaken his meaning. Mr Norrell would certainly do magic; he would do it in Hurtfew Abbey and the results would be seen in York. "Gentlemen," said Childermass to Dr Foxcastle, "do not like to leave their comfortable firesides unless they must. I dare say if you, sir, could have managed the seeing part of the business from your own drawing-room you would not be here in the cold and wet."

Dr Foxcastle drew in his breath sharply and bestowed on John Childermass a look that said that he thought John Childermass very insolent.

Childermass did not seem much dismayed by Dr Foxcastle's opinion of him, indeed he looked rather entertained by it. He said, "It is time, sirs. You should take your stations within the Church. You would be sorry, I am sure, to miss anything when so much hangs upon it."

It was twenty minutes past the hour and gentlemen of the York society were already filing into the Cathedral by the door in the south transept. Several looked about them before going inside, as if taking a last fond farewell of a world they were not quite sure of seeing again.

3

The stones of York

February 1807

A GREAT OLD CHURCH in the depths of winter is a discouraging place at the best of times; the cold of a hundred winters seems to have been preserved in its stones and to seep out of them. In the cold, dank, twilight interior of the Cathedral the gentlemen of the York society were obliged to stand and wait to be astonished, without any assurance that the surprize when it came would be a pleasant one.

Mr Honeyfoot tried to smile cheerfully at his companions, but for a gentleman so practised in the art of a friendly smile it was a very poor attempt.

Upon the instant bells began to toll. Now these were nothing more than the bells of St Michael-le-Belfrey telling the half hour, but inside the Cathedral they had an odd, far-away sound like the bells of another country. It was not at all a cheerful sound. The gentlemen of the York society knew very well how bells often went with magic and in particular with the magic of those unearthly beings, *fairies*; they knew how, in the old days, silvery bells would often sound just as some Englishman or Englishwoman of particular virtue or beauty was about to be stolen away by fairies to live in strange, ghostly lands for ever. Even the Raven King – who was not a fairy, but an Englishman – had a somewhat regrettable habit of abducting men and women and taking them to live with him in

35

his castle in the Other Lands.[1] Now, had you and I the power to seize by magic any human being that took our fancy and the power to keep that person by our side through all eternity, and had we all the world to chuse from, then I dare say our choice might fall on someone a little more captivating than a member of the Learned Society of York Magicians, but this comforting thought did not occur to the gentlemen inside York Cathedral and several of them began to wonder how angry Dr Foxcastle's letter had made Mr Norrell and they began to be seriously frightened.

As the sounds of the bells died away a voice began to speak from somewhere high up in the gloomy shadows above their heads. The magicians strained their ears to hear it. Many of them were now in such a state of highly-strung nervousness that they imagined that instructions were being given to them as in a fairy-tale. They

---

[1] The well-known ballad "The Raven King" describes just such an abduction.

Not long, not long my father said
Not long shall you be ours
The Raven King knows all too well
Which are the fairest flowers

The priest was all too worldly
Though he prayed and rang his bell
The Raven King three candles lit
The priest said it was well

Her arms were all too feeble
Though she claimed to love me so
The Raven King stretched out his hand
She sighed and let me go

This land is all too shallow
It is painted on the sky
And trembles like the wind-shook rain
When the Raven King goes by

For always and for always
I pray remember me
Upon the moors, beneath the stars
With the King's wild company

thought that perhaps mysterious prohibitions were being related to them. Such instructions and prohibitions, the magicians knew from the fairy-tales, are usually a little queer, but not very difficult to conform to – or so it seems at first sight. They generally follow the style of: "Do not eat the last candied plum in the blue jar in the corner cupboard," or "Do not beat your wife with a stick made from wormwood." And yet, as all fairy-tales relate, circumstances always conspire against the person who receives the instructions and they find themselves in the middle of doing the very thing that was forbidden to them and a horrible fate is thereby brought upon their heads.

At the very least the magicians supposed that their doom was being slowly recited to them. But it was not at all clear what language the voice was speaking. Once Mr Segundus thought he heard a word that sounded like *"maleficient"* and another time *"interficere"* a Latin word meaning "to kill". The voice itself was not easy to understand; it bore not the slightest resemblance to a human voice – which only served to increase the gentlemen's fear that fairies were about to appear. It was extraordinarily harsh, deep and rasping; it was like two rough stones being scraped together and yet the sounds that were produced were clearly intended to be speech – indeed *were* speech. The gentlemen peered up into the gloom in fearful expectation, but all that could be seen was the small, dim shape of a stone figure that sprang out from one of the shafts of a great pillar and jutted into the gloomy void. As they became accustomed to the queer sound they recognized more and more words; old English words and old Latin words all mixed up together as if the speaker had no conception of these being two distinct languages. Fortunately, this abominable muddle presented few difficulties to the magicians, most of whom were accustomed to unravelling the ramblings and writings of the scholars of long ago. When translated into clear, comprehensible English it was something like this: *Long, long ago,* (said the voice), *five hundred years ago or more, on a winter's day at twilight, a young man entered the Church with a young girl with ivy leaves in her hair. There was no one else there but the stones. No one to see him strangle her but the stones. He let her fall dead upon the stones and no one saw but the stones. He was never punished for his sin because there were no witnesses but the stones. The years went by and whenever the man entered the Church and stood among the congregation the stones cried out that this was the man who had murdered the girl with the ivy leaves wound into her hair, but no one ever heard us. But it is not too late! We know where he is buried! In the corner of the south transept! Quick! Quick! Fetch picks! Fetch shovels! Pull up the paving stones. Dig up his bones! Let them be smashed with the shovel! Dash his skull against the pillars and break it! Let the stones have vengeance too! It is not too late! It is not too late!*

Hardly had the magicians had time to digest this and to wonder some more who it was that spoke, when another stony voice began. This time the voice seemed to issue from the chancel and it spoke only English; yet it was a queer sort of English full of ancient and forgotten words. This voice complained of some soldiers who had entered the Church and broken some windows. A hundred years later they had come again and smashed a rood screen, erased the faces of the saints, carried off plate. Once they had sharpened their arrowheads on the brim of the font; three hundred years later they had fired their pistols in the chapter house. The second voice did not appear to understand that, while a great Church may stand for millennia, men cannot live so long. "They delight in destruction!" it cried. "And they themselves deserve only to be destroyed!" Like the first, this speaker seemed to have stood in the Church for countless years and had, presumably, heard a great many sermons and prayers, yet the sweetest of Christian virtues – mercy, love, meekness – were unknown to him. And all the while the first voice continued to lament the dead girl with ivy leaves in her hair and the two gritty voices clashed together in a manner that was very disagreeable.

Mr Thorpe, who was a valiant gentleman, peeped into the chancel alone, to discover who it was that spoke. "It is a statue," he said.

And then the gentlemen of the York society peered up again into the gloom above their heads in the direction of the first unearthly voice. And this time very few of them had any doubts that it was the little stone figure that spoke, for as they watched they could perceive its stubby stone arms that it waved about in its distress.

Then all the other statues and monuments in the Cathedral began to speak and to say in their stony voices all that they had seen in their stony lives and the noise was, as Mr Segundus later told Mrs Pleasance, beyond description. For York Cathedral had many little carved people and strange animals that flapped their wings.

Many complained of their neighbours and perhaps this is not so surprizing since they had been obliged to stand together for so many hundreds of years. There were fifteen stone kings that stood each upon a stone pedestal in a great stone screen. Their hair was tightly curled as if it had been put into curl papers and never brushed out – and Mrs Honeyfoot could never see them without declaring that she longed to take a hairbrush to each of their royal heads. From the first moment of their being able to speak the kings began quarrelling and scolding each other – for the pedestals were all of a height, and kings – even stone ones – dislike above all things to be made equal to others. There was besides a little group of queer figures with linked arms that looked out with stone eyes from atop an ancient column. As soon as the spell took effect each of these tried to push the others away from him, as if even stone arms begin to ache after a century or so and stone people begin to tire of being shackled to each other.

One statue spoke what seemed to be Italian. No one knew why this should be, though Mr Segundus discovered later that it was a copy of a work by Michael Angel. It seemed to be describing an entirely different church, one where vivid black shadows contrasted sharply with brilliant light. In other words it was describing what the parent-statue in Rome could see.

Mr Segundus was pleased to observe that the magicians, though very frightened, remained within the walls of the Church. Some were so amazed by what they saw that they soon forgot their fear entirely and ran about to discover more and more miracles, making observations, writing down notes with pencils in little memorandum books as if they had forgotten the perfidious document which from today would prevent them studying magic. For a long time the magicians of York (soon, alas, to be magicians no more!) wandered through the aisles and saw marvels. And at every moment their ears were assaulted by the hideous cacophony of a thousand stone voices all speaking together.

In the chapter house there were stone canopies with many little stone heads with strange headgear that all chattered and cackled together. Here were marvellous stone carvings of a hundred English trees: hawthorn, oak, blackthorn, wormwood, cherry and bryony. Mr Segundus found two stone dragons no longer than his forearm, which slipped one after the other, over and under and between stone hawthorn branches, stone hawthorn leaves, stone hawthorn roots and stone hawthorn tendrils. They moved, it seemed, with as much ease as any other creature and yet the sound of so many stone muscles moving together under a stone skin, that scraped stone ribs, that clashed against a heart made of stone – and the sound of stone claws rattling over stone branches – was quite intolerable and Mr Segundus wondered that they could bear it. He observed a little cloud of gritty dust, such as attends the work of a stonecutter, that surrounded them and rose up in the air; and he believed that if the spell allowed them to remain in motion for any length of time they would wear themselves away to a sliver of limestone.

Stone leaves and herbs quivered and shook as if tossed in the breeze and some of them so far emulated their vegetable counterparts as to grow. Later, when the spell had broken, strands of stone ivy and stone rose briars would be discovered wound around chairs and lecterns and prayer-books where no stone ivy or briars had been before.

But it was not only the magicians of the York society who saw wonders that day. Whether he had intended it or not Mr Norrell's magic had spread beyond the Cathedral close and into the city. Three statues from the west front of the Cathedral had been taken to Mr Taylor's workshops to be mended. Centuries of Yorkshire rain had worn down these images and no one knew any longer what great personages they were intended to represent. At half past ten one of Mr Taylor's masons had just raised his chisel to the face of one of these statues intending to fashion it into the likeness of a pretty saintess; at that moment the statue cried out aloud and raised its arm to ward off the chisel, causing the poor workman to fall down in a swoon. The statues were later returned to the exterior of the Cathedral untouched, their faces worn as flat as biscuits and as bland as butter.

Then all at once there seemed a change in the sound and one by one the voices stopped until the magicians heard the bells of St Michael-le-Belfrey ring for the half hour again. The first voice (the voice of the little figure high up in the darkness) continued for some time after the others had fallen silent, upon its old theme of the undiscovered murderer (*It is not too late! It is not too late!*) until it too fell silent.

The world had changed while the magicians had been inside the Church. Magic had returned to England whether the magicians wished it to or not. Other changes of a more prosaic nature had also occurred: the sky had filled with heavy, snow-laden clouds. These were scarcely grey at all, but a queer mixture of slate-blue and sea-green. This curious coloration made a kind of twilight such as one imagines is the usual illumination in fabled kingdoms under the sea.

Mr Segundus felt very tired by his adventure. Other gentlemen had been more frightened than he; he had seen magic and thought it wonderful beyond any thing he had imagined, and yet now that it was over his spirits were greatly agitated and he wished very much to be allowed to go quietly home without speaking to any one. While he was in this susceptible condition he found himself halted and addressed by Mr Norrell's man of business.

"I believe, sir," said Mr Childermass, "that the society must now be broken up. I am sorry for it."

Now it may have been due entirely to Mr Segundus's lowness of spirits, but he suspected that, in spite of Childermass's manner which was very respectful, in some other part of Childermass's person he was laughing at the York magicians. Childermass was one of that uncomfortable class of men whose birth is lowly and who are destined all their lives to serve their betters, but whose clever brains and quick abilities make them wish for recognition and rewards far beyond their reach. Sometimes, by some strange combination of happy circumstances, these men find their own path to greatness, but more often the thought of what might have been turns them sour; they become unwilling servants and perform their tasks no better – or worse – than their less able fellows. They become insolent, lose their places and end badly.

"I beg your pardon, sir," said Childermass, "but I have a question to put to you. I hope you will not think it impertinent, but I would like to know if you ever look into a London paper?"

Mr Segundus replied that he did.

"Indeed? That is most interesting. I myself am fond of a newspaper. But I have little leisure for reading – except such books as come my way in the course of my duties for Mr Norrell. And what sort of thing does one find in a London paper nowadays? – you will excuse my asking, sir, only Mr Norrell, who never looks at a paper of any sort, put the question to me yesterday and I did not think myself qualified to answer it."

"Well," said Mr Segundus, a little puzzled, "there are all sorts of things. What did you wish to know? There are accounts of the actions of His Majesty's Navy against the French; speeches of the Government; reports of scandals and divorces. Is this what you meant?"

"Oh yes!" said Childermass. "You explain it very well, sir. I wonder," he continued, growing thoughtful, "whether provincial news is ever reported in the London papers? — whether (for example) today's remarkable occurrences might merit a paragraph?"

"I do not know," said Mr Segundus. "It seems to me quite possible but then, you know, Yorkshire is so far from London — perhaps the London editors will never get to hear of what has happened."

"Ah," said Mr Childermass; and then was silent.

Snow began to fall; a few flakes at first — then rather more than a few; until a million little flakes were drifting down from a soft, heavy greenish-grey sky. All the buildings of York became a little fainter, a little greyer in the snow; the people all seemed a little smaller; the cries and shouts, the footsteps and hoofsteps, the creaks of carriages and the slammings of doors were all a little more distant. And all these things became somehow less important until all the world contained was the falling snow, the sea-green sky, the dim, grey ghost of York Cathedral — and Childermass.

And all this time Childermass said nothing. Mr Segundus wondered what more he required — all his questions had been answered. But Childermass waited and watched Mr Segundus with his queer black eyes, as if he were waiting for Mr Segundus to say one thing more — as if he fully expected that Mr Segundus would say it — indeed as if nothing in the world were more certain.

"If you wish," said Mr Segundus, shaking the snow from his cape, "I can remove all the uncertainty from the business. I can write a letter to the editor of *The Times* informing him of Mr Norrell's extraordinary feats."

"Ah! That is generous indeed!" said Childermass. "Believe me, sir, I know very well that not every gentleman would be so magnanimous in defeat. But it is no more than I expected. For I told Mr Norrell that I did not think there could be a more obliging gentleman than Mr Segundus."

"Not at all," said Mr Segundus, "it is nothing."

The Learned Society of York Magicians was disbanded and its members were obliged to give up magic (all except Mr Segundus) – and, though some of them were foolish and not all of them were entirely amiable, I do not think that they deserved such a fate. For what is a magician to do who, in accordance with a pernicious agreement, is not allowed to study magic? He idles about his house day after day, disturbs his niece (or wife, or daughter) at her needlework and pesters the servants with questions about matters in which he never took an interest before – all for the sake of having someone to talk to, until the servants complain of him to their mistress. He picks up a book and begins to read, but he is not attending to what he reads and he has got to page 22 before he discovers it is a *novel* – the sort of work which above all others he most despises – and he puts it down in disgust. He asks his niece (or wife, or daughter) ten times a day what o'clock it is, for he cannot believe that time can go so slowly – and he falls out with his pocket watch for the same reason.

Mr Honeyfoot, I am glad to say, fared a little better than the others. He, kind-hearted soul, had been very much affected by the story that the little stone figure high up in the dimness had related. It had carried the knowledge of the horrid murder in its small stone heart for centuries, it remembered the dead girl with the ivy leaves in her hair when no one else did, and Mr Honeyfoot thought that its faithfulness ought to be rewarded. So he wrote to the Dean and to the Canons and to the Archbishop, and he made himself very troublesome until these important personages agreed to allow Mr Honeyfoot to dig up the paving stones of the south transept. And when this was done Mr Honeyfoot and the men he had employed uncovered some bones in a leaden coffin, just as the little stone figure had said they would. But then the Dean said that he could not authorize the removal of the bones from the Cathedral (which was what Mr Honeyfoot wanted) on the evidence of the little stone figure; there was no precedent for such a thing. Ah! said Mr Honeyfoot but there was, you know; and the argument raged for a number of years and, as a consequence, Mr Honeyfoot really had no leisure to repent signing Mr Norrell's document.[2]

The library of the Learned Society of York Magicians was sold to Mr Thoroughgood of Coffee-yard. But somehow no one thought to mention this to Mr Segundus and he only learnt about it in a round-about fashion when Mr Thoroughgood's shopboy told a friend (that was a clerk in Priestley's linen-drapers) and the friend chanced to mention it to Mrs Cockcroft of the George Inn and she told Mrs Pleasance who was Mr Segundus's landlady. As soon as Mr Segundus heard of it he ran down through the snowy streets to Mr Thoroughgood's shop without troubling to put on his hat or his coat or his boots. But the books were already gone. He inquired of Mr Thoroughgood who had bought them. Mr Thoroughgood begged Mr Segundus's pardon but he feared he could not divulge the name of the gentleman; he did not think the

---

[2] The example cited by Mr Honeyfoot was of a murder that had taken place in 1279 in the grim moor town of Alston. The body of a young boy was found in the churchyard hanging from a thorn-tree that stood before the church-door. Above the door was a statue of the Virgin and Child. So the people of Alston sent to Newcastle, to the Castle of the Raven King and the Raven King sent two magicians to make the Virgin and the Jesus-Child speak and say how they had seen a stranger kill the boy, but for what reason they did not know. And after that, whenever a stranger came to the town, the people of Alston would drag him before the church-door and ask "Is this him?" but always the Virgin and Child replied that it was not. Beneath the Virgin's feet were a lion and a dragon who curled around each other in a most puzzling manner and bit each other's necks. These creatures had been carved by someone who had never seen a lion or a dragon, but who had seen a great many dogs and sheep and something of the character of a dog and a sheep had got into his carving. Whenever some poor fellow was brought before the Virgin and Child to be examined the lion and the dragon would cease biting each other and look up like the Virgin's strange watchdogs and the lion would bark and the dragon would bleat angrily.

Years went by and the townspeople who remembered the boy were all dead, and the likelihood was that the murderer was too. But the Virgin and Child had somehow got into the habit of speaking and whenever some unfortunate stranger passed within the compass of their gaze they would still turn their stone heads and say, "It is not him." And Alston acquired the reputation of an eerie place and people would not go there if they could help it.

gentleman wished his name to be generally known. Mr Segundus, hatless and coatless and breathless, with water-logged shoes and mud-splashes on his stockings and the eyes of everybody in the shop upon him, had some satisfaction in telling Mr Thoroughgood that it did not signify whether Mr Thoroughgood told him or not, for he believed he knew the gentleman anyway.

Mr Segundus did not lack curiosity about Mr Norrell. He thought about him a great deal and often talked of him with Mr Honeyfoot.[3] Mr Honeyfoot was certain that everything that had happened could be explained by an earnest wish on Mr Norrell's part to bring back magic to England. Mr Segundus was more doubtful and began to look about him to try if he could discover any acquaintance of Norrell's that might be able to tell him something more.

A gentleman in Mr Norrell's position with a fine house and a large estate will always be of interest to his neighbours and, unless those neighbours are very stupid, they will always contrive to know a little of what he does. Mr Segundus discovered a family in Stonegate who were cousins to some people that had a farm five miles from Hurtfew Abbey – and he befriended the Stonegate-family and persuaded them to hold a dinner-party and to invite their cousins to come to it. (Mr Segundus grew quite shocked at his own skill in thinking up these little stratagems.) The cousins duly arrived and were all most ready to talk about their rich and peculiar neighbour who had bewitched York Cathedral, but the

---

[3] To aid his better understanding of Mr Norrell's character and of Mr Norrell's magical powers Mr Segundus wrote a careful description of the visit to Hurtfew Abbey. Unfortunately he found his memory on this point peculiarly unclear. Whenever he returned to read what he had written he discovered that he now remembered things differently. Each time he began by crossing out words and phrases and putting in new ones, and he ended by re-writing completely. After four or five months he was obliged to admit to himself that he no longer knew what Mr Honeyfoot had said to Mr Norrell, or what Mr Norrell had said in reply, or what he – Mr Segundus – had seen in the house. He concluded that to attempt to write any thing upon the subject was futile, and he threw what he had written into the fire.

beginning and the end of their information was that Mr Norrell was about to leave Yorkshire and go to London.

Mr Segundus was surprized to hear this, but more than that he was surprized at the effect this news had upon his own spirits. He felt oddly discomfited by it – which was very ridiculous, he told himself; Norrell had never shewn any interest in him or done him the least kindness. Yet Norrell was Mr Segundus's only colleague now. When he was gone Mr Segundus would be the only magician, the last magician in Yorkshire.

4

The Friends of English Magic

Early spring 1807

CONSIDER, IF YOU WILL, a man who sits in his library day after day; a small man of no particular personal attractions. His book is on the table before him. A fresh supply of pens, a knife to cut new nibs, ink, paper, notebooks – all is conveniently to hand. There is always a fire in the room – he cannot do without a fire, he feels the cold. The room changes with the season: he does not. Three tall windows open on a view of English countryside which is tranquil in spring, cheerful in summer, melancholy in autumn and gloomy in winter – just as English landscape should be. But the changing seasons excite no interest in him – he scarcely raises his eyes from the pages of his book. He takes his exercise as all gentlemen do; in dry weather his long walk crosses the park and skirts a little wood; in wet weather there is his short walk in the shrubbery. But he knows very little of shrubbery or park or wood. There is a book waiting for him upon the library table; his eyes fancy they still follow its lines of type, his head still runs upon its argument, his fingers itch to take it up again. He meets his neighbours twice or thrice a quarter – for this is England where a man's neighbours will never suffer him to live entirely bereft of society, let him be as dry and sour-faced as he may. They pay him visits, leave their cards with his servants, invite him to dine or to dance at assembly-balls. Their intentions are largely charitable – they have a notion that it is bad for a man to be always alone – but they also have some curiosity to discover whether he has changed at all since they last saw him. He has not. He has nothing to say to them and is considered the dullest man in Yorkshire.

Yet within Mr Norrell's dry little heart there was as lively an ambition to bring back magic to England as would have satisfied even Mr Honeyfoot, and it was with the intention of bringing that ambition to a long-postponed fulfilment that Mr Norrell now proposed to go to London.

Childermass assured him that the time was propitious and Childermass knew the world. Childermass knew what games the children on street-corners are playing – games that all other grown-ups have long since forgotten. Childermass knew what old people by firesides are thinking of, though no one has asked them in years. Childermass knew what young men hear in the rattling of the drums and the tooting of the pipes that makes them leave their homes and go to be soldiers – and he knew the half-eggcupful of glory and the barrelful of misery that await them. Childermass could look at a smart attorney in the street and tell you what he had in his coat-tail pockets. And all that Childermass knew made him smile; and some of what he knew made him laugh out loud; and none of what he knew wrung from him so much as ha'pennyworth of pity.

So when Childermass told his master, "Go to London. Go now," Mr Norrell believed him.

"The only thing I do not quite like," said Mr Norrell, "is your plan to have Segundus write to one of the London newspapers upon our behalf. He is certain to make errors in what he writes – have you thought of that? I dare say he will try his hand at interpretation. These third-rate scholars can never resist putting in something of themselves. He will make guesses – wrong guesses – at the sorts of magic I employed at York. Surely there is enough confusion surrounding magic without our adding to it. Must we make use of Segundus?"

Childermass bent his dark gaze upon his master and his even darker smile, and replied that he believed they must. "I wonder, sir," he said, "if you have lately heard of a naval gentleman of the name of Baines?"

"I believe I know the man you mean," said Mr Norrell.

"Ah!" said Childermass. "And how did you come to hear of him?"

A short silence.

"Well then," said Mr Norrell reluctantly, "I suppose that I have seen Captain Baines's name in one of the newspapers."

"Lieutenant Hector Baines served on *The King of the North*, a frigate," said Childermass. "At twenty-one years of age he lost a leg and two or three fingers in an action in the West Indies. In the same battle the Captain of *The King of the North* and many of the seamen died. Reports that Lieutenant Baines continued to command the ship and issue orders to his crew while the ship's doctor was actually sawing at his leg are, I dare say, a good deal exaggerated, but he certainly brought a fearfully damaged ship out of the Indies, attacked a Spanish ship full of bounty, gained a fortune and came home a hero. He jilted the young lady to whom he was engaged and married another. This, sir, is the Captain's history as it appeared in *The Morning Post*. And now I shall tell you what followed. Baines is a northerner like you, sir, a man of obscure birth with no great friends to make life easy for him. Shortly after his marriage he and his bride went to London to stay at the house of some friends in Seacoal-lane, and while they were there they were visited by people of all ranks and stations. They ate their dinner at viscountesses' tables, were toasted by Members of Parliament, and all that influence and patronage can do for Captain Baines was promised to him. This success, sir, I attribute to the general approbation and esteem which the report in the newspaper gained for him. But perhaps you have friends in London who will perform the same services for you without troubling the editors of the newspapers?"

"You know very well that I do not," said Mr Norrell impatiently.

In the meantime, Mr Segundus laboured very long over his letter and it grieved him that he could not be more warm in his praise of Mr Norrell. It seemed to him that the readers of the London newspaper would expect him to say something of Mr Norrell's personal virtues and would wonder why he did not.

In due course the letter appeared in *The Times* entitled: "EX-TRAORDINARY OCCURRENCES IN YORK: AN APPEAL TO THE FRIENDS OF ENGLISH MAGIC." Mr Segundus ended his description of the magic at York by saying that the Friends of English Magic must surely bless that love of extreme retirement which marked Mr Norrell's character – for it had fostered his studies and had at last borne fruit in the shape of the wonderful magic at York Cathedral – but, said Mr Segundus, he appealed to the Friends of English Magic to join him in begging Mr Norrell not to return to a life of solitary study but to take his place upon the wider stage of the Nation's affairs and so begin a new chapter in the History of English Magic.

AN APPEAL TO THE FRIENDS OF ENGLISH MAGIC had a most sensational effect, particularly in London. The readers of *The Times* were quite thunderstruck by Mr Norrell's achievements. There was a general desire to see Mr Norrell; young ladies pitied the poor old gentlemen of York who had been so frightened by him, and wished very much to be as terrified themselves. Clearly such an opportunity as this was scarcely likely to come again; Mr Norrell determined to establish himself in London with all possible haste. "You must get me a house, Childermass," he said. "Get me a house that says to those that visit it that magic is a respectable profession – no less than Law and a great deal more so than Medicine."

Childermass inquired drily if Mr Norrell wished him to seek out architecture expressive of the proposition that magic was as respectable as the Church?

Mr Norrell (who knew there were such things as jokes in the world or people would not write about them in books, but who had never actually been introduced to a joke or shaken its hand) considered a while before replying at last that no, he did not think they could quite claim that.

So Childermass (perhaps thinking that nothing in the world is so respectable as money) directed his master to a house in Hanover-square among the abodes of the rich and prosperous. Now I do not know what may be your opinion yet to say the truth I do not much care for the south side of Hanover-square; the houses are so tall and thin – four storeys at least – and all the tall, gloomy windows are so regular, and every house so exactly resembles its neighbours that they have something of the appearance of a high wall blocking out the light. Be that as it may, Mr Norrell (a less fanciful person than I) was satisfied with his new house, or at least as satisfied as any gentleman could be who for more than thirty years has lived in a large country-house surrounded by a park of mature timber, which is in its turn surrounded by a good estate of farms and woods – a gentleman, in other words, whose eye has never been offended by the sight of any other man's property whenever he looked out of the window.

"It is certainly a small house, Childermass," he said, "but I do not complain. My own comfort, as you know, I do not regard."

Childermass replied that the house was larger than most.

"Indeed?" said Mr Norrell, much surprized. Mr Norrell was particularly shocked by the smallness of the library, which could not be made to accommodate one third of the books he considered indispensable; he asked Childermass how people in London housed their books? Perhaps they did not read?

Mr Norrell had been in London not above three weeks when he received a letter from a Mrs Godesdone, a lady of whom he had never heard before.

". . . I know it is very *shoking* that I should write to you upon no acquaintance whatsoever & no doubt you say to yourself who is

52

this impertinent creachure? I did not now there was such a person in existence! and consider me shokingly bold etc. etc. but Drawlight is a dear freind of mine and assures me that you are the sweetest-natured creachure in the world and will not mind it. I am most impatient for the pleasure of your acquaintance and would consider it the greatest honour in the world if you would consent to give us the pleasure of your company at an evening-party on Thursday se'night. Do not let the apprehension of meeting with a croud prevent you from coming – I detest a croud of all things and only my most intimate freinds will be invited to meet you . . ."

It was not the sort of letter to make any very favourable impression upon Mr Norrell. He read it through very rapidly, put it aside with an exclamation of disgust and took up his book again. A short while later Childermass arrived to attend to the morning's business. He read Mrs Godesdone's letter and inquired what answer Mr Norrell intended to return to it?

"A refusal," said Mr Norrell.

"Indeed? And shall I say that you have a prior engagement?" asked Childermass.

"Certainly, if you wish," said Mr Norrell.

"And *do* you have a prior engagement?" asked Childermass.

"No," said Mr Norrell.

"Ah!" said Childermass. "Then perhaps it is the overabundance of your engagements on other days that makes you refuse this one? You fear to be too tired?"

"I have no engagements. You know very well that I do not." Mr Norrell read for another minute or two before remarking (apparently to his book), "You are still here."

"I am," said Childermass.

"Well then," said Mr Norrell, "what is it? What is the matter?"

"I had thought you were come to London to shew people what a modern magician looked like. It will be a slow business if you are to stay at home all the time."

Mr Norrell said nothing. He picked up the letter and looked at it. "Drawlight," he said at last. "What does she mean by that? I know no one of that name."

"I do not know what she means," said Childermass, "but I do know this: at present it will not do to be too nice."

At eight o'clock on the evening of Mrs Godesdone's party Mr Norrell in his best grey coat was seated in his carriage, wondering about Mrs Godesdone's dear friend, Drawlight, when he was roused to a realization that the carriage was no longer moving. Looking out of the window he saw a great lamp-lit chaos of people, carriages and horses. Thinking that everyone else must find the London streets as confusing as he did, he naturally fell into the supposition that his coachman and footman had lost their way and, banging on the roof of the carriage with his stick, he cried, "Davey! Lucas! Did not you hear me say Manchester-street? Why did you not make sure of the way before we set off?"

Lucas, on the box-seat, called down that they were already in Manchester-street, but must wait their turn – there was a long line of carriages that were to stop at the house before them.

"Which house?" cried Mr Norrell.

The house they were going to, said Lucas.

"No, no! You are mistaken," said Mr Norrell. "It is to be a small gathering."

But on his arrival at Mrs Godesdone's house Mr Norrell found himself instantly plunged into the midst of a hundred or so of Mrs Godesdone's most intimate friends. The hall and reception rooms were crowded with people and more were arriving at every moment. Mr Norrell was very much astonished, yet what in the world was there to be surprized at? It was a fashionable London party, no different from any other that might be held at any of half a dozen houses across Town every day of the week.

And how to describe a London party? Candles in lustres of cut-glass are placed everywhere about the house in dazzling profusion; elegant mirrors triple and quadruple the light until night outshines day; many-coloured hot-house fruits are piled up in stately pyramids upon white-clothed tables; divine creatures, resplendent with jewels, go about the room in pairs, arm in arm, admired by all who see them. Yet the heat is over-powering, the pressure and noise almost as bad; there is nowhere to sit and scarce anywhere to stand. You may see your dearest friend in another part of the room; you may have a world of things to tell him – but how in the world will you ever reach him? If you are fortunate then perhaps you will discover him later in the crush and shake his hand as you are both hurried past each other. Surrounded by cross, hot strangers, your chance of rational conversation is equal to what it would be in an African desert. Your only wish is to preserve your favourite gown from the worst ravages of the crowd. Every body complains of the heat and the suffocation. Every body declares it to be entirely insufferable. But if it is all misery for the guests, then what of the wretchedness of those who have not been invited? Our sufferings are nothing to theirs! And we may tell each other tomorrow that it was a delightful party.

It so happened that Mr Norrell arrived at the same moment as a very old lady. Though small and disagreeable-looking she was clearly someone of importance (she was all over diamonds). The servants clustered round her and Mr Norrell proceeded into the house, unobserved by any of them. He entered a room full of people where he discovered a cup of punch upon a little table. While he was drinking the punch it occurred to him that he had told no one his name and consequently no one knew he was here. He found himself in some perplexity as to how to proceed. His fellow-guests were occupied in greeting their friends, and as for approaching one of the servants and announcing himself, Mr Norrell felt quite unequal to the task; their proud faces and air of indescribable superiority unnerved him. It was a great pity that one or two of the late members of the Society of York Magicians were not there to see him looking so all forlorn and ill at ease; it might have cheered them up immeasurably. But it is the same with all of us. In familiar surroundings our manners are cheerful and easy, but only transport us to places where we know no one and no one knows us, and Lord! how uncomfortable we become!

Mr Norrell was wandering from room to room, wishing only to go away again, when he was stopped in mid-perambulation by the sound of his own name and the following enigmatic words: ". . . assures me that he is never to be seen without a mystic robe of midnight blue, adorned with otherlandish symbols! But Drawlight – who knows this Norrell very well – says that . . ."

The noise of the room was such that it is to be marvelled at that Mr Norrell heard anything at all. The words had been spoken by a young woman and Mr Norrell looked frantically about him to try and discover her, but without success. He began to wonder what else was being said about him.

He found himself standing near to a lady and a gentleman. *She* was unremarkable enough – a sensible-looking woman of forty or fifty – *he*, however, was a style of man not commonly seen in Yorkshire. He was rather small and was dressed very carefully in a good black coat and linen of a most exquisite whiteness. He had a little pair of silver spectacles that swung from a black velvet ribbon around his neck. His features were very regular and rather good; he had short, dark hair and his skin was very clean and white – except that about his cheeks there was the faintest suggestion of rouge. But it was his eyes that were remarkable: large, well-shaped, dark and so very brilliant as to have an almost liquid appearance. They were fringed with the longest, darkest eyelashes. There were many little feminine touches about him that he had contrived for himself, but his eyes and eyelashes were the only ones which nature had given him.

Mr Norrell paid good attention to their conversation to discover if they were talking about him.

". . . the advice that I gave Lady Duncombe about her own daughter," said the small man. "Lady Duncombe had found a most unexceptional husband for her daughter, a gentleman with nine hundred a year! But the silly girl had set her heart upon a penniless Captain in the Dragoons, and poor Lady Duncombe was almost frantic. 'Oh, your ladyship!' I cried the instant that I heard about it, 'Make yourself easy! Leave everything to me. I do not set up as any very extraordinary genius, as your ladyship knows, but my odd talents are exactly suited to this sort of thing.' Oh, madam! you will laugh when you hear how I contrived matters! I dare say no one else in the world would have thought of such a ridiculous scheme! I took Miss Susan to Gray's in Bond-street where we both spent a very agreeable morning in trying on necklaces and earrings. She has passed most of her life in Derbyshire and has not been accustomed to really *remarkable* jewels. I do not think she had ever thought *seriously* upon such things before. Then Lady Duncombe and I dropt one or two hints that in marrying Captain Hurst she would put it quite out of her power to make such delightful purchases ever again, whereas if she married Mr Watts she might make her choice of the best of them. I next took pains to get acquainted with Captain Hurst and persuaded him to accompany me to Boodle's where – well I will not deceive you, madam – where there is gambling!" The small man giggled. "I lent him a little money to try his luck – it was not my own money you understand. Lady Duncombe had given it to me for the purpose. We went three or four times and in a remarkably short space of time the Captain's debts were – well, madam, *I* cannot see how he will ever get clear of them! Lady Duncombe and I represented to him that it is one thing to expect a young woman to marry upon a small income, but quite another to expect her to take a man encumbered with debts. He was not inclined to listen to us at first. At first he made use of – what shall I say? – some rather *military* expressions. But in the end he was obliged to admit the justice of all we said."

Mr Norrell saw the sensible-looking woman of forty or fifty give the small man a look of some dislike. Then she bowed, very slightly and coldly, and passed without a word away into the crowd; the small man turned in the other direction and immediately hailed a friend.

Mr Norrell's eye was next caught by an excessively pretty young woman in a white-and-silver gown. A tall, handsome-looking man was talking to her and she was laughing very heartily at everything he said.

". . . and what if he should discover two dragons – one red and one white – beneath the foundations of the house, locked in eternal struggle and symbolizing the future destruction of Mr Godesdone? I dare say," said the man slyly, "you would not mind it if he did."

She laughed again, even more merrily than before, and Mr Norrell was surprized to hear in the next instant someone address her as "Mrs Godesdone".

Upon reflection Mr Norrell thought that he ought to have spoken to her but by then she was nowhere to be seen. He was sick of the noise and sight of so many people and determined to go quietly away, but it so happened that just at that moment the crowds about the door were particularly impenetrable; he was caught up in the current of people and carried away to quite another part of the room. Round and round he went like a dry leaf caught up in a drain; in one of these turns around the room he discovered a quiet corner near a window. A tall screen of carved ebony inlaid with mother-of-pearl half-hid – ah! what bliss was this! – a bookcase. Mr Norrell slipped behind the screen, took down John Napier's *A Plaine Discouerie of the Whole Revelation of St John* and began to read.

He had not been there very long when, happening to glance up, he saw the tall, handsome man who had been speaking to Mrs Godesdone and the small, dark man who had gone to such trouble to destroy the matrimonial hopes of Captain Hurst. They were discoursing energetically, but the press and flow of people around them was so great that, without any ceremony, the tall man got hold of the small man's sleeve and pulled him behind the screen and into the corner which Mr Norrell occupied.

"He is not here," said the tall man, giving each word an emphasis with a poke of his finger in the other's shoulder. "Where are the fiercely burning eyes that you promised us? Where the trances that none of us can explain? Has any one been cursed? – I do not think so. You have called him up like a spirit from the vasty deep, and he has not come."

"I was with him only this morning," said the small man defiantly, "to hear of the wonderful magic that he has been doing recently and he said then that he would come."

"It is past midnight. He will not come now." The tall man smiled a very superior smile. "Confess, you do not know him."

Then the small man smiled in rivalry of the other's smile (these two gentlemen positively jousted in smiles) and said, "No one in London knows him better. I shall confess that I am a little – a very little – disappointed."

"Ha!" cried the tall man. "It is the opinion of the room that we have all been most abominably imposed upon. We came here in the expectation of seeing something very extraordinary, and instead we have been obliged to provide our own amusement." His eye happening to light upon Mr Norrell, he said, "*That* gentleman is reading a book."

The small man glanced behind him and in doing so happened to knock his elbow against *A Plaine Discouverie of the Whole Revelation of St John*. He gave Mr Norrell a cool look for filling up so very small a space with so very large a book.

"I have said that I am disappointed," continued the small man, "but I am not at all surprized. You do not know him as I do. Oh! I can assure you he has a pretty shrewd notion of his value. No one can have a better. A man who buys a house in Hanover-square knows the style in which things ought to be done. Oh, yes! He has bought a house in Hanover-square! You had not heard that, I dare say? He is as rich as a Jew. He had an old uncle called Haythornthwaite who died and left him a world of money. He has – among other trifles – a good house and a large estate – that of Hurtfew Abbey in Yorkshire."

"Ha!" said the tall man drily. "He was in high luck. Rich old uncles who die are in shockingly short supply."

"Oh, indeed!" cried the small man. "Some friends of mine, the Griffins, have an amazingly rich old uncle to whom they have paid all sorts of attentions for years and years – but though he was at least a hundred years old when they began, he is not dead yet and it seems he intends to live for ever to spite them, and all the Griffins are growing old themselves and dying one by one in a state of the most bitter disappointment. Yet I am sure that *you*, my dear Lascelles, need not concern yourself with any such vexatious old persons – your fortune is comfortable enough, is it not?"

The tall man chose to disregard this particular piece of impertinence and instead remarked coolly, "I believe that gentleman wishes to speak to you."

The gentleman in question was Mr Norrell who, quite amazed to hear his fortune and property discussed so openly, had been waiting to speak for some minutes past. "I beg your pardon," he said.

"Yes?" said the small man sharply.

"I am Mr Norrell."

The tall man and the small man gave Mr Norrell two very broad stares.

After a silence of some moments the small gentleman, who had begun by looking offended, had passed through a stage of looking blank and was beginning to look puzzled, asked Mr Norrell to repeat his name.

This Mr Norrell did, whereupon the small gentleman said, "I do beg your pardon, but . . . Which is to say . . . I hope you will excuse my asking so impertinent a question, but is there at your house in Hanover-square someone all dressed in black, with a thin face like a twisted hedge-root?"

Mr Norrell thought for a moment and then he said, "Childermass. You mean Childermass."

"Oh, Childermass!" cried the small man, as if all was now perfectly plain. "Yes, of course! How stupid of me! That is Childermass! Oh, Mr Norrell! I can hardly begin to express my delight in making your acquaintance. My name, sir, is Drawlight."

"Do you know Childermass?" asked Mr Norrell, puzzled.

"I . . ." Mr Drawlight paused. "I have seen such a person as I described coming out of your house and I . . . Oh, Mr Norrell! Such a noodle I am upon occasion! I mistook him for you! Pray do not be offended, sir! For now that I behold you, I plainly see that whereas *he* has the wild, romantic looks one associates with magicians, *you* have the meditative air of a scholar. Lascelles, does not Mr Norrell have the grave and sober bearing of a scholar?"

The tall man said, without much enthusiasm, that he supposed so.

"Mr Norrell, my friend, Mr Lascelles," said Drawlight.

Mr Lascelles made the slightest of bows.

"Oh, Mr Norrell!" cried Mr Drawlight. "You cannot imagine the torments I have suffered tonight, in wondering whether or not you would come! At seven o'clock my anxieties upon this point were so acute that I could not help myself! I actually went down to the Glasshouse-street boiling-cellar expressly to inquire of Davey and Lucas to know their opinions! Davey was certain that you would not come, which threw me, as you may imagine, into the utmost despair!"

"Davey and Lucas!" said Mr Norrell in tones of the greatest astonishment. (These, it may be remembered, were the names of Mr Norrell's coachman and footman.)

"Oh, yes!" said Mr Drawlight. "The Glasshouse-street boiling-cellar is where Davey and Lucas occasionally take their mutton, as I dare say you know." Mr Drawlight paused in his flow of chatter, just long enough for Mr Norrell to murmur that he had not known that.

"I have been most industriously talking up your extraordinary powers to all my wide acquaintance," continued Mr Drawlight. "I have been your John the Baptist, sir, preparing the way for you! – and I felt no hesitation in declaring that you and I were great friends for I had a presentiment from the first, my dear Mr Norrell, that we would be; and as you see I was quite right, for now here we are, chatting so comfortably to one another!"

5

Drawlight

Spring to autumn 1807

E ARLY NEXT MORNING Mr Norrell's man of business, Childermass, answered a summons to attend his master in the breakfast-room. He found Mr Norrell pale-faced and in a state of some nervous agitation.

"What is the matter?" asked Childermass.

"Oh!" cried Mr Norrell, looking up. "You dare to ask me that! You, who have so neglected your duties that any scoundrel may put a watch upon my house and question my servants without fear of disturbance! Aye, and get answers to those questions, too! What do I employ you for, I should like to know, if not to protect me from such impertinence as this?"

Childermass shrugged. "You mean Drawlight, I suppose."

A short, astonished silence.

"You knew of it?" cried Mr Norrell. "Good God, man! What were you thinking of? Have you not told me a hundred times that, in order to secure my privacy, the servants must be kept from gossiping?"

"Oh! certainly!" said Childermass. "But I am very much afraid, sir, that you must give up some of your habits of privacy. Retirement and seclusion are all very well in Yorkshire, but we are not in Yorkshire any more."

"Yes, yes!" said Mr Norrell irritably. "I know that we are not.

But that is not the question. The question is: what does this Drawlight want?"

"To have the distinction of being the first gentleman in London to make the acquaintance of a magician. That is all."

But Mr Norrell was not to be reasoned out of his fears. He rubbed his yellow-white hands nervously together, and directed fearful glances into the shadowy corners of the room as though suspecting them of harbouring other Drawlights, all spying upon him. "He did not look like a scholar in those clothes," he said, "but that is no guarantee of any thing. He wore no rings of power or allegiance but still . . ."

"I do not well understand you," said Childermass. "Speak plainly."

"Might he not have some *skill* of his own, do you suppose?" said Mr Norrell. "Or perhaps he has friends who are jealous of my success! Who are his associates? What is his education?"

Childermass smiled a long smile that went all up one side of his face. "Oh! You have talked yourself into a belief that he is the agent of some other magician. Well, sir, he is not. You may depend upon me for that. Far from neglecting your interests, after we received Mrs Godesdone's letter I made some inquiries about the gentleman – as many, I dare say, as he has made about you. It would be an odd sort of magician, I think, that employed such a creature as he is. Besides, if such a magician had existed you would have long since found him out, would not you? – and discovered the means to part him from his books and put an end to his scholarship? You have done it before, you know."

"You know no harm of this Drawlight then?"

Childermass raised an eyebrow and smiled his sideways smile. "Upon the contrary," he said.

"Ah!" cried Mr Norrell, "I knew it! Well then, I shall certainly make a point of avoiding his society."

"Why?" asked Childermass. "I did not say so. Have I not just told you that he is no threat to you? What is it to you that he is a bad man? Take my advice, sir, make use of the tool which is to hand."

Then Childermass related to Mr Norrell what he had discovered about Drawlight: how he belonged to a certain breed of gentlemen, only to be met with in London, whose main occupation is the wearing of expensive and fashionable clothes; how they pass their lives in ostentatious idleness, gambling and drinking to excess and spending months at a time in Brighton and other fashionable watering places; how in recent years this breed seemed to have reached a sort of perfection in Christopher Drawlight. Even his dearest friends would have admitted that he possessed not a single good quality.[1]

Despite Mr Norrell's tuttings and suckings-in of air at every new revelation, there is no doubt that this conversation did him good. When Lucas entered the room ten minutes later with a pot of chocolate, he was composedly eating toast and preserves and appeared entirely different from the anxious, fretful creature he had been earlier that morning.

A loud rap was heard at the door and Lucas went to answer it. A light tread was next heard upon the stairs and Lucas re-appeared to announce, "Mr Drawlight!"

"Ah, Mr Norrell! How do you do, sir?" Mr Drawlight entered the room. He wore a dark blue coat, and carried an ebony stick with a silver knob. He appeared to be in excellent spirits, and bowed and smiled and walked to and fro so much that five minutes later there was scarcely an inch of carpet in the room that he had not stood upon, a table or chair he had not lightly and caressingly

---

[1] He had once found himself in a room with Lady Bessborough's long-haired white cat. He happened to be dressed in an immaculate black coat and trousers, and was therefore thoroughly alarmed by the cat's stalking round and round and making motions as if it proposed to sit upon him. He waited until he believed himself to be unobserved, then he picked it up, opened a window and tossed it out. Despite falling three storeys to the ground, the cat survived, but one of its legs was never quite right afterwards and it always evinced the greatest dislike to gentlemen in black clothes.

touched, a mirror he had not danced across, a painting that he had not for a moment smiled upon.

Mr Norrell, though confident now that his guest was no great magician or great magician's servant, was still not much inclined to take Childermass's advice. His invitation to Mr Drawlight to sit down at the breakfast-table and take some chocolate was of the coldest sort. But sulky silences and black looks had no effect upon Mr Drawlight whatsoever, since he filled up the silences with his own chatter and was too accustomed to black looks to mind them.

"Do you not agree with me, sir, that the party last night was the most charming in the world? Though, if I may say so, I think you were quite right to leave when you did. I was able to go round afterwards and tell everyone that the gentleman that they had just espied walking out of the room was indeed Mr Norrell! Oh! believe me, sir, your departure was not unobserved. The Honourable Mr Masham was quite certain he had just caught sight of your esteemed shoulder, Lady Barclay thought she had seen a neat grey curl of your venerable wig, and Miss Fiskerton was quite ecstatic to think that her gaze had rested momentarily upon the tip of your scholarly nose! And the little that they have seen of you, sir, has made them desire more. They long to view the complete man!"

"Ah!" said Mr Norrell, with some satisfaction.

Mr Drawlight's repeated assurances that the ladies and gentle-men at Mrs Godesdone's party had been utterly enchanted by Mr Norrell went some way to diminish Mr Norrell's prejudices against his guest. According to Mr Drawlight, Mr Norrell's company was like seasoning: the smallest pinch of it could add a relish to the entire dish. Mr Drawlight made himself so agreeable that Mr Norrell grew by degrees more communicative.

"And to what fortunate circumstance, sir," asked Mr Draw-light, "do we owe the happiness of your society? What brings you to London?"

"I have come to London in order to further the cause of modern magic. I intend, sir, to bring back magic to Britain," answered Mr Norrell gravely. "I have a great deal to communicate to the Great Men of our Age. There are many ways in which I may be of service to them."

Mr Drawlight murmured politely that he was sure of it.

"I may tell you, sir," said Mr Norrell, "that I heartily wish this duty had fallen to the lot of some other magician." Mr Norrell sighed and looked as noble as his small, pinched features would allow. It is an extraordinary thing that a man such as Mr Norrell – a man who had destroyed the careers of so many of his fellow-magicians – should be able to convince himself that he would rather all the glory of his profession belonged to one of them, but there is no doubt that Mr Norrell believed it when he said it.

Mr Drawlight murmured sympathetically. Mr Drawlight was sure that Mr Norrell was too modest. Mr Drawlight could not suppose for a moment that anyone could be better suited to the task of bringing back magic to Britain than Mr Norrell.

"But I labour under a disadvantage, sir," said Mr Norrell.

Mr Drawlight was surprized to hear it.

"I do not know the world, sir. I know that I do not. I have a scholar's love of silence and solitude. To sit and pass hour after hour in idle chatter with a roomful of strangers is to me the worst sort of torment – but I dare say there will be a good deal of that sort of thing. Childermass assures me that there will be." Mr Norrell looked wistfully at Drawlight as if hopeful that Drawlight might contradict him.

"Ah!" Mr Drawlight considered a moment. "And that is exactly why I am so happy that you and I have become friends! I do not pretend to be a scholar, sir; I know next to nothing of magicians or magical history, and I dare say that, from time to time, you may find my society irksome, but you must set any little irritations of that nature against the great good that I may do you in taking you about and shewing you to people. Oh, Mr Norrell, sir! You cannot imagine how useful I may be to you!"

Mr Norrell declined to give his word there and then to accompany Mr Drawlight to all the places that Mr Drawlight said were so delightful and to meet all those people whose friendship, Mr Drawlight said, would add a new sweetness to Mr Norrell's existence, but he did consent to go with Mr Drawlight that evening to a dinner at Lady Rawtenstall's house in Bedford-square.

Mr Norrell got through the dinner with less fatigue than he expected, and so agreed to meet Mr Drawlight upon the morrow at Mr Plumtree's house. With Mr Drawlight as his guide, Mr Norrell entered society with greater confidence than before. His engagements became numerous; he was busy from eleven o'clock in the morning to past midnight. He paid morning-visits; he ate his dinner in dining-parlours all over the Town; he attended evening-parties, balls and concerts of Italian music; he met baronets, viscounts, viscountesses, and honourable thises and thats; he was to be met with walking down Bond-street, arm-in-arm with Mr Drawlight; he was observed taking the air in a carriage in Hyde-park with Mr Drawlight and Mr Drawlight's dear friend, Mr Lascelles.

On days when Mr Norrell did not dine abroad Mr Drawlight took his mutton at Mr Norrell's house in Hanover-square – which Mr Norrell imagined Mr Drawlight must be very glad to do, for Childermass had told him that Mr Drawlight had scarcely any money. Childermass said that Drawlight lived upon his wits and his debts; none of his great friends had ever been invited to visit him at home, because home was a lodging above a shoemaker's in Little Ryder-street.

Like every new house, the house in Hanover-square – which had seemed perfection at first – was soon discovered to be in need of every sort of improvement. Naturally, Mr Norrell was impatient to have it all accomplished as soon as possible, but when he appealed to Drawlight to agree with him that the London workmen were extraordinarily slow, Drawlight took the opportunity to ascertain all Mr Norrell's plans for colours, wallpapers, carpets, furniture and ornaments, and to find fault with all of them. They argued the point for a quarter of an hour and then Mr Drawlight ordered Mr Norrell's carriage to be got ready and directed Davey to take him and Mr Norrell straight to Mr Ackermann's shop in the Strand. There Mr Drawlight shewed Mr Norrell a book which contained a picture by Mr Repton of an empty, old-fashioned parlour, where a stony-faced old person from the time of Queen Elizabeth stared out of a painting on the wall and the empty chairs all gaped at each other like guests at a party who discover they have nothing to say to one another. But on the next page, ah! what changes had been wrought by the noble arts of joinery, paper-hanging and upholstery! Here was a picture of the same parlour, new-furnished and improved beyond all recognition! A dozen or so fashionably-dressed ladies and gentlemen had been enticed into the smart new apartment by the prospect of refreshing their spirits by reclining in elegant postures upon the chairs, or walking in the vine-clad conservatory which had mysteriously appeared on the other side of a pair of French windows. The moral, as Mr Drawlight explained it, was that if Mr Norrell hoped to win friends for the cause of modern magic, he must insert a great many more French windows into his house.

Under Mr Drawlight's tutelage Mr Norrell learnt to prefer picture-gallery reds to the respectable dull greens of his youth. In the interests of modern magic, the honest materials of Mr Norrell's house were dressed up with paint and varnish, and made to represent things they were not – like actors upon a stage. Plaster was painted to resemble wood, and wood was painted to resemble different sorts of wood. By the time it came to select the appoint-ments for the dining-parlour, Mr Norrell's confidence in Draw-light's taste was so complete that Drawlight was commissioned to chuse the dinner-service without reference to any one else.

"You will not regret it, my dear sir!" cried Drawlight, "for three weeks ago I chose a set for the Duchess of B—— and she declared the moment she saw it that she never in her life saw anything half so charming!"

On a bright May morning Mr Norrell was seated in a drawing-room in Wimpole-street at the house of a Mrs Littleworth. Among the people gathered there were Mr Drawlight and Mr Lascelles. Mr Lascelles was exceedingly fond of Mr Norrell's society, indeed he came second only to Mr Drawlight in this respect, but his reasons for courting Mr Norrell's notice were quite different. Mr Lascelles was a clever, cynical man who thought it the most ridiculous thing in the world that a scholarly old gentleman should have talked himself into the belief that he could perform magic. Consequently, Mr Lascelles took great pleasure in asking Mr Norrell questions about magic whenever the opportunity arose so that he might amuse himself with the answers.

"And how do you like London, sir?" he asked.

"Not at all," said Mr Norrell.

"I am sorry to hear it," said Mr Lascelles. "Have you discovered any brother-magicians to talk to?"

Mr Norrell frowned and said he did not believe there were any magicians in London, or if so, then all his researches had not been able to uncover them.

"Ah, sir!" cried Mr Drawlight. "There you are mistaken! You have been most abominably misinformed! We have magicians in London – Oh! forty at least. Lascelles, would not you agree that we have hundreds of magicians in London? One may see them upon practically every street corner. Mr Lascelles and I will be very happy to make you acquainted with them. They have a sort of king whom they call Vinculus – a tall, ragged scarecrow of a man who has a little booth just outside St Christopher Le Stocks, all splashed with mud, with a dirty yellow curtain and, if you give him two pennies, he will prophesy."

"Vinculus's fortunes are nothing but calamities," observed Mr Lascelles, laughing. "Thus far he has promised me drowning, madness, the destruction by fire of all my property and a natural daughter who will do me great injury in my old age by her spitefulness."

"I shall be glad to take you, sir," said Drawlight to Mr Norrell. "I am as fond as any thing of Vinculus."

"Take care if you do go, sir," advised Mrs Littleworth. "Some of these men can put one in a dreadful fright. The Cruickshanks brought a magician – a very dirty fellow – to the house to shew their friends some tricks, but when he got there it seemed he did not know any – and so they would not pay him. In a great rage he swore that he would turn the baby into a coal scuttle; and then they were in great confusion because the baby was nowhere to be found – though no new coal scuttles had appeared, just the old familiar ones. They searched the house from top to bottom and Mrs Cruikshank was half-dead with anxiety and the physician was sent for – until the nursemaid appeared with the baby at the door and it came out that she had taken it to shew her mother in James-street."

Despite such enticements as these, Mr Norrell declined Mr Drawlight's kind offer to take him to see Vinculus in his yellow booth.

"And what is your opinion of the Raven King, Mr Norrell?" asked Mrs Littleworth eagerly.

"I have none. He is a person I never think of."

"Indeed?" remarked Mr Lascelles. "You will excuse my saying so, Mr Norrell, but that is rather an extraordinary statement. I never met a magician yet who did not declare that the Black King was the greatest of them all – the magician *par excellence*! A man who could, had he so desired, have wrested Merlin from the tree, spun the old gentleman on his head and put him back in again."[2]

Mr Norrell said nothing.

"But surely," continued Mr Lascelles, "none of the other *Aureates* could rival his achievements? Kingdoms in all the worlds

<hr />

[2] Merlin is presumed to have been imprisoned in a hawthorn tree by the sorceress, Nimue.

that ever were.[3] Bands of human knights and fairy knights to carry out his bidding. Magic woods that walked about. To say nothing of his longevity – a three-hundred-year reign – and at the end of it we are told that he was still, in appearance at least, a young man."

Mr Norrell said nothing.

"But perhaps you think that the histories lie? I have frequently heard it suggested that the Raven King never existed – that he was not one magician at all, but a long train of magicians, all looking much the same. Perhaps that is what you think?"

Mr Norrell looked as if he would prefer to remain silent, but the directness of Mr Lascelles's question obliged him to give a reply. "No," he said at last, "I am quite certain that he existed. But I cannot consider his influence upon English magic as any thing other than deplorable. His magic was of a particularly pernicious sort and nothing would please me more than that he should be forgot as completely as he deserves."

"And what of your fairy-servants, sir?" said Mr Lascelles. "Are they visible only to yourself? Or may other people perceive them?"

Mr Norrell sniffed and said he had none.

"What none?" exclaimed a lady in a carnation-pink gown, much surprised.

"You are wise, Mr Norrell," said Mr Lascelles. "Tubbs *versus* Starhouse must stand as a warning to all magicians."[4]

---

[3] Mr Lascelles exaggerates. The Raven King's kingdoms were never more than three in number.

[4] Tubbs *versus* Starhouse: a famous case brought before the Quarter Sessions at Nottingham a few years ago.

A Nottinghamshire man called Tubbs wished very much to see a fairy and, from thinking of fairies day and night, and from reading all sorts of odd books about them, he took it into his head that his coachman was a fairy.

The coachman (whose name was Jack Starhouse) was dark and tall and scarcely ever said a word which discomfited his fellow-servants and made them think him proud. He had only recently entered Mr Tubbs's household, and said that previously he had been coachman to an old man called Browne at a place called Coldmicklehill in the north. He had one great talent: he could make any creature love him. The horses were always very willing when he had the reins and never cross or fidgety at all, and he could command cats

71

"Mr Tubbs was no magician," said Mr Norrell. "Nor did I ever hear that he claimed to be one. But had he been the greatest magician in Christendom, he would still have been wrong to wish for the company of fairies. A more poisonous race or one more

---

[4] *cont'd* in a way that the people of Nottinghamshire had never seen before. He had a whispering way of talking to them; any cat he spoke to would stay quite still with an expression of faint surprize on its face as if it had never heard such good sense in all its life nor ever expected to again. He could also make them dance. The cats that belonged to Mr Tubbs's household were as grave and mindful of their dignity as any other set of cats, but Jack Starhouse could make them dance wild dances, leaping about upon their hind legs and casting themselves from side to side. This he did by strange sighs and whistlings and hissings.

One of the other servants observed that if only cats had been good for any thing – which they were not – then all this might have had some point to it. But Starhouse's wonderful mastery was not useful, nor did it entertain his fellow-servants; it only made them uncomfortable.

Whether it were this or his handsome face with the eyes a little too wide apart that made Mr Tubbs so certain he was a fairy I do not know, but Mr Tubbs began to make inquiries about the coachman in secret.

One day Mr Tubbs called Starhouse to his study. Mr Tubbs said that he had learnt that Mr Browne was very ill – had been ill for all the time Starhouse had claimed to work for him – and had not gone out for years and years. So Mr Tubbs was curious to know what he had needed a coachman for.

For a little while Jack Starhouse said nothing. Then he admitted that he had not been in Mr Browne's employ. He said he had worked for another family in the neighbourhood. He had worked hard, it had been a good place, he had been happy; but the other servants had not liked him, he did not know why, it had happened to him before. One of the other servants (a woman) had told lies about him and he had been dismissed. He had seen Mr Browne once years ago. He said he was very sorry that he had lied to Mr Tubbs, but he had not known what else to do.

Mr Tubbs explained that there was no need to invent further stories. He knew that Starhouse was a fairy and said he was not to fear; he would not betray him; he only wished to talk to him about his home and people.

At first Starhouse did not at all understand what Mr Tubbs meant, and when finally he did understand, it was in vain that he protested that he was a human being and an Englishman, Mr Tubbs did not believe him.

After this, whatever Starhouse was doing, wherever he went, he would find Mr Tubbs waiting for him with a hundred questions about fairies and Faerie. Starhouse was made so unhappy by this treatment (though Mr Tubbs was always kind and courteous), that he was obliged to give up his place. While yet unemployed, he met with a man in an ale-house in Southwell who persuaded him to bring an action against his former master for defamation of character. In a famous ruling Jack Starhouse became the first man to be declared human under English law.

inimical to England has never existed. There have been far too
many magicians too idle or ignorant to pursue a proper course of
study, who instead bent all their energies upon acquiring a fairy-
servant – and when they had got such a servant they depended
upon him to complete all their business for them. English history is
full of such men and some, I am glad to say, were punished for it as
they deserved. Look at Bloodworth.''[5]

---

[4] *cont'd* But this curious episode ended unhappily for both Tubbs and
Starhouse. Tubbs was punished for his harmless ambition to see a fairy by
being made an object of ridicule everywhere. Unflattering caricatures of him
were printed in the London, Nottingham, Derby and Sheffield papers, and
neighbours with whom he had been on terms of the greatest goodwill and
intimacy for years declined to know him any more. While Starhouse quickly
discovered that no one wished to employ a coachman who had brought an
action against his master; he was forced to accept work of a most degrading
nature and very soon fell into great poverty.

The case of Tubbs *versus* Starhouse is interesting not least because it serves
as an illustration of the widely-held belief that fairies have not left England
completely. Many Englishmen and women think that we are surrounded by
fairies every day of our lives. Some are invisible and some masquerade as
Christians and may in fact be known to us. Scholars have debated the matter
for centuries but without reaching any conclusion.

[5] Simon Bloodworth's fairy-servant came to him quite out of the blue offering
his services and saying he wished to be known as "Buckler". As every English
schoolchild nowadays can tell you, Bloodworth would have done better to
have inquired further and to have probed a little deeper into who, precisely,
Buckler was, and why, exactly, he had come out of Faerie with no other aim
than to become the servant of a third-rate English magician.

Buckler was very quick at all sorts of magic and Bloodworth's business in
the little wool-town of Bradford on Avon grew and prospered. Only once did
Buckler cause any sort of difficulty when, in a sudden fit of rage, he destroyed
a little book belonging to Lord Lovel's chaplain.

The longer Buckler remained with Bloodworth the stronger he became and
the first thing that Buckler did when he became stronger was to change his
appearance: his dusty rags became a suit of good clothes; a rusty pair of
scissars that he had stolen from a locksmith in the town became a sword; his
thin, piebald fox-face became a pale and handsome human one; and he grew
very suddenly two or three feet taller. This, he was quick to impress on Mrs
Bloodworth and her daughters, was his true appearance – the other merely
being an enchantment he had been under.

On a fine May morning in 1310 when Bloodworth was away from home
Mrs Bloodworth discovered a tall cupboard standing in the corner of her
kitchen where no cupboard had ever been before. When she asked Buckler
about it, he said immediately that it was a magical cupboard and that he had

Mr Norrell made many new acquaintances, but kindled no pure flame of friendship in the hearts of any. In general, London found him disappointing. He did no magic, cursed no one, foretold nothing. Once at Mrs Godesdone's house he was heard to remark that he thought it might rain, but this, if a prophecy, was a disappointing one, for it did not rain – indeed no rain fell until the

[5] *cont'd*   brought it there. He said that he had always thought that it was a pity that magic was not more commonly used in England; he said it pained him to see Mrs Bloodworth and her daughters washing and sweeping and cooking and cleaning from dawn to dusk when they ought, in his opinion, to be sitting on cushions in jewel–spangled gowns eating comfits. This, thought Mrs Bloodworth, was very good sense. Buckler said how he had often reproved her husband for his failure to make Mrs Bloodworth's life pleasant and easy, but Bloodworth had not paid him any attention. Mrs Bloodworth said that she was not a bit surprized.

Buckler said that if she stepped inside the cupboard she would find herself in a magical place where she could learn spells that would make any work finished in an instant, make her appear beautiful in the eyes of all who beheld her, make large piles of gold appear whenever she wished it, make her husband obey her in all things, etc., etc.

How many spells were there? asked Mrs Bloodworth.

About three, thought Buckler.

Were they hard to learn?

Oh no! Very easy.

Would it take long?

No, not long, she would be back in time for Mass.

Seventeen people entered Buckler's cupboard that morning and were never seen again in England; among them were Mrs Bloodworth, her two youngest daughters, her two maids and two manservants, Mrs Bloodworth's uncle and six neighbours. Only Margaret Bloodworth, Bloodworth's eldest daughter, refused to go.

The Raven King sent two magicians from Newcastle to investigate the matter and it is from their written accounts that we have this tale. The chief witness was Margaret who told how, on his return, "my poor father went purposely into the cupboard to try if he could rescue them, tho' I begged him not to. He has not come out again."

Two hundred years later Dr Martin Pale was journeying through Faerie. At the castle of John Hollyshoes (an ancient and powerful fairy-prince) he discovered a human child, about seven or eight years old, very pale and starved-looking. She said her name was Anne Bloodworth and she had been in Faerie, she thought, about two weeks. She had been given work to do washing a great pile of dirty pots. She said she had been washing them steadily since she arrived and when she was finished she would go home to see her parents and sisters. She thought she would be finished in a day or two.

following Saturday. He hardly ever spoke of magic, and when he did it was like a history lesson and no one could bear to listen to him. He rarely had a good word to say for any other magician, except once when he praised a magician of the last century, Francis Sutton-Grove.[6]

"But I thought, sir," said Mr Lascelles, "that Sutton-Grove was unreadable. I have always heard that *De Generibus Artium* was entirely unreadable."

"Oh!" said Mr Norrell, "how it fares as an amusement for ladies and gentlemen I do not know, but I do not think that the serious student of magic can value Sutton-Grove too highly. In Sutton-Grove he will find the first attempt to define those areas of magic that the modern magician ought to study, all laid out in lists and tables. To be sure, Sutton-Grove's system of classification is often erroneous – perhaps that is what you mean by 'unreadable'? – nevertheless I know of no more pleasant sight in the world than a dozen or so of his lists; the student may run his eye over them and think 'I know this,' or, 'I have this still to do,' and there before him is work enough for four, perhaps five years."

The tale of the statues in the Cathedral of York grew so stale in

---

[6] Francis Sutton-Grove (1682–1765), theoretical magician. He wrote two books *De Generibus Artium Magicarum Anglorum*, 1741, and *Prescriptions and Descriptions*, 1749. Even Mr Norrell, Sutton-Grove's greatest (and indeed only) admirer, thought that *Prescriptions and Descriptions* (wherein he attempted to lay down rules for practical magic) was abominably bad, and Mr Norrell's pupil, Jonathan Strange, loathed it so much that he tore his copy into pieces and fed it to a tinker's donkey (see *Life of Jonathan Strange* by John Segundus, 1820, pub. John Murray).

De Generibus Artium Magicarum Anglorum was reputed to be the dreariest book in the canon of English magic (which contains many tedious works). It was the first attempt by an Englishman to define the areas of magic that the modern magician ought to study; according to Sutton-Grove these numbered thirty-eight thousand, nine hundred and forty-five and he listed them all under different heads. Sutton-Grove foreshadows the great Mr Norrell in one other way: none of his lists make any mention of the magic traditionally ascribed to birds or wild animals, and Sutton-Grove purposely excludes those kinds of magic for which it is customary to employ fairies, e.g. bringing back the dead.

the retelling that people began to wonder if Mr Norrell had ever done anything else and Mr Drawlight was obliged to invent some new examples.

"But what can this magician do, Drawlight?" asked Mrs Godesdone one evening when Mr Norrell was not present.

"Oh, madam!" cried Drawlight. "What can he not do? Why! It was only a winter or so ago that in York – which as you may know, madam, is Mr Norrell's native city – a great storm came out of the north and blew everybody's washing into the mud and the snow – and so the aldermen, thinking to spare the ladies of the town the labour of washing everything again, applied to Mr Norrell – and he sent a troop of fairies to wash it all anew – and all the holes in people's shirts and nightcaps and petticoats were mended and all the frayed edges were made whole and good again and everybody said that they had never seen such a dazzling whiteness in all their days!"

This particular story became very popular and raised Mr Norrell in everyone's estimation for several weeks that summer, and consequently when Mr Norrell spoke, as he sometimes did, of modern magic, most of his audience supposed that this was the sort of thing he must mean.

But if the ladies and gentlemen whom Mr Norrell met in London's drawing-rooms and dining-parlours were generally disappointed in *him*, then he was becoming equally dissatisfied with *them*. He complained constantly to Mr Drawlight of the frivolous questions that they put to him, and said that the cause of English magic had not been furthered one whit by the hours he had spent in their company.

One dull Wednesday morning at the end of September Mr Norrell and Mr Drawlight were seated together in the library in Hanover-square. Mr Drawlight was in the middle of a long tale of something that Mr F. had said in order to insult Lord S., and what Lady D. had thought about it all, when Mr Norrell suddenly said, "I would be grateful, Mr Drawlight, if you could advise me on the following important point: has any body informed the Duke of Portland of my arrival in London?"[7]

"Ah! sir," cried Drawlight, "only you, with your modest nature, could suppose it possible. I assure you *all* the Ministers have heard of the extraordinary Mr Norrell by now."

"But if that is the case," said Mr Norrell, "then why has his Grace sent me no message? No, I begin to think that they must be entirely ignorant of my existence – and so, Mr Drawlight, I would be grateful if you could inform me of any connexions in Government that you may have to whom I could apply."

"The Government, sir?" replied Mr Drawlight.

"I came here to be useful," said Mr Norrell, plaintively. "I had hoped by now to play some distinguished part in the struggle against the French."

"If you feel yourself neglected, sir, then I am heartily sorry for it!" cried Drawlight. "But there is no need, I do assure you. There are ladies and gentlemen all over Town who would be happy to see any little tricks or illusions you might like to shew us one evening after dinner. You must not be afraid of overwhelming us – our nerves are all pretty strong."

Mr Norrell said nothing.

"Well, sir," said Mr Drawlight, with a smooth smile of his white teeth and a conciliatory look in his dark, liquid eyes, "we must not argue about it. I only wish I were able to oblige you but, as you see, it is entirely out of my power. The Government has its sphere. I have mine."

In fact Mr Drawlight knew several gentlemen in various Government posts who might be very glad to meet Mr Drawlight's friend and to listen to what that friend might have to say, in return for a promise from Mr Drawlight never to tell one or two curious things he knew about them. But the truth was that Mr Drawlight could see no advantage to himself in introducing Mr Norrell to any

---

[7] Duke of Portland, Prime Minister and First Lord of the Treasury 1807–09.

of these gentlemen; he preferred to keep Mr Norrell in the drawing-rooms and dining-parlours of London where he hoped, in time, to persuade him to perform those little tricks and what-not that Mr Drawlight's acquaintance longed to see.

Mr Norrell began writing urgent letters to gentlemen in Government, which he shewed to Mr Drawlight before giving them to Childermass to deliver, but the gentlemen in Government did not reply. Mr Drawlight had warned Mr Norrell that they would not. Gentlemen in Government are generally kept pretty busy.

A week or so later Mr Drawlight was invited to a house in Soho-square to hear a famous Italian soprano, newly arrived from Rome. Naturally, Mr Norrell was invited too. But on arriving at the house Drawlight could not find the magician among the crowd. Lascelles was leaning upon the mantelpiece in conversation with some other gentlemen. Drawlight went up to him and inquired if he knew where Mr Norrell was.

"Oh!" said Mr Lascelles. "He is gone to pay a visit to Sir Walter Pole. Mr Norrell has important information which he wishes conveyed to the Duke of Portland immediately. And Sir Walter Pole is the man that Mr Norrell intends to honour with the message."

"Portland?" cried another gentleman. "What? Are the Ministers got so desperate as that? Are they consulting magicians?"

"You have run away with a wrong idea," smiled Mr Lascelles. "It is all Norrell's own doing. He intends to offer his services to the Government. It seems he has a plan to defeat the French by magic. But I think it highly improbable that he will persuade the Ministers to listen to him. What with the French at their throats on the Continent, and everybody else at their throats in Parliament – I doubt if a more harassed set of gentlemen is to be found anywhere, or one with less attention to spare for a Yorkshire gentleman's eccentricities."

Like the hero of a fairy-tale Mr Norrell had discovered that the power to do what he wished had been his own all along. Even a magician must have relations, and it so happened that there was a distant connexion of Mr Norrell (on his mother's side) who had once made himself highly disagreeable to Mr Norrell by writing him a letter. To prevent such a thing ever occurring again Mr Norrell had made this man a present of eight hundred pounds (which was what the man wanted), but I am sorry to say that this failed to suppress Mr Norrell's mother's relative, who was steeped in villainy, and he had written a *second* letter to Mr Norrell in which he heaped thanks and praise upon his benefactor and declared that, ". . . henceforth I shall consider myself and my friends as belonging to your interest and we hold ourselves ready to vote at the next election in accordance with your noble wishes, and if, in time to come, it should appear that any service of mine might be useful to you, your commands will only honour, and elevate in the opinion of the World, your humble and devoted servant, Wendell Markworthy."

Thus far Mr Norrell had never found it necessary to elevate Mr Markworthy in the opinion of the world by honouring him with any commands, but it now appeared (it was Childermass that had found it out) that Mr Markworthy had used the money to secure for himself and his brother clerkships in the East India Company. They had gone to India and ten years later had returned very rich men. Having never received any instructions from Mr Norrell, his first patron, as to which way to vote, Mr Markworthy had followed the lead of Mr Bonnell, his superior at the East India Company, and had encouraged all his friends to do the same. He had made himself very useful to Mr Bonnell, who was in turn a great friend of the politician, Sir Walter Pole. In the busy worlds of trade and government this gentleman owes that one a favour, while he in his turn is owed a favour by someone else, and so on until a chain is formed of promises and obligations. In this case the chain extended all the way from Mr Norrell to Sir Walter Pole and Sir Walter Pole was now a Minister.

6

"Magic is not respectable, sir."

October 1807

I<small>T WAS A</small> difficult time to be a Minister.

The war went from bad to worse and the Government was universally detested. As each fresh catastrophe came to the public's notice some small share of blame might attach itself to this or that person, but in general everyone united in blaming the Ministers, and they, poor things, had no one to blame but each other – which they did more and more frequently.

It was not that the Ministers were dull-witted – upon the contrary there were some brilliant men among them. Nor were they, upon the whole, bad men; several led quite blameless domestic lives and were remarkably fond of children, music, dogs, landscape painting. Yet so unpopular was the Government that, had it not been for the careful speeches of the Foreign Secretary, it would have been almost impossible to get any piece of business through the House of Commons.

The Foreign Secretary was a quite peerless orator. No matter how low the Government stood in the estimation of everyone, when the Foreign Secretary stood up and spoke – ah! how different everything seemed then! How quickly was every bad thing discovered to be the fault of the previous administration (an evil set of men who wedded general stupidity to wickedness of purpose). As for the present Ministry, the Foreign Secretary said that not since the days of Antiquity had the world seen gentlemen so virtuous, so misunderstood and so horribly misrepresented by their enemies. They were all as wise as Solomon, as noble as Caesar and as courageous as Mark Antony; and no one in the world so much resembled Socrates in point of honesty as the Chancellor of the Exchequer. But in spite of all these virtues and abilities none of the Ministers' plans to defeat the French ever seemed to come to anything and even their cleverness was complained of. Country gentlemen who read in their newspapers the speeches of this or that Minister would mutter to themselves that he was certainly a clever fellow. But the country gentlemen were not made comfortable by this thought. The country gentlemen had a strong suspicion that cleverness was somehow unBritish. That sort of restless, unpredictable brilliance belonged most of all to Britain's arch-enemy, the Emperor Napoleon Buonaparte; the country gentlemen could not approve it.

Sir Walter Pole was forty-two and, I am sorry to say, quite as clever as any one else in the Cabinet. He had quarrelled with most of the great politicians of the age at one time or another and once, when they were both very drunk, had been struck over the head with a bottle of madeira by Richard Brinsley Sheridan. Afterwards Sheridan remarked to the Duke of York, "Pole accepted my apologies in a handsome, gentleman-like fashion. Happily he is such a plain man that one scar more or less can make no significant difference."

To my mind he was not so very plain. True, his features were all extremely bad; he had a great face half as long again as other faces, with a great nose (quite sharp at the end) stuck into it, two dark eyes like clever bits of coal and two little stubby eyebrows like very small fish swimming bravely in a great sea of face. Yet, taken together, all these ugly parts made a rather pleasing whole. If you had seen that face in repose (proud and not a little melancholy), you would have imagined that it must always look so, that no face in existence could be so ill-adapted to express feeling. But you could not have been more wrong.

81

Nothing was more characteristic of Sir Walter Pole than *Surprize*. His eyes grew large, his eyebrows rose half an inch upon his face and he leant suddenly backwards and altogether he resembled nothing so much as a figure in the engravings of Mr Rowlandson or Mr Gillray. In public life *Surprize* served Sir Walter very well. "But, surely," he cried, "You cannot mean to say —!" And, always supposing that the gentleman who was so foolish as to suggest — in Sir Walter's hearing was no friend or yours, or if you have that sort of mischief in you that likes to see blunt wits confounded by sharp ones, you would be entertained. On days when he was full of cheerful malice Sir Walter was better than a play in Drury-lane. Dull gentlemen in both Houses grew perplexed, and avoided him when they could. (Old Lord So-and-so waves his stick at Sir Walter as he trots down the little stone passage that connects the House of Commons to the Horse-Guards, and cries over his shoulder, "I will not speak to you, sir! You twist my words! You give me meanings I never intended!")

Once, while making a speech to a mob in the City, Sir Walter had memorably likened England and her politicians to an orphaned young lady left in the care of a pack of lecherous, avaricious old men. These scoundrels, far from offering the young lady protection from the wicked world, stole her inheritance and plundered her house. And if Sir Walter's audience stumbled on some of his vocabulary (the product of an excellent classical education) it did not much matter. All of them were capable of imagining the poor young lady standing on her bed in her petti-coats while the leading Whig politicians of the day ransacked her closets and sold off all her bits of things to the rag man. And all the young gentlemen found themselves pleasantly shocked by the picture.

Sir Walter had a generous spirit and was often kind-hearted. He told someone once that he hoped his enemies all had reason to fear him and his friends reason to love him – and I think that upon the whole they did. His cheerful manner, his kindness and cleverness, the great station he now held in the world – these were even more to his credit as he maintained them in the face of problems that would almost certainly have brought down a lesser man. Sir Walter was distressed for money. I do not mean that he merely lacked for cash. Poverty is one thing, Sir Walter's debts quite another. Miserable situation! – and all the more bitter since it was no fault of his: *he* had never been extravagant and he had certainly never been foolish, but he was the son of one imprudent man and the grandson of another. Sir Walter had been born in debt. Had he been a different sort of man, then all might have been well. Had he been at all inclined to the Navy then he might have made his fortune in prize money; had he loved farming he might have improved his lands and made his money with corn. Had he even been a Minister fifty years before he might have lent out Treasury-money at twenty per cent interest and pocketed the profit. But what can a modern politician do? – he is more likely to spend money than make it.

Some years ago his friends in Government had got him the position of Secretary-in-Ordinary to the Office of Supplication, for which he received a special hat, a small piece of ivory and seven hundred pounds a year. There were no duties attached to the place because no one could remember what the Office of Supplication was supposed to do or what the small piece of ivory was for. But then Sir Walter's friends went out and new Ministers came in, declaring that they were going to abolish sinecures, and among the many offices and places which they pruned from the tree of Government was the Office of Supplication.

By the spring of 1807 it seemed as if Sir Walter's political career must be pretty much at an end (the last election had cost him almost two thousand pounds). His friends were almost frantic. One of those friends, Lady Winsell, went to Bath where, at a concert of Italian music, she made the acquaintance of some people called Wintertowne, a widow and her daughter. A week later Lady Winsell wrote to Sir Walter: "It is exactly what I have always wished for you. Her mother is all for a great marriage and will make no difficulties – or at least if she does then I rely upon *you* to charm them away. As for the money! I tell you, my dear friend, when they named the sum that is to be hers, tears sprang into my eyes! What would you say to one thousand a year? I will say nothing of the young person herself – when you have seen her you shall praise her to me much more ably than ever I could to you."

At about three o'clock upon the same day that Mr Drawlight attended the recital by the Italian lady, Lucas, Mr Norrell's footman, knocked upon the door of a house in Brunswick-square where Mr Norrell had been summoned to meet Sir Walter. Mr Norrell was admitted to the house and was shown to a very fine room upon the first floor.

The walls were hung with a series of gigantic paintings in gilded frames of great complexity, all depicting the city of Venice, but the day was overcast, a cold stormy rain had set in, and Venice – that city built of equal parts of sunlit marble and sunlit sea – was drowned in a London gloom. Its aquamarine-blues and cloud-whites and glints of gold were dulled to the greys and greens of drowned things. From time to time the wind flung a little sharp rain against the window (a melancholy sound) and in the grey light the well-polished surfaces of tulipwood *chiffoniers* and walnut writing-tables had all become black mirrors, darkly reflecting one another. For all its splendour, the room was peculiarly comfortless; there were no candles to light the gloom and no fire to take off the chill. It was as if the housekeeping was under the direction of someone with excellent eyesight who never felt the cold.

Sir Walter Pole rose to receive Mr Norrell and begged the honour of presenting Mrs Wintertowne and her daughter, Miss Wintertowne. Though Sir Walter spoke of *two* ladies, Mr Norrell could perceive only *one*, a lady of mature years, great dignity and magisterial aspect. This puzzled Mr Norrell. He thought Sir Walter must be mistaken, and yet it would be rude to contradict

Sir Walter so early in the interview. In a state of some confusion, Mr Norrell bowed to the magisterial lady.

"I am very glad to meet you, sir," said Sir Walter. "I have heard a great deal about you. It seems to me that London talks of very little else but the extraordinary Mr Norrell," and, turning to the magisterial lady, Sir Walter said, "Mr Norrell is a magician, ma'am, a person of great reputation in his native county of Yorkshire."

The magisterial lady stared at Mr Norrell.

"You are not at all what I expected, Mr Norrell," remarked Sir Walter. "I had been told you were a *practical* magician – I hope you are not offended, sir – it is merely what I was told, and I must say that it is a relief to me to see that you are nothing of the sort. London is plagued with a great number of mock-sorcerers who trick the people out of their money by promising them all sorts of unlikely things. I wonder, have you seen Vinculus, who has a little booth outside St Christopher Le Stocks? He is the worst of them. You are a *theoretical* magician, I imagine?" Sir Walter smiled encouragingly. "But they tell me that you have something to ask me, sir."

Mr Norrell begged Sir Walter's pardon but said that he was indeed a practical magician; Sir Walter looked surprised. Mr Norrell hoped very earnestly that he would not by this admission lose Sir Walter's good opinion.

"No, no. By no means," murmured Sir Walter politely.

"The misapprehension under which you labour," said Mr Norrell, "by which I mean, of course, the belief that all practical magicians must be charlatans – arises from the shocking idleness of English magicians in the last two hundred years. I have performed one small feat of magic – which the people in York were kind enough to say they found astounding – and yet I tell you, Sir Walter, any magician of modest talent might have done as much. This general lethargy has deprived our great nation of its best support and left us defenceless. It is this deficiency which I hope to supply. Other magicians may be able to neglect their duty, but I cannot; I am come, Sir Walter, to offer you my help in our present difficulties."

"Our present difficulties?" said Sir Walter. "You mean the war?" He opened his small black eyes very wide. "My dear Mr Norrell! What has the war to do with magic? Or magic to do with the war? I believe I have heard what you did in York, and I hope the housewives were grateful, but I scarcely see how we can apply such magic to the war! True, the soldiers get very dirty, but then, you know," and he began to laugh, "they have other things of think of."

Poor Mr Norrell! He had not heard Drawlight's story of how the fairies had washed the people's clothes and it came as a great shock to him. He assured Sir Walter that he had never in his life washed linen – not by magic nor by any other means – and he told Sir Walter what he had really done. But, curiously, though Mr Norrell was able to work feats of the most breath-taking wonder, he was only able to describe them in his usual dry manner, so that Sir Walter was left with the impression that the spectacle of half a thousand stone figures in York Cathedral all speaking together had been rather a dull affair and that he had been fortunate in being elsewhere at the time. "Indeed?" he said. "Well, that is most interesting. But I still do not quite understand how . . ."

Just at that moment someone coughed, and the moment that Sir Walter heard the cough he stopped speaking as if to listen.

Mr Norrell looked round. In the furthest, most shadowy corner of the room a young woman in a white gown lay upon a sopha, with a white shawl wrapped tightly around her. She lay quite still. One hand pressed a handkerchief to her mouth. Her posture, her stillness, everything about her conveyed the strongest impression of pain and ill-health.

So certain had Mr Norrell been that the corner was unoccupied, that he was almost as startled by her sudden appearance as if she had come there by someone else's magic. As he watched she was seized by a fit of coughing that continued for some moments, and during that time Sir Walter appeared most uncomfortable. He did not look at the young woman (though he looked everywhere else in the room). He picked up a gilt ornament from a little table by his side, turned it over, looked at its underneath, put it down again. Finally he coughed – a brief clearing of the throat as though to suggest that everyone coughed – coughing was the most natural thing in the world – coughing could never, under any circumstances, be cause for alarm. The young woman upon the sopha came at last to the end of her own coughing fit, and lay quite still and quiet, though her breathing did not seem to come easily.

Mr Norrell's gaze travelled from the young lady to the great, gloomy painting that hung above her and he tried to recollect what he had been speaking of.

"It is a marriage," said the majestic lady.

"I beg your pardon, madam?" said Mr Norrell.

But the lady only nodded in the direction of the painting and bestowed a stately smile upon Mr Norrell.

The painting which hung above the young lady shewed, like every other picture in the room, Venice. English cities are, for the most part, built upon hills; their streets rise and fall, and it occurred to Mr Norrell that Venice, being built upon the sea, must be the flattest, as well as the queerest, city in the world. It was the flatness which made the painting look so much like an exercise in perspective; statues, columns, domes, palaces, and cathedrals stretched away to where they met a vast and melancholy sky, while the sea that lapped at the walls of those buildings was crowded with ornately carved and gilded barges, and those strange black Venetian vessels that so much resemble the slippers of ladies in mourning.

"It depicts the symbolic marriage of Venice to the Adriatic," said the lady (whom we must now presume to be Mrs Wintertowne), "a curious Italian ceremony. The paintings which you see

87

in this room were all bought by the late Mr Wintertowne during his travels on the Continent; and when he and I were married they were his wedding-gift to me. The artist – an Italian – was then quite unknown in England. Later, emboldened by the patronage he received from Mr Wintertowne, he came to London."

Her manner of speech was as stately as her person. After each sentence she paused to give Mr Norrell time to be impressed by the information it contained.

"And when my dear Emma is married," she continued, "these paintings shall be my wedding-present to her and Sir Walter."

Mr Norrell inquired if Miss Wintertowne and Sir Walter were to be married soon.

"In ten days' time!" answered Mrs Wintertowne triumphantly.

Mr Norrell offered his congratulations.

"You are a magician, sir?" said Mrs Wintertowne. "I am sorry to hear it. It is a profession I have a particular dislike to." She looked keenly at him as she said so, as though her disapproval might in itself be enough to make him renounce magic instantly and take up some other occupation.

When he did not she turned to her prospective son-in-law. "My own stepmother, Sir Walter, placed great faith in a magician. After my father's death he was always in the house. One could enter a room one was quite sure was empty and find him in a corner half hidden by a curtain. Or asleep upon the sopha with his dirty boots on. He was the son of a leather tanner and his low origins were frankly displayed in all he did. He had long, dirty hair and a face like a dog, but he sat at our table like a gentleman. My stepmother deferred to him in all she did and for seven years he governed our lives completely."

"And your own opinion was disregarded, ma'am?" said Sir Walter. "I am surprised at that!"

Mrs Wintertowne laughed. "I was only a child of eight or nine when it began, Sir Walter. His name was Dreamditch and he told us constantly how happy he was to be our friend, though my

brother and I were equally constant in assuring him that we considered him no friend of ours. But he only smiled at us like a dog that has learned how to smile and does not know how to leave off. Do not misunderstand me, Sir Walter. My stepmother was in many ways an excellent woman. My father's esteem for her was such that he left her six hundred a year and the care of his three children. Her only weakness was foolishly to doubt her own capabilities. My father believed that, in understanding and in knowledge of right and wrong and in many other things, women are men's equals and I am entirely of his opinion. My stepmother should not have shrunk from the charge. When Mr Wintertowne died *I* did not."

"No, indeed, ma'am," murmured Sir Walter.

"Instead," continued Mrs Wintertowne, "she placed all her faith in the magician, Dreamditch. He had not an ounce of magic in him and was consequently obliged to invent some. He made rules for my brother, my sister and me, which, he assured my stepmother, would keep us safe. We wore purple ribbons tied tightly round our chests. In our room six places were laid at the table, one for each of us and one for each of the spirits which Dreamditch said looked after us. He told us their names. What do you suppose they were, Sir Walter?"

"I have not the least idea in the world, ma'am."

Mrs Wintertowne laughed. "Meadowlace, Robin Summerfly and Buttercup. My brother, Sir Walter, who resembled myself in independence of spirit, would often say in my stepmother's hearing, 'Damn Meadowlace! Damn Robin Summerfly! Damn Buttercup!' and she, poor silly woman, would plead very piteously with him to stop. They did us no good those fairy spirits. My sister became ill. Often I went to her room and found Dreamditch there, stroking her pale cheeks and unresisting hand with his long yellow unclean fingernails. He was almost weeping, the fool. He would have saved her if he could. He made spells, but she died. A beautiful child, Sir Walter. For years I hated my stepmother's magician. For years I thought him a wicked man, but in the end, Sir Walter, I knew him to be nothing but a sad and pitiful fool."

Sir Walter turned in his chair. "Miss Wintertowne!" he said. "You spoke – but I did not hear what it was you said."

"Emma! What is it?" cried Mrs Wintertowne.

There was a soft sigh from the sopha. Then a quiet, clear voice said, "I said that you were quite wrong, Mama."

"Am I, my love?" Mrs Wintertowne, whose character was so forceful and whose opinions were handed down to people in the manner of Moses distributing the commandments, did not appear in the least offended when her daughter contradicted her. Indeed she seemed almost pleased about it.

"Of course," said Miss Wintertowne, "we must have magicians. Who else can interpret England's history to us and in particular her northern history, her black northern King? Our common historians cannot." There was silence for a moment. "I am fond of history," she said.

"I did not know that," said Sir Walter.

"Ah, Sir Walter!" cried Mrs Wintertowne. "Dear Emma does not waste her energies upon novels like other young women. Her reading has been extensive; she knows more of biography and poetry than any young woman I know."

"Yet I hope," said Sir Walter eagerly, leaning over the back of his chair to speak to his betrothed, "that you like novels as well, and then, you know, we could read to each other. What is your opinion of Mrs Radcliffe? Of Madame d'Arblay?"

But what Miss Wintertowne thought of these distinguished ladies Sir Walter did not discover for she was seized by a second fit of coughing which obliged her to struggle – with an appearance of great effort – into a sitting position. He waited some moments for an answer, but when her coughing had subsided she lay back on the sopha as before, with looks of pain and exhaustion, and closed her eyes.

Mr Norrell wondered that no one thought to go to her assistance. There seemed to be a sort of conspiracy in the room to deny that the poor young woman was ill. No one asked if they could bring her anything. No one suggested that she go to bed, which Mr Norrell – who was often ill himself – imagined would be by far the best thing for her.

"Mr Norrell," said Sir Walter, "I cannot claim to understand what this help is that you offer us . . ."

"Oh! As to particulars," Mr Norrell said, "I know as little of warfare as the generals and the admirals do of magic, and yet . . ."

". . . but whatever it is," continued Sir Walter, "I am sorry to say that it will not do. Magic is not respectable, sir. It is not," Sir Walter searched for a word, "serious. The Government cannot meddle with such things. Even this innocent little chat that you and I have had today, is likely to cause us a little embarrassment when people get to hear of it. Frankly, Mr Norrell, had I understood better what you were intending to propose today, I would not have agreed to meet you."

Sir Walter's manner as he said all this was far from unkind, but, oh, poor Mr Norrell! To be told that magic was not serious was a very heavy blow. To find himself classed with the Dreamditches and the Vinculuses of this world was a crushing one. In vain he protested that he had thought long and hard about how to make magic respected once more; in vain he offered to shew Sir Walter a long list of recommendations concerning the regulation of magic in England. Sir Walter did not wish to see them. He shook his head and smiled, but all he said was: "I am afraid, Mr Norrell, that I can do nothing for you."

When Mr Drawlight arrived at Hanover-square that evening he was obliged to listen to Mr Norrell lamenting the failure of all his hopes of succeeding with Sir Walter Pole.

"Well, sir, what did I tell you?" cried Drawlight. "But, oh! Poor Mr Norrell! How unkind they were to you! I am very sorry for it. But I am not in the least surprized! I have always heard that those Wintertownes were stuffed full of pride!"

But there was, I regret to say, a little duplicity in Mr Drawlight's nature and it must be said that he was not quite as sorry as he professed to be. This display of independence had provoked him and he was determined to punish Mr Norrell for it. For the next week Mr Norrell and Mr Drawlight attended only the quietest dinners and, without quite arranging matters so that Mr Norrell would find himself the guest of Mr Drawlight's shoemaker or the old lady who dusts the monuments in Westminster Abbey, Mr Drawlight took care that their hosts were people of as little consequence, influence, or fashion, as possible. In this way Drawlight hoped to create in Mr Norrell the impression that not only the Poles and Wintertownes slighted him, but the whole world, so that Mr Norrell might be brought to understand who was his true friend, and might become a little more accommodating when it came to performing those small tricks of magic that Drawlight had been promising for many months now.

Such were the hopes and schemes that animated the heart of Mr Norrell's dearest friend but, unfortunately for Mr Drawlight, so cast down was Mr Norrell by Sir Walter's rejection that he scarcely noticed the change in the style of entertainments and Drawlight succeeded in punishing no one but himself.

Now that Sir Walter was quite beyond Mr Norrell's reach, Mr Norrell became more and more convinced that Sir Walter was exactly the patron he wished for. A cheerful, energetic man, with pleasant, easy manners, Sir Walter Pole was everything that Mr Norrell was not. Therefore, reasoned Mr Norrell, Sir Walter Pole would have achieved everything that he *could* not. The influential men of the Age would have listened to Sir Walter.

"If only he had listened to me," sighed Mr Norrell one evening as he and Drawlight dined alone. "But I could not find the words to convince him. Of course I wish now that I had asked you or Mr Lascelles to come with me. Men of the world prefer to be talked to by other men of the world. I know that now. Perhaps I should have done some magic to shew him – turned the teacups into rabbits or the teaspoons into goldfish. At least then he would have believed me. But I do not think the old lady would have been pleased if I had done that. I do not know. What is your opinion?"

But Drawlight, who had begun to believe that if anyone had ever died of boredom then he was almost certain to expire within the next quarter of an hour, found that he had lost the will to speak and the best he could manage was a withering smile.

7

An opportunity unlikely to occur again

October 1807

"WELL, SIR! YOU have your revenge!" cried Mr Drawlight appearing quite suddenly in the library in Hanover-square.

"My revenge!" said Mr Norrell. "What do you mean?"

"Oh!" said Mr Drawlight. "Sir Walter's bride, Miss Wintertowne, is dead. She died this very afternoon. They were to be married in two days' time, but, poor thing, she is quite dead. A thousand pounds a year! – Imagine his despair! Had she only contrived to remain alive until the end of the week, what a difference it would have made! His need of the money is quite desperate – he is all to pieces. I should not be at all surprized if we were to hear tomorrow that he has cut his throat."

Mr Drawlight leant for a moment upon the back of a good, comfortable chair by the fire and, looking down, discovered a friend. "Ah, Lascelles, I declare. There you are behind the newspaper I see. How do you do?"

Meanwhile Mr Norrell stared at Mr Drawlight. "The young woman is dead, you say?" he said in amazement. "The young woman that I saw in that room? I can scarcely believe it. This is very unexpected."

"Oh! Upon the contrary," said Drawlight, "nothing was more probable."

"But the wedding!" said Mr Norrell. "All the necessary arrangements! They could not have known how ill she was."

"But I assure you," said Drawlight, "they did know. Everyone knew. Why! there was a fellow called Drummond, who saw her at Christmas at a private ball in Leamington Spa, and wagered Lord Carlisle fifty pounds that she would be dead within a month."

Mr Lascelles tutted in annoyance and put down his newspaper. "No, no," he said, "that was not Miss Wintertowne. You are thinking of Miss Hookham-Nix, whose brother has threatened to shoot her, should she bring disgrace upon the family – which everyone supposes she must do sooner or later. But it happened at Worthing – and it was not Lord Carlisle who took the bet but the Duke of Exmoor."

Drawlight considered this a moment. "I believe you are right," he said at last. "But it does not matter, for everyone *did* know that Miss Wintertowne was ill. Except of course the old lady. *She* thought her daughter perfection – and what can Perfection have to say to ill-health? Perfection is only to be admired; Perfection has only to make a great marriage. But the old lady has never allowed that Perfection might be ill – she could never bear to hear the subject mentioned. For all Miss Wintertowne's coughs and swoonings upon the ground and lyings-down upon the sopha, I never heard that any physician ever came near her."

"Sir Walter would have taken better care of her," said Lascelles, shaking out his newspaper before he began once more to read it. "One may say what one likes about his politics, but he is a sensible man. It is a pity she could not have lasted till Thursday."

"But, Mr Norrell," said Drawlight turning to their friend, "you look quite pale and sick! You are shocked, I dare say, at the spectacle of a young and innocent life cut off. Your good feelings, as ever, do you credit, sir – and I am entirely of your opinion – the thought of the poor young lady crushed out of existence like a lovely flower beneath someone's boot – well, sir, it cuts my heart like a knife – I can hardly bear to think of it. But then, you know, she was very ill and must have died at some time or other – and by your own account she was not very kind to *you*. I know it is not the fashion to say so, but I am the sternest advocate in the world for young people giving respectful attention to scholarly old persons such as yourself. Impudence, and sauciness, and everything of that sort I hate."

But Mr Norrell did not appear to hear the comfort his friend was so kind as to give him and when at last he spoke his words seemed chiefly addressed to himself, for he sighed deeply and murmured, "I never thought to find magic so little regarded here." He paused and then said in a quick, low voice, "It is a very dangerous thing to bring someone back from the dead. It has not been done in three hundred years. I could not attempt it!"

This was rather extraordinary and Mr Drawlight and Mr Lascelles looked round at their friend in some surprize.

"Indeed, sir," said Mr Drawlight, "and no one proposes that you should."

"Of course I know the form of it," continued Mr Norrell as if Drawlight had not spoken, "but it is precisely the sort of magic that I have set my face against! – It relies so much upon . . . It relies so much . . . That is to say the outcome must be entirely unpredictable. – Quite out of the magician's power to determine. No! I shall not attempt it. I shall not even think of it."

There was a short silence. But despite the magician's resolve to think no more about the dangerous magic, he still fidgeted in his chair and bit his finger-ends and breathed very quick and exhibited other such signs of nervous agitation.

"My dear Mr Norrell," said Drawlight slowly, "I believe I begin to perceive your meaning. And I must confess that I think the idea an excellent one! You have in mind a great act of magic, a testimony to your extraordinary powers! Why, sir! Should you succeed all the Wintertownes and Poles in England will be on your doorstep soliciting the acquaintance of the wonderful Mr Norrell!"

"And if he should fail," observed Mr Lascelles, drily, "every one else in England will be shutting his door against the notorious Mr Norrell."

"My dear Lascelles," cried Drawlight, "what nonsense you talk! Upon my word, there is nothing in the world so easy to explain as failure – it is, after all, what every body does all the time."

Mr Lascelles said that that did not follow at all, and they were just beginning to argue about it when an anguished cry burst from the lips of their friend, Mr Norrell.

"Oh, God! What shall I do? What shall I do? I have laboured all these months to make my profession acceptable in the eyes of men and still they despise me! Mr Lascelles, you know the world, tell me . . ."

"Alas, sir," interrupted Mr Lascelles quickly, "I make a great point of never giving advice to any one." And he went back to his newspaper.

"My dear Mr Norrell!" said Drawlight (who did not wait to be asked for *his* opinion). "Such an opportunity is hardly likely to occur again . . ." (A potent argument this, and one which caused Mr Norrell to sigh very deeply.) ". . . and I must say I do not think that I could forgive myself if I allowed you to pass it by. With one stroke you return to us that sweet young woman – whose death no one can hear of without shedding a tear; you restore a fortune to a worthy gentleman; *and* you re-establish magic as a power in the realm for generations to come! Once you have proved the virtue of your skills – their utility and so forth – who will be able to deny magicians their dues of veneration and praise? They will be quite as much respected as admirals, a great deal more than generals, and probably as much as archbishops and lord chancellors! I should not be at all surprised if His Majesty did not immediately set up a convenient arrangement of degrees with magicians-in-ordinary and magicians-canonical, non-stipendiary magicians and all that sort of thing. And you, Mr Norrell, at the top as Arch-Magician! And all this with one stroke, sir! With one stroke!"

Drawlight was pleased with this speech; Lascelles, rustling the paper in his irritation, clearly had a great many things to say in contradiction of Drawlight, but had put it out of his power to say any of them by his declaration that he never gave advice.

"There is scarcely any form of magic more dangerous!" said Mr Norrell in a sort of horrified whisper. "It is dangerous to the magician and dangerous to the subject."

"Well, sir," said Drawlight reasonably, "I suppose you are the best judge of the danger as it applies to yourself, but the subject, as you term her, is dead. What worse can befall her?"

Drawlight waited a moment for a reply to this interesting question, but Mr Norrell made none.

"I shall now ring for the carriage," Drawlight declared and did so. "I shall go immediately to Brunswick-square. Have no fear, Mr Norrell, I have every expectation that all our proposals will meet with most ready acquiesence on all sides. I shall return within the hour!"

After Drawlight had hurried away, Mr Norrell sat for a quarter of an hour or so simply staring in front of him and though Lascelles did not believe in the magic that Mr Norrell said would be done (nor, therefore, in the danger that Mr Norrell said would be braved) he was glad that he could not see what Mr Norrell seemed to see.

Then Mr Norrell roused himself and took down five or six books in a great hurry and opened them up – presumably searching out those passages which were full of advice for magicians who wished to awaken dead young ladies. This occupied him until another three-quarters of an hour had passed, when a little bustle could be heard outside the library, and Mr Drawlight's voice preceded him into the room.

". . . the greatest favour in the world! So very much obliged to you . . ." Mr Drawlight danced through the library-door, his face one immense smile. "All is well, sir! Sir Walter did hold back a little at first, but all is well! He asked me to convey to you his gratitude for your kind attention, but he did not think that it could do any good. *I* said that if he were thinking of the thing getting out afterwards and being talked about, then he need not fear at all, for we had no wish to see him embarrassed – and that Mr Norrell's one desire was to be of service to him and that Lascelles and I were discretion itself – but he said he did not mind about that, for people would always laugh at a Minister, only he had rather Miss Wintertowne were left sleeping now – which he thought more respectful of her present situation. My dear Sir Walter! cried I, how can you say so? You cannot mean that a rich and beautiful young lady would gladly quit this life on the very eve of her marriage – when you yourself were to be the happy man! Oh! Sir Walter! – I said – *you* may not believe in Mr Norrell's magic, but what can it hurt to try? Which the old lady saw the sense of immediately and added her arguments to mine – and she told me of a magician she had known in her childhood, a most talented person and a devoted friend to all her family, who had prolonged her sister's life several years beyond what any one had expected. I tell you, Mr Norrell, nothing can express the gratitude Mrs Wintertowne feels at your goodness and she begs me to say to you that you are to come immediately – and Sir Walter himself says that he can see no sense in putting it off – so I told Davey to wait at the door and on no account to go anywhere else. Oh! Mr Norrell, it is to be a night of reconciliations! All misunderstandings, all unfortunate constructions which may have been placed on one or two ill-chosen words – all, all are to be swept away! It is to be quite like a play by Shakespeare!"

Mr Norrell's greatcoat was fetched and he got into the carriage; and from the expression of surprize upon his face when the carriage-doors opened and Mr Drawlight jumped in one side and Mr Lascelles jumped in the other I am tempted to suppose that he had not originally intended that those two gentlemen should accompany him to Brunswick-square.

Lascelles threw himself into the carriage, snorting with laughter and saying that he had never in his life heard of anything so ridiculous and comparing their snug drive through the London streets in Mr Norrell's carriage to ancient French and Italian fables in which fools set sail in milk-pails to fetch the moon's reflection from the bottom of a duckpond – all of which might well have offended Mr Norrell had Mr Norrell been in spirits to attend to him.

When they arrived at Brunswick-square they found, gathered upon the steps, a little crowd of people. Two men ran out to catch the horses' heads and the light from the oil-lamp above the steps shewed the crowd to be a dozen or so of Mrs Wintertowne's servants all on the look-out for the magician who was to bring back their young lady. Human nature being what it is, I dare say there may have been a few among them who were merely curious to see what such a man might look like. But many shewed in their pale faces signs that they had been grieving and these were, I think, prompted by some nobler sentiment to keep their silent vigil in the cold midnight street.

One of them took a candle and went before Mr Norrell and his friends to shew them the way, for the house was very dark and cold. They were upon the staircase when they heard Mrs Wintertowne's voice calling out from above, "Robert! Robert! Is it Mr Norrell? Oh! Thank God, sir!" She appeared before them very suddenly in a doorway. "I thought you would never come!" And then, much to Mr Norrell's consternation, she took both his hands in her own and, pressing them hard, entreated him to use his most potent spells to bring Miss Wintertowne back to life. Money was not to be thought of. He might name his price! Only say that he would return her darling child to her. He must promise her that he would!

Mr Norrell cleared his throat and was perhaps about to embark upon one of his long, uninteresting expositions of the philosophy of modern magic, when Mr Drawlight glided forward, took Mrs Wintertowne's hands and rescued them both.

"Now I beg of you, my dear madam," cried Drawlight, "to be

101

more tranquil! Mr Norrell is come, as you see, and we must try what his power may do. He begs that you will not mention payment again. Whatever he does tonight will be done for friendship's sake . . ." And here Mr Drawlight stood upon tiptoes and lifted his chin to look over Mrs Wintertowne's shoulder to where Sir Walter Pole was standing within the room. Sir Walter had just risen from his chair and stood a little way off, regarding the newcomers. In the candlelight he was pale and hollow-eyed and there was about him a kind of gauntness which had not been there before. Mere common courtesy said that he ought to have come forward to speak to them, but he did not do so.

It was curious to observe how Mr Norrell hesitated in the doorway and exhibited great unwillingness to be conducted further into the house until he had spoken to Sir Walter. "But I must just speak to Sir Walter! Just a few words with Sir Walter! – I shall do my utmost for you, Sir Walter!" he called out from the door. "Since the young lady is, ahem!, not long gone from us, I may say that the situation is promising. Yes, I think I may go so far as to say that the situation is a promising one. I shall go now, Sir Walter, and do my work. I hope, in due course, I shall have the honour of bringing you good news!"

All the assurances that Mrs Wintertowne begged for – and did not get – from Mr Norrell, Mr Norrell was now anxious to bestow upon Sir Walter who clearly did not want them. From his sanctuary in the drawing-room Sir Walter nodded and then, when Mr Norrell still lingered, he called out hoarsely, "Thank you, sir. Thank you!" And his mouth stretched out in a curious way. It was, perhaps, meant for a smile.

"I wish with all my heart, Sir Walter," called out Mr Norrell, "that I might invite you to come up with me and to see what it is I do, but the curious nature of this particular magic demands solitude. I will, I hope, have the honour of shewing you some magic upon another occasion."

Sir Walter bowed slightly and turned away.

Mrs Wintertowne was at that moment speaking to her servant, Robert, and Drawlight took advantage of this slight distraction to pull Mr Norrell to one side and whisper frantically in his ear: "No, no, sir! Do not send them away! My advice is to gather as many of them around the bed as can be persuaded to come. It is, I assure you, the best guarantee of our night's exploits being generally broadcast in the morning. And do not be afraid of making a little bustle to impress the servants – your best incantations if you please! Oh! What a noodle-head I am! Had only I thought to bring some Chinese powders to throw in the fire! I don't suppose that you have any about you?"

Mr Norrell made no reply to this but asked to be brought without delay to where Miss Wintertowne was.

But though the magician particularly asked to be taken there alone, his dear friends, Mr Drawlight and Mr Lascelles, were not so unkind as to leave him to face this great crisis of his career alone and consequently the three of them together were conducted by Robert to a chamber upon the second floor.

8

A gentleman with thistle-down hair

October 1807

T HERE WAS NO one there.

Which is to say there was someone there. Miss Wintertowne lay upon the bed, but it would have puzzled philosophy to say now whether she were someone or no one at all.

They had dressed her in a white gown and hung a silver chain about her neck; they had combed and dressed her beautiful hair and put pearl-and-garnet earrings in her ears. But it was extremely doubtful whether Miss Wintertowne cared about such things any more. They had lit candles and laid a good fire in the hearth, they had put roses about the room, which filled it with a sweet perfume, but Miss Wintertowne could have lain now with equal composure in the foulest-smelling garret in the city.

"And she was quite tolerable to look at, you say?" said Mr Lascelles.

"You never saw her?" said Drawlight. "Oh! she was a heavenly creature. Quite divine. An angel."

"Indeed? And such a pinched-looking ruin of a thing now! I shall advise all the good-looking women of my acquaintance not to die," said Mr Lascelles. He leaned closer. "They have closed her eyes," he said.

"Her eyes were perfection," said Drawlight, "a clear dark grey, with long, dark eye-lashes and dark eye-brows. It is a pity you never saw her – she was exactly the sort of creature you would have admired." Drawlight turned to Mr Norrell. "Well, sir, are you ready to begin?"

Mr Norrell was seated in a chair next to the fire. The resolute, businesslike manner, which he had adopted on his arrival at the house, had disappeared; instead he sat with neck bowed, sighing heavily, his gaze fixed upon the carpet. Mr Lascelles and Mr Drawlight looked at him with that degree of interest appropriate to the character of each – which is to say that Mr Drawlight was all fidgets and bright-eyed anticipation, and Mr Lascelles all cool, smiling scepticism. Mr Drawlight took a few respectful steps back from the bed so that Mr Norrell might more conveniently approach it and Mr Lascelles leant against a wall and crossed his arms (an attitude he often adopted in the theatre).

Mr Norrell sighed again. "Mr Drawlight, I have already said that this particular magic demands complete solitude. I must ask you to wait downstairs."

"Oh, but, sir!" protested Drawlight. "Surely such intimate friends as Lascelles and I can be no inconvenience to you? We are the quietest creatures in the world! In two minutes' time you will have quite forgotten that we are here. And I must say that I consider our presence as absolutely essential! For who will broadcast the news of your achievement tomorrow morning if not Lascelles and myself? Who will describe the ineffable grandeur of the moment when your magicianship triumphs and the young woman rises from the dead? Or the unbearable pathos of the moment when you are forced to admit defeat? You will not do it half so well yourself, sir. You know that you will not."

"Perhaps," said Mr Norrell. "But what you suggest is entirely impossible. I will not, *cannot* begin until you leave the room."

Poor Drawlight! He could not force the magician to begin the magic against his will, but to have waited so long to see some magic and then to be excluded! It was almost more than he could bear. Even Mr Lascelles was a little disappointed for he had hoped to witness something very ridiculous that he could laugh at.

When they had gone Mr Norrell rose wearily from his seat and took up a book that he had brought with him. He opened it at a place he had marked with a folded letter and placed it upon a little table so that it would be to hand if he needed to consult it. Then he began to recite a spell.

It took effect almost immediately because suddenly there was something green where nothing green had been before and a fresh, sweet smell as of woods and fields wafted through the room. Mr Norrell stopped speaking.

Someone was standing in the middle of the room: a tall, handsome person with pale, perfect skin and an immense amount of hair, as pale and shining as thistle-down. His cold, blue eyes glittered and he had long dark eye-brows, which terminated in an upward flourish. He was dressed exactly like any other gentleman, except that his coat was of the brightest green imaginable – the colour of leaves in early summer.

"*O Lar!*" began Mr Norrell in a quavering voice. "*O Lar! Magnum opus est mihi tuo auxilio. Haec virgo mortua est et familia eius eam ad vitam redire vult.*"[1] Mr Norrell pointed to the figure on the bed.

At the sight of Miss Wintertowne the gentleman with the thistle-down hair suddenly became very excited. He spread wide his hands in a gesture of surprized delight and began to speak Latin very rapidly. Mr Norrell, who was more accustomed to seeing Latin written down or printed in books, found that he could not follow the language when it was spoken so fast, though he did recognize a few words here and there, words such as "*formosa*" and "*venusta*" which are descriptive of feminine beauty.

Mr Norrell waited until the gentleman's rapture had subsided and then he directed the gentleman's attention to the mirror above

---

[1] "O Fairy. I have great need of your help. This virgin is dead and her family wish her to be returned to life."

the mantelpiece. A vision appeared of Miss Wintertowne walking along a narrow rocky path, through a mountainous and gloomy landscape. "*Ecce mortua inter terram et caelum!*" declared Mr Norrell. "*Scito igitur, O Lar, me ad hanc magnam operam te elegisse quia . . .*"[2]

"Yes, yes!" cried the gentleman suddenly breaking into English. "You elected to summon *me* because my genius for magic exceeds that of all the rest of my race. Because I have been the servant and confidential friend of Thomas Godbless, Ralph Stokesey, Martin Pale *and* of the Raven King. Because I am valorous, chivalrous, generous and as handsome as the day is long! That is all quite understood! It would have been madness to summon anyone else! We both know who *I* am. The question is: who in the world are *you?*"

"I?" said Mr Norrell, startled. "I am the greatest magician of the Age!"

The gentleman raised one perfect eye-brow as if to say he was surprised to hear it. He walked around Mr Norrell slowly, considering him from every angle. Then, most disconcerting of all, he plucked Mr Norrell's wig from his head and looked underneath, as if Mr Norrell were a cooking pot on the fire and he wished to know what was for dinner.

"I . . . I am the man who is destined to restore magic to England!" stammered Mr Norrell, grabbing back his wig and replacing it, slightly askew, upon his head.

"Well, obviously you are *that!*" said the gentleman. "Or I should not be here! You do not imagine that I would waste my time upon a three-penny hedge-sorcerer, do you? But *who* are you? That is what I wish to know. What magic have you done? Who was your master? What magical lands have you visited? What enemies have you defeated? Who are your allies?"

Mr Norrell was extremely surprised to be asked so many questions and he was not at all prepared to answer them. He

---

[2] "Here is the dead woman between earth and heaven! Know then, O Fairy, that I have chosen you for this great task because . . ."

wavered and hesitated before finally fixing upon the only one to which he had a sensible answer. "I had no master. I taught myself."

"How?"

"From books."

"Books!" (This in a tone of the utmost contempt.)

"Yes, indeed. There is a great deal of magic in books nowadays. Of course, most of it is nonsense. No one knows as well as I how much nonsense is printed in books. But there is a great deal of useful information too and it is surprizing how, after one has learnt a little, one begins to see . . ."

Mr Norrell was beginning to warm to his subject, but the gentleman with the thistle-down hair had no patience to listen to other people talk and so he interrupted him.

"Am I the first of my race that you have seen?"

"Oh, yes!"

This answer seemed to please the gentleman with the thistle-down hair and he smiled. "So! Should I agree to restore this young woman to life, what would be my reward?"

Mr Norrell cleared his throat. "What sort of thing . . . ?" he said, a little hoarsely.

"Oh! That is easily agreed!" cried the gentleman with the thistle-down hair. "My wishes are the most moderate things in the world. Fortunately I am utterly free from greed and sordid ambition. Indeed, you will find that my proposal is much more to your advantage than mine – such is my unselfish nature! I simply wish to be allowed to aid you in all your endeavours, to advise you upon all matters and to guide you in your studies. Oh! and you must take care to let all the world know that your greatest achievements are due in larger part to me!"

Mr Norrell looked a little ill. He coughed and muttered some-thing about the gentleman's generosity. "Were I the sort of magician who is eager to entrust all his business to another person, then your offer would be most welcome. But unfortunately . . . I fear . . . In short I have no notion of employing you – or indeed any other member of your race – ever again."

A long silence.

"Well, this is ungrateful indeed!" declared the gentleman, coldly. "I have put myself to the trouble of paying you this visit. I have listened with the greatest good nature to your dreary conversation. I have borne patiently with your ignorance of the proper forms and etiquette of magic. And now you scorn my offer of assistance. Other magicians, I may say, have endured all sorts of torments to gain my help. Perhaps I would do better to speak to the other one. Perhaps he understands better than you how to address persons of high rank and estate?" The gentleman glanced about the room. "I do not see him. Where is he?"

"Where is who?"

"The other one."

"The other what?"

"Magician!"

"Magici . . ." Mr Norrell began to form the word but it died upon his lips. "No, no! There is no other magician! I am the only one. I assure you I am the only one. Why should you think that . . . ?"

"*Of course* there is another magician!" declared the gentleman, as if it were perfectly ridiculous to deny anything quite so obvious. "He is your dearest friend in all the world!"

"I have no friends," said Mr Norrell.

He was utterly perplexed. Whom might the fairy mean? Childermass? Lascelles? *Drawlight?*

"He has red hair and a long nose. And he is very conceited – as are all Englishmen!" declared the gentleman with the thistle-down hair.

This was no help. Childermass, Lascelles and Drawlight were all very conceited in their ways, Childermass and Lascelles both had long noses, but none of them had red hair. Mr Norrell could make nothing of it and so he returned, with a heavy sigh, to the matter in hand. "You will not help me?" he said. "You will not bring the young woman back from the dead?"

"I did not say so!" said the gentleman with the thistle-down hair, in a tone which suggested that he wondered why Mr Norrell should think *that*. "I must confess," he continued, "that in recent centuries I have grown somewhat bored of the society of my family and servants. My sisters and cousins have many virtues to recommend them, but they are not without faults. They are, I am sorry to say, somewhat boastful, conceited and proud. This young woman," he indicated Miss Wintertowne, "she had, I dare say, all the usual accomplishments and virtues? She was graceful? Witty? Vivacious? Capricious? Danced like sunlight? Rode like the wind? Sang like an angel? Embroidered like Penelope? Spoke French, Italian, German, Breton, Welsh and many other languages?"

Mr Norrell said he supposed so. He believed that those were the sorts of things young ladies did nowadays.

"Then she will be a charming companion for me!" declared the gentleman with the thistle-down hair, clapping his hands together.

Mr Norrell licked his lips nervously. "What exactly are you proposing?"

"Grant me half the lady's life and the deal is done."

"Half her life?" echoed Mr Norrell.

"Half," said the gentleman with the thistle-down hair.

"But what would her friends say if they learnt I had bargained away half her life?" asked Mr Norrell.

"Oh! They will never know any thing of it. You may rely upon me for that," said the gentleman. "Besides, she has no life now. Half a life is better than none."

Half a life did indeed seem a great deal better than none. With half a life Miss Wintertowne might marry Sir Walter and save him from bankruptcy. Then Sir Walter might continue in office and lend his support to all Mr Norrell's plans for reviving English magic. But Mr Norrell had read a great many books in which were described the dealings of other English magicians with persons of

111

this race and he knew very well how deceitful they could be. He thought he saw how the gentleman intended to trick him.

"How long is a life?" he asked.

The gentleman with the thistle-down hair spread his hands in a gesture of the utmost candour. "How long would you like?"

Mr Norrell considered. "Let us suppose she had lived until she was ninety-four. Ninety-four would have been a good age. She is nineteen now. That would be another seventy-five years. If you were to bestow upon her another seventy-five years, then I see no reason why you should not have half of it."

"Seventy-five years then," agreed the gentleman with the thistle-down hair, "exactly half of which belongs to me."

Mr Norrell regarded him nervously. "Is there any thing more we must do?" he asked. "Shall we sign something?"

"No, but I should take something of the lady's to signify my claim upon her."

"Take one of these rings," suggested Mr Norrell, "or this necklace about her neck. I am sure I can explain away a missing ring or necklace."

"No," said the gentleman with the thistle-down hair. "It ought to be something . . . Ah! I know!"

Drawlight and Lascelles were seated in the drawing-room where Mr Norrell and Sir Walter Pole had first met. It was a gloomy enough spot. The fire burnt low in the grate and the candles were almost out. The curtains were undrawn and no one had put up the shutters. The rattle of the rain upon the windows was very melancholy.

"It is certainly a night for raising the dead," remarked Mr Lascelles. "Rain and trees lash the window-panes and the wind moans in the chimney – all the appropriate stage effects, in fact. I am frequently struck with the play-writing fit and I do not know that tonight's proceedings might not inspire me to try again – a tragi-comedy, telling of an impoverished minister's desperate attempts to gain money by any means, beginning with a mercenary marriage and ending with sorcery. I should think it might be received very well. I believe I shall call it, *'Tis Pity She's a Corpse*."

Lascelles paused for Drawlight to laugh at this witticism, but Drawlight had been put out of humour by the magician's refusal to allow him to stay and witness the magic, and all he said was: "Where do you suppose they have all gone?"

"I do not know."

"Well, considering all that you and I have done for them, I think we have deserved better than this! It is scarcely half an hour since they were so full of their gratitude to us. To have forgotten us so soon is very bad! And we have not been offered so much as a bit of cake since we arrived. I dare say it is rather too late for dinner – though I for one am famished to death!" He was silent a moment. "The fire is going out too," he remarked.

"Then put some more coals on," suggested Lascelles.

"What! And make myself all dirty?"

One by one all the candles went out and the light from the fire grew less and less until the Venetian paintings upon the walls became nothing but great squares of deepest black hung upon walls of a black that was slightly less profound. For a long time they sat in silence.

"That was the clock striking half-past one o'clock!" said Drawlight suddenly. "How lonely it sounds! Ugh! All the horrid things one reads of in novels always happen just as the church bell tolls or the clock strikes some hour or other in a dark house!"

"I cannot recall an instance of any thing very dreadful happening at half-past one," said Lascelles.

At that moment they heard footsteps on the stairs – which quickly became footsteps in the passageway. The drawing-room door was pushed open and someone stood there, candle in hand.

Drawlight grasped for the poker.

But it was Mr Norrell.

"Do not be alarmed, Mr Drawlight. There is nothing to be afraid of."

Yet Mr Norrell's face, as he raised up his candlestick, seemed to tell a different story; he was very pale and his eyes were wide and not yet emptied, it seemed, of the dregs of fear. "Where is Sir Walter?" he asked. "Where are the others? Miss Wintertowne is asking for her mama."

Mr Norrell was obliged to repeat the last sentence twice before the other two gentlemen could be made to understand him.

Lascelles blinked two or three times and opened his mouth as if in surprize, but then, recovering himself, he shut his mouth again and assumed a supercilious expression; this he wore for the remainder of the night, as if he regularly attended houses where young ladies were raised from the dead and considered this particular example to have been, upon the whole, a rather dull affair. Drawlight, in the meantime, had a thousand things to say and I dare say he said all of them, but unfortunately no one had attention to spare just then to discover what they were.

Drawlight and Lascelles were sent to find Sir Walter. Then Sir Walter fetched Mrs Wintertowne, and Mr Norrell led that lady, tearful and trembling, to her daughter's room. Meanwhile the news of Miss Wintertowne's return to life began to penetrate other parts of the house; the servants learnt of it and were overjoyed and full of gratitude to Mr Norrell, Mr Drawlight and Mr Lascelles. A butler and two manservants approached Mr Drawlight and Mr Lascelles and begged to be allowed to say that if ever Mr Drawlight or Mr Lascelles could benefit from any small service that the butler or the manservants might be able to render them, they had only to speak.

Mr Lascelles whispered to Mr Drawlight that he had not realized before that doing kind actions would lead to his being addressed in such familiar terms by so many low people – it was most unpleasant – he would take care to do no more. Fortunately the low people were in such glad spirits that they never knew they had offended him.

It was soon learnt that Miss Wintertowne had left her bed and, leaning upon Mr Norrell's arm, had gone to her own sitting-room where she was now established in a chair by her fire and that she had asked for a cup of tea.

Drawlight and Lascelles were summoned upstairs to a pretty little sitting-room where they found Miss Wintertowne, her mother, Sir Walter, Mr Norrell and some of the servants.

One would have thought from their looks that it had been Mrs Wintertowne and Sir Walter who had journeyed across several supernatural worlds during the night, they were so grey-faced and drawn; Mrs Wintertowne was weeping and Sir Walter passed his hand across his pale brow from time to time like someone who had seen horrors.

Miss Wintertowne, on the other hand, appeared quite calm and collected, like a young lady who had spent a quiet, uneventful evening at home. She was sitting in a chair in the same elegant gown that she had been wearing when Drawlight and Lascelles had seen her last. She rose and smiled at Drawlight. "I think, sir, that you and I scarcely ever met before, yet I have been told how much I owe to you. But I fear it is a debt quite beyond any repaying. That I am here at all is in a large part due to your energy and insistence. Thank you, sir. Many, many thanks."

And she held out both her hands to him and he took them.

"Oh! Madam!" he cried, all bows and smiles. "It was, I do assure you, the greatest hon . . ."

And then he stopped and was silent a moment. "Madam?" he said. He gave a short, embarrassed laugh (which was odd enough in itself – Drawlight was not easily embarrassed). He did not let go of her hands, but looked around the room as if in search of someone to help him out of a difficulty. Then he lifted one of her own hands and shewed it to her. She did not appear in any way alarmed by what she saw, but she did look surprised; she raised the hand so that her mother could see it.

The little finger of her left hand was gone.

9

Lady Pole

October 1807

IT HAS BEEN remarked (by a lady infinitely cleverer than the present author) how kindly disposed the world in general feels to young people who either die or marry. Imagine then the interest that surrounded Miss Wintertowne! No young lady ever had such advantages before: for she died upon the Tuesday, was raised to life in the early hours of Wednesday morning, and was married upon the Thursday; which some people thought too much excitement for one week.

The desire to see her was quite universal. The full stretch of most people's information was that she had lost a finger in her passage from one world to the next and back again. This was most tantalizing; was she changed in any other way? No one knew.

On Wednesday morning (which was the morning that followed her happy revival) the principals in this marvellous adventure seemed all in a conspiracy to deprive the Town of news; morning-callers at Brunswick-square learnt only that Miss Wintertowne and her mother were resting; in Hanover-square it was exactly the same – Mr Norrell was very much fatigued – it was entirely impossible that he see any body; and as for Sir Walter Pole, no body was quite certain where to find him (though it was strongly suspected that he was at Mrs Wintertowne's house in Brunswick-square). Had it not been for Mr Drawlight and Mr Lascelles (benevolent souls!) the Town would have been starved of information of any sort, but they drove diligently about London making their appearance in a quite impossible number of drawing-rooms, morning-rooms, dining-rooms and card-rooms. It is impossible to say how many dinners Drawlight was invited to sit down to that day – and it is fortunate that he was never at any time much of an eater or he might have done some lasting damage to his digestion. Fifty times or more he must have described how, after Miss Wintertowne's restoration, Mrs Wintertowne and he had wept together; how Sir Walter Pole and he had clasped each other's hand; how Sir Walter had thanked him most gratefully and how he had begged Sir Walter not to think of it; and how Mrs Wintertowne had insisted that Mr Lascelles and he both be driven home in her very own carriage.

Sir Walter Pole had left Mrs Wintertowne's house at about seven o'clock and had gone back to his lodgings to sleep for a few hours, but at about midday he returned to Brunswick-square just as the Town had supposed. (How our neighbours find us out!) By this time it had become apparent to Mrs Wintertowne that her daughter now enjoyed a certain celebrity; that she had, as it were, risen to public eminence overnight. As well as the people who left their cards at the door, great numbers of letters and messages of congratulation were arriving every hour for Miss Wintertowne, many of them from people of whom Mrs Wintertowne had never heard. "Permit me, madam," wrote one, "to entreat you to shake off the oppression of that shadowy vale which has been revealed to you."

That unknown persons should think themselves entitled to comment upon so private a matter as a death and a resurrection, that they should vent their curiosity in letters to her daughter was a circumstance to excite Mrs Wintertowne's utmost displeasure; she had a great deal to say in censure of such vulgar, ill-bred beings, and upon his arrival at Brunswick-square Sir Walter was obliged to listen to all of it.

"My advice, ma'am," he said, "is to think no more about it. As we politicians well know a policy of dignity and silence is our best defence against this sort of impertinence."

"Ah! Sir Walter!" cried his mother-in-law to be. "It is very gratifying to me to discover how frequently our opinions agree! Dignity and silence. Quite. I do not think we can ever be too discreet upon the subject of poor, dear Emma's sufferings. After tomorrow I for one am determined never to speak of it again."

"Perhaps," said Sir Walter, "I did not mean to go so far. Because, you know, we must not forget Mr Norrell. We shall always have a standing reminder of what has happened in Mr Norrell. I fear he must often be with us – after the service he has done us we can scarcely ever shew him consideration enough." He paused and then added with a wry twist of his ugly face, "Happily Mr Norrell himself has been so good as to indicate how he thinks *my* share of the obligation might best be discharged." This was a reference to a conversation which Sir Walter and Mr Norrell had had at four o'clock that morning, when Mr Norrell had waylaid Sir Walter upon the stairs and talked to him at great length about his plans to baffle the French by magic.

Mrs Wintertowne said that she would, of course, be glad to distinguish Mr Norrell with marks of special respect and consideration; any one might know how highly she regarded him. Quite apart from his great magicianship – which, said Mrs Wintertowne, there was no need to mention when he came to the house – he seemed a very good sort of old gentleman.

"Indeed," said Sir Walter. "But for now our most pressing concern must be that Miss Wintertowne should not undertake more than she is equal to – and it was of this that I particularly wished to speak to you. I do not know what may be your opinion but it seems to me that it would be as well to put off the wedding for a week or two."

Mrs Wintertowne could not approve of such a plan; all the arrangements were made and so much of the wedding-dinner cooked. Soup, jellies, boiled meats, pickled sturgeon and so forth were all ready; what was the good of letting it all spoil now, only to have it all to do over again in a week or so? Sir Walter had nothing to say to arguments of domestic economy, and so he suggested that they ask Miss Wintertowne to say whether or not she felt strong enough.

And so they rose from their seats in the icy drawing-room (where this conversation had taken place) and went up to Miss Wintertowne's sitting-room on the second-floor where they put the question to her.

"Oh!" said she. "I never felt better in my life. I feel very strong and well. Thank you. I have been out already this morning. I do not often walk. I rarely feel equal to exercise, but this morning I felt as if the house were a prison. I longed to be outside."

Sir Walter looked very concerned. "Was that wise?" He turned to Mrs Wintertowne. "Was that well done?"

Mrs Wintertowne opened her mouth to protest but her daughter only laughed and exclaimed, "Oh! Mama knew nothing of it, I assure you. I went out while she was asleep in her room. Barnard went with me. And I walked round Brunswick-square twenty times. Twenty! – is not that the most ridiculous thing you ever heard? But I was possessed of such a desire to walk! Indeed I would have run, I think, if it were at all possible, but in London, you know . . ." She laughed again. "I wanted to go further but Barnard would not let me. Barnard was in a great flutter and worry lest I should faint away in the road. She would not let me go out of sight of the house."

They stared at her. It was – apart from anything else – probably the longest speech Sir Walter had ever heard her utter. She was sitting very straight with a bright eye and blooming complexion – the very picture of health and beauty. She spoke so rapidly and with such expression; she looked so cheerful and was so exceedingly animated. It was as if Mr Norrell had not only restored her to life, but to twice or thrice the amount of life she had had before.

It was very odd.

"Of course," said Sir Walter, "if you feel well enough to take exercise, then I am sure that no one would wish to prevent you – nothing is so likely to make you strong, and to ensure your continuing health, as regular exercise. But perhaps, for the present, it would be as well not to go out without telling any one. You should have someone more than Barnard to guard you. From tomorrow, you know, I may claim that honour for myself."

"But you will be busy, Sir Walter," she reminded him. "You will have all your Government business to attend to."

"Indeed, but . . ."

"Oh! I know that you will be pretty constantly engaged with business affairs. I know I must not expect anything else."

She seemed so cheerfully resigned to his neglecting her that he could not help opening his mouth to protest – but the justice of what she said prevented him from saying a word. Ever since he had first seen her at Lady Winsell's house in Bath he had been greatly struck by her beauty and elegance – and had quickly concluded that it would be a very good thing, not only to marry her as soon as it could conveniently be contrived, but also to get better acquainted with her – for he had begun to suspect that, setting aside the money, she might suit him very well as a wife. He thought that an hour or so of conversation might accomplish a great deal towards setting them upon that footing of perfect unreserve and confidence which was so much to be desired between husband and wife. He had high hopes that such a tête-à-tête would soon provide ample proofs of their mutual sympathies and tastes. Several things she had said had encouraged him to hope that it might be so. And being a man – and a clever one – and forty-two years old, he naturally had a great deal of information and a great many opinions upon almost every subject you care to mention, which he was eager to communicate to a lovely woman of nineteen – all of which, he thought, she could not fail but to find quite enthralling. But, what with *his* great preoccupation with business and *her* poor health they had yet to have this interesting conversation; and now she told him that she expected things to continue much the same after they were married. She did not appear to resent it. Instead, with her new, lively spirits, she seemed quite entertained that he should ever have deceived himself that matters could be otherwise.

Unfortunately he was already late for an appointment with the Foreign Secretary so he took Miss Wintertowne's hand (her whole, right hand) and kissed it very gallantly; told her how much he looked forward to the morrow that would make him the happiest of men; attended politely – hat in hand – to a short speech by Mrs Wintertowne upon the subject; and left the house resolving to consider the problem further – just as soon, in fact, as he could find the time.

Upon the following morning the wedding did indeed take place at St George's Hanover-square. It was attended by almost all of His Majesty's Ministers, two or three of the Royal Dukes, half a dozen admirals, a bishop and several generals. But I am sorry to say that, vital as such great men must always be to a Nation's peace and prosperity, on the day that Miss Wintertowne married Sir Walter Pole, no body cared tuppence for any of them. The man who drew most eyes, the man whom every body whispered to his neighbour to point out to him, was the magician, Mr Norrell.

10

The difficulty of finding
employment for a magician

October 1807

S IR WALTER INTENDED to introduce the subject of magic
among the other Ministers by degrees, allowing them to
grow gradually accustomed to the idea before proposing
that they make trial of Mr Norrell in the war. He was afraid that
they would oppose him; he was sure that Mr Canning would be
sarcastic, that Lord Castlereagh would be uncooperative, and the
Earl of Chatham merely bemused.

But all of these fears were entirely unfounded. The Ministers, he soon
discovered, were quite as alive to the novelty of the situation as any one
else in London. The next time the cabinet met at Burlington House[1]

---

[1] Burlington House in Piccadilly was the London residence of the Duke of
Portland, the First Minister of the Treasury (whom many people nowadays
like to call the *Prime Minister* in the French style). It had been erected in an
Age when English noblemen were not afraid to rival their Monarch in
displays of power and wealth and it had no equal for beauty anywhere in
the capital. As for the Duke himself, he was a most respectable old person,
but, poor man, he did not accord with any body's idea of what a Prime
Minister ought to be. He was very old and sick. Just at present he lay in a
curtained room somewhere in a remote part of the house, stupefied by
laudanum and dying by degrees. He was of no utility whatsoever to his
country and not much to his fellow Ministers. The only advantage of his
leadership as far as they could see was that it allowed them to use his
magnificent house as their meeting-place and to employ his magnificent
servants to fetch them any little thing they might fancy out of his cellar. (They
generally found that governing Great Britain was a thirsty business.)

122

they declared themselves eager to employ England's only magician. But it was by no means clear what ought to be done with him. It had been two hundred years since the English Government had last commissioned a magician and they were a little out of the habit of it.

"*My* chief problem," explained Lord Castlereagh, "is in finding men for the Army – a quite impossible task, I assure you; the British are a peculiarly unmilitary race. But I have my eye on Lincolnshire; I am told that the pigs in Lincolnshire are particularly fine and by eating them the population grows very stout and strong. Now what would suit me best would be a general spell cast over Lincolnshire so that three or four thousand young men would all at once be filled with a lively desire to become soldiers and fight the French." He looked at Sir Walter rather wistfully. "Would your friend know of such a spell, Sir Walter, do you think?"

Sir Walter did not know but he said he would ask Mr Norrell.

Later that same day Sir Walter called upon Mr Norrell and put the question to him. Mr Norrell was delighted. He did not believe that anyone had ever proposed such a piece of magic before and begged Sir Walter to convey his compliments to Lord Castlereagh as the possessor of a most original brain. As to whether or not it were possible; "The difficulty lies in confining the application of the spell to Lincolnshire – and to young men. There is a danger that if we were successful – which I flatter myself we would be – then Lincolnshire – and several of the neighbouring counties – might be entirely emptied of people."

Sir Walter went back to Lord Castlereagh and told him no.

The next magic which the Ministers proposed pleased Mr Norrell a great deal less. The resurrection of Lady Pole engrossed the thoughts of everyone in London and the Ministers were by no means exempt from the general fascination. Lord Castlereagh began it when he asked the other Ministers who was it that Napoleon Buonaparte had feared most in all the world? Who had always seemed to know what the wicked French emperor would do next? Who had inflicted so resounding a defeat upon the French that they dare not stick their French noses out of their ports? Who had united in one person all the virtues that make up an Englishman? Who else, said Lord Castlereagh, but Lord Nelson? Clearly the first thing to be done was to bring back Lord Nelson from the dead. Lord Castlereagh begged Sir Walter's pardon – perhaps he had not understood something – but why they were wasting time talking about it?

Whereupon Mr Canning, an energetic and quarrelsome person, replied quickly that of course Lord Nelson was sadly missed, Nelson had been the Nation's hero, Nelson had done everything Lord Castlereagh said he did. But when all was said and done – and Mr Canning meant no disrespect to the Navy, that most glorious of British institutions – Nelson had only been a sailor, whereas the late Mr Pitt had been everything.[2] If anyone dead was going to be brought back to life then really there was no choice – it must be Pitt.

Lord Chatham (who was also the late Mr Pitt's brother) naturally seconded this proposal but he wondered why they had to make a choice – why not resurrect both Pitt and Nelson? It would only be a question of paying the magician twice and there could not be any objection to that, he supposed?

Then other Ministers proposed other dead gentlemen as candidates for restoration until it seemed that half the vaults in England might be emptied. Very soon they had quite a long list and were, as usual, starting to argue about it.

"This will not do," said Sir Walter. "We must begin somewhere and it seems to me that every one of us was helped to his present position by the friendship of Mr Pitt. We would do very wrong to give some other gentleman the preference."

---

[2] William Pitt the Younger (1759–1806). It is very doubtful that we will ever see his like again, for he became Prime Minister at the age of twenty-four and led the country from that day forth, with just one brief interval of three years, until his death.

A messenger was sent to fetch Mr Norrell from Hanover-square to Burlington House. Mr Norrell was led into the magnificent painted saloon where the Ministers were sitting. Sir Walter told him that they were contemplating another resurrection.

Mr Norrell turned very pale and muttered something of how his special regard for Sir Walter had compelled him to undertake a sort of magic which otherwise he would not have attempted – he really had no wish to make a second attempt – the Ministers did not know what they were asking.

But when Mr Norrell understood better *who* it was that they proposed as a candidate, he looked a great deal relieved and was heard to say something about the condition of the *body*.

Then the Ministers thought how Mr Pitt had been dead for almost two years, and that, devoted as they had been to Pitt in his life, they really had very little desire to see him in his present condition. Lord Chatham (Mr Pitt's brother) remarked sadly that poor William would certainly have come a good deal unravelled by now.

The subject was not mentioned again.

A week or so later Lord Castlereagh proposed sending Mr Norrell to the Netherlands or possibly Portugal – places where the Ministers entertained faint hopes of gaining some foothold against Buonaparte – where Mr Norrell might do magic under the direction of the generals and the admirals. So Admiral Paycocke, an ancient red-faced seaman, and Captain Harcourt-Bruce of the 20th Light Dragoons were dispatched as a joint military and naval expedition to Hanover-square to take an observation of Mr Norrell.

Captain Harcourt-Bruce was not only dashing, handsome and brave, he was also rather romantic. The reappearance of magic in England thrilled him immensely. He was a great reader of the more exciting sort of history – and his head was full of ancient battles in which the English were outnumbered by the French and doomed to die, when all at once would be heard the sound of strange, unearthly music, and upon a hilltop would appear the Raven King in his tall, black helmet with its mantling of raven-feathers streaming in the wind; and he would gallop down the hillside on his tall, black horse with a hundred human knights and a hundred fairy knights at his back, and he would defeat the French by magic.

That was Captain Harcourt-Bruce's idea of a magician. *That* was the sort of thing which he now expected to see reproduced on every battlefield on the Continent. So when he saw Mr Norrell in his drawing-room in Hanover-square, and after he had sat and watched Mr Norrell peevishly complain to his footman, first that the cream in his tea was too creamy, and next that it was too watery – well, I shall not surprize you when I say he was somewhat disappointed. In fact he was so downcast by the whole under-taking that Admiral Paycocke, a bluff old gentleman, felt rather sorry for him and only had the heart to laugh at him and tease him very moderately about it.

Admiral Paycocke and Captain Harcourt-Bruce went back to the Ministers and said it was absolutely out of the question to send Mr Norrell anywhere; the admirals and the generals would never forgive the Government if they did it. For some weeks that autumn it seemed the Ministers would never be able to find employment for their only magician.

11

Brest

November 1807

I N THE FIRST week of November a squadron of French ships
was preparing to leave the port of Brest which lies on the west
coast of Brittany in France. The intention of the French was
to cruise about the Bay of Biscay looking for British ships to
capture or, if they were unable to do that, to prevent the British
from doing any thing which they appeared to want to do.

The wind blew steadily off the land. The French sailors made
their preparations quickly and efficiently and the ships were
almost ready when heavy black clouds appeared suddenly and
a rain began to fall.

Now it was only natural that such an important port as Brest
should contain a great number of people who studied the winds
and the weather. Just as the ships were about to set sail several of
these persons hurried down to the docks in great excitement to
warn the sailors that there was something very queer about the
rain: the clouds, they said, had come from the north, whereas the
wind was blowing from the east. The thing was impossible, but it
had happened. The captains of the ships just had time to be
astonished, incredulous or unnerved – as their characters dictated
– when another piece of news reached them.

Brest harbour consists of an inner bay and an outer, the inner
bay being separated from the open sea by a long thin peninsula. As

the rain grew heavier the French officers in charge of the ships learnt that a great fleet of British ships had appeared in the outer bay.

How many ships were there? The officers' informants did not know. More than could be easily counted – perhaps as many as a hundred. Like the rain, the ships had seemingly arrived in a single instant out of an empty sea. What sort of ships were they? Ah! That was the strangest thing of all! The ships were all ships of the line, heavily armed two- and three-decked warships.

This was astonishing news. The ships' great number and their great size was, in truth, more puzzling than their sudden appearance. The British Navy blockaded Brest continually, but never with more than twenty-five ships at a time, of which only ten or twelve were ships of the line, the remainder being agile little frigates, sloops and brigs.

So peculiar was this tale of a hundred ships that the French captains did not believe it until they had ridden or rowed to Lochrist or Camaret Saint-Julien or other places where they could stand upon the clifftops and see the ships for themselves.

Days went by. The sky was the colour of lead and the rain continued to fall. The British ships remained stubbornly where they were. The people of Brest were in great dread lest some of the ships might attempt to come up to the town and bombard it. But the British ships did nothing.

Stranger still was the news that came from other ports in the French Empire, from Rochefort, Toulon, Marseilles, Genoa, Venice, Flushing, Lorient, Antwerp and a hundred other towns of lesser importance. They too were blockaded by British fleets of a hundred or so warships. It was impossible to comprehend. Added together these fleets contained more warships than the British possessed. Indeed they contained more warships than there were upon the face of the earth.

The most senior officer at Brest at that time was Admiral Desmoulins. He had a servant, a very small man no bigger than an eight-year-old child, and as dark as a European can be. He looked as if he had been put into the oven and baked for too long and was now rather overdone. His skin was the colour of a coffee-bean and the texture of a dried-up rice-pudding. His hair was black, twisted and greasy like the spines and quills you may observe on the less succulent parts of roasted chickens. His name was Perroquet (which means parrot). Admiral Desmoulins was very proud of Perroquet; proud of his size, proud of his cleverness, proud of his agility and most of all, proud of his colour. Admiral Desmoulins often boasted that he had seen blacks who would appear fair next to Perroquet.

It was Perroquet who sat in the rain for four days studying the ships through his eye-glass. Rain spurted from his child-size bicorn hat as if from two little rainspouts; it sank into the capes of his child-size coat, making the coat fearfully heavy and turning the wool into felt; and it ran in little streams down his baked, greasy skin; but he paid it not the slightest attention.

After four days Perroquet sighed, jumped to his feet, stretched himself, took off his hat, gave his head a good scratch, yawned and said, "Well, my Admiral, they are the queerest ships I have ever seen and I do not understand them."

"In what way, Perroquet?" asked the Admiral.

Gathered on the cliffs near Camaret Saint-Julien with Perroquet were Admiral Desmoulins and Captain Jumeau, and rain spurted from *their* bicorn hats and turned the wool of *their* coats into felt and filled their boots with half an inch of water.

"Well," said Perroquet, "the ships sit upon the sea as if they were becalmed and yet they are not becalmed. There is a strong westerly wind which ought by rights to blow them on to these rocks, but does it? No. Do the ships beat off? No. Do they reduce sail? No. I cannot count the number of times the wind has changed since I have sat here, but what have the men on those ships done? Nothing."

Captain Jumeau, who disliked Perroquet and was jealous of his influence with the Admiral, laughed. "He is mad, my Admiral. If the British were really as idle or ignorant as he says, their ships would all be heaps of broken spars by now."

"They are more like pictures of ships," mused Perroquet, paying the Captain no attention, "than the ships themselves. But a queerer thing still, my Admiral, is that ship, the three-decker at the northernmost tip of the line. On Monday it was just like the others but now its sails are all in tatters, its mizzen mast is gone and there is a ragged hole in its side."

"Huzza!" cried Captain Jumeau. "Some brave French crew has inflicted this damage while we stand here talking."

Perroquet grinned. "And do you think, Captain, that the British would permit one French ship to go up to their hundred ships and blow one of them to bits and then sail calmly away again? Ha! I should like to see you do it, Captain, in your little boat. No, my Admiral, it is my opinion that the British ship is melting."

"Melting!" declared the Admiral in surprize.

"The hull bulges like an old woman's knitting bag," said Perroquet. "And the bowsprit and the spritsail yard are drooping into the water."

"What idiotic nonsense!" declared Captain Jumeau. "How can a ship melt?"

"I do not know," said Perroquet, thoughtfully. "It depends upon what it is made of."

"Jumeau, Perroquet," said Admiral Desmoulins, "I believe that our best course will be to sail out and examine those ships. If the British fleet seems likely to attack, we will turn back, but in the meantime perhaps we may learn something."

So Perroquet and the Admiral and Captain Jumeau set sail in the rain with a few brave men; for sailors, though they face hardship with equanimity, are superstitious, and Perroquet was not the only person in Brest who had noticed the queerness of the British ships.

After they had gone some way, our adventurers could see that the strange ships were entirely grey and that they glittered; even under that dark sky, even in all that drenching rain they shone. Once, for a moment, the clouds parted and a ray of sunlight struck the sea. The ships disappeared. Then the clouds closed and the ships were there again.

"Dear God!" cried the Admiral. "What does all this mean?"

"Perhaps," said Perroquet uneasily, "the British ships have all been sunk and these are their ghosts."

Still the strange ships glittered and shone, and this led to some discussion as to what they might be made of. The Admiral thought perhaps iron or steel. (Metal ships indeed! The French are, as I have often supposed, a very whimsical nation.)

Captain Jumeau wondered if they might not be of silver paper.

"Silver paper!" exclaimed the Admiral.

"Oh, yes!" said Captain Jumeau. "Ladies, you know, take silver paper and roll it into quills and make little baskets of it, which they then decorate with flowers and fill with sugar plums."

The Admiral and Perroquet were surprised to hear this, but Captain Jumeau was a handsome man, and clearly knew more of the ways of ladies than they did.

But if it took one lady an evening to make a basket, how many ladies would it take to make a fleet? The Admiral said it made his head hurt to think of it.

The sun came out again. This time, since they were closer to ships, they could see how the sunlight shone *through* them and made them colourless until they were just a faint sparkle upon the water.

"Glass," said the Admiral, and he was near to the mark, but it was clever Perroquet who finally hit upon the truth.

"No, my Admiral, it is the rain. They are made of rain."

As the rain fell from the heavens the drops were made to flow together to form solid masses – pillars and beams and sheets, which someone had shaped into the likeness of a hundred ships.

Perroquet and the Admiral and Captain Jumeau were consumed with curiosity to know who could have made such a thing and they agreed he must be a master-rainsmith.

"But not only a master-rainsmith!" exclaimed the Admiral, "A master-puppeteer! See how they bob up and down upon the water! How the sails billow and fall!"

"They are certainly the prettiest things that ever I saw, my Admiral," agreed Perroquet, "but I repeat what I said before; he knows nothing of sailing or seamanship, whoever he is."

For two hours the Admiral's wooden ship sailed in and out of the rain-ships. Being ships of rain they made no sound at all – no creaking of timber, no slap of sail in the wind, no call of sailor to his mate. Several times groups of smooth-faced men of rain came to the ship's rail to gaze out at the wooden ship with its crew of flesh-and-blood men, but what the rain-sailors were thinking, no one could tell. Yet the Admiral, the Captain and Perroquet felt themselves to be perfectly safe, for, as Perroquet remarked, "Even if the rain-sailors wish to fire upon us, they only have rain-cannonballs to do it with and we will only get wet."

Perroquet and the Admiral and Captain Jumeau were lost in admiration. They forgot that they had been tricked, forgot that they had wasted a week and that for a week the British had been slipping into ports on the Baltic coast and ports on the Portuguese coast and all sorts of other ports where the Emperor Napoleon Buonaparte did not want them to go. But the spell which held the ships in place appeared to be weakening (which presumably explained the melting ship at the northernmost point of the fleet). After two hours it stopped raining and in the same moment the spell broke, which Perroquet and the Admiral and Captain Jumeau knew by a curious twist of their senses, as if they had tasted a string quartet, or been, for a moment, deafened by the sight of the colour blue. For the merest instant the rain-ships became mist-ships and then the breeze gently blew them apart.

The Frenchmen were alone upon the empty Atlantic.

12

The Spirit of English Magic
urges Mr Norrell to the Aid of Britannia

December 1807

O N A DAY in December two great draycarts happened to
collide in Cheapside. One, which was loaded with
barrels of sherry-wine, overturned. While the draymen
argued about which of them was to blame, some passers-by
observed that sherry-wine was leaking from one of the barrels.
Soon a crowd of drinkers gathered with glasses and pint-pots to
catch the sherry, and hooks and bars to make holes in those casks
which were still undamaged. The draycarts and crowd had soon
so effectively stopt up Cheapside that queues of carriages formed
in all the neighbouring streets, Poultry, Threadneedle-street,
Bartholomew-lane and, in the other direction, Aldersgate, Newgate
and Paternoster-row. It became impossible to imagine how the knot
of carriages, horses and people would ever get undone again.

Of the two draymen one was handsome and the other was fat
and, having made up their quarrel, they became a sort of Bacchus
and Silenus to the revel. They decided to entertain both themselves and their followers by opening all the carriage-doors to see
what the rich people were doing inside. Coachmen and footmen
tried to prevent this impertinence but the crowd were too many to
be held off and too drunk to mind the blows of the whip which the
crosser sort of coachmen gave them. In one of these carriages the

fat drayman discovered Mr Norrell and cried, "What! Old Norrell!" The draymen both climbed into the carriage to shake Mr Norrell's hand and breathe sherry fumes all over him and assure him that they would lose no time in moving everything out of the way so that he – the hero of the French Blockade – might pass. Which promise they kept and respectable people found their horses unhitched and their carriages pushed and shoved into tanners' yards and other nasty places, or backed into dirty brick-lanes where they got stuck fast and all the varnish was scraped off; and when the draymen and their friends had made this triumphal path for Mr Norrell they escorted him and his carriage along it, as far as Hanover-square, cheering all the way, flinging their hats in the air and making up songs about him.

Everyone, it seemed, was delighted with what Mr Norrell had done. A large part of the French Navy had been tricked into remaining in its ports for eleven days and during that time the British had been at liberty to sail about the Bay of Biscay, the English Channel and the German Sea, just as it pleased and a great many things had been accomplished. Spies had been deposited in various parts of the French Empire and other spies brought back to England with news about what Buonaparte was doing. British merchant ships had unloaded their cargoes of coffee and cotton and spices in Dutch and Baltic ports without any interference.

Napoleon Buonaparte, it was said, was scouring France to find a magician of his own – but with no success. In London the Ministers were quite astonished to find that, for once, they had done something the Nation approved.

Mr Norrell was invited to the Admiralty, where he drank madeira-wine in the Board Room. He sat in a chair close to the fire and had a long comfortable chat with the First Lord of the Admiralty, Lord Mulgrave, and the First Secretary to the Admiralty, Mr Horrocks. Above the fireplace there were carvings of nautical instruments and garlands of flowers which Mr Norrell greatly admired. He described the beautiful carvings in the library at Hurtfew Abbey; "And yet," said Mr Norrell, "I envy you, my lord. Indeed I do. Such a fine representation of the instruments of your profession! I wish that I might have done the same. Nothing looks so striking. Nothing, I believe, inspires a man with such eagerness to begin his day's work as the sight of his instruments neatly laid out – or their images in good English oak as we have here. But really a magician has need of so few tools. I will tell you a little trick, my lord, the more apparatus a magician carries about with him – coloured powders, stuffed cats, magical hats and so forth – the greater the fraud you will eventually discover him to be!"

And what, inquired Mr Horrocks politely, were the few tools that a magician did require?

"Why! Nothing really," said Mr Norrell. "Nothing but a silver basin for seeing visions in."

"Oh!" cried Mr Horrocks. "I believe I would give almost any thing to see *that* magic done – would not you, my lord? Oh, Mr Norrell, might we prevail upon you to shew us a vision in a silver basin?"

Usually Mr Norrell was the last man in the world to satisfy such idle curiosity, but he had been so pleased with his reception at the Admiralty (for the two gentlemen paid him a world of compliments) that he agreed almost immediately and a servant was dispatched to find a silver basin; "A silver basin about a foot in diameter," said Mr Norrell, "which you must fill with clean water."

The Admiralty had lately sent out orders for three ships to rendezvous south of Gibraltar and Lord Mulgrave had a great curiosity to know whether or not this had occurred; would Mr Norrell be able to find it out? Mr Norrell did not know, but promised to try. When the basin was brought and Mr Norrell bent over it, Lord Mulgrave and Mr Horrocks felt as if nothing else could have so conjured up the ancient glories of English magic;

they felt as if they were living in the Age of Stokesey, Godbless and the Raven King.

A picture appeared upon the surface of the water in the silver basin, a picture of three ships riding the waves of a blue sea. The strong, clear light of the Mediterranean shone out into the gloomy December room and lit up the faces of the three gentlemen who peered into the bowl.

"It moves!" cried Lord Mulgrave in astonishment.

It did indeed. The sweetest white clouds imaginable were gliding across the blue sky, the ships rode the waves and tiny people could be seen moving about them. Lord Mulgrave and Mr Horrocks had no difficulty in recognizing HMS *Catherine of Winchester*, HMS *Laurel* and HMS *Centaur*.

"Oh, Mr Norrell!" cried Mr Horrocks. "The *Centaur* is my cousin's ship. Can you shew me Captain Barry?"

Mr Norrell fidgeted about and drew in his breath with a sharp hiss and stared fiercely at the silver basin, and by and by appeared a vision of a pink-faced, gold-haired, overgrown cherub of a man walking about a quarterdeck. This, Mr Horrocks assured them, was his cousin, Captain Barry.

"He looks very well, does he not?" cried Mr Horrocks. "I am glad to know he is in such good health."

"Where are they? Can you tell?" Lord Mulgrave asked Mr Norrell.

"Alas," said Mr Norrell, "this art of making pictures is the most imprecise in the world.[1] I am delighted to have had the honour of shewing your lordship some of His Majesty's ships. I am yet more pleased that they are the ones you want – which is frankly more than I expected – but I fear I can tell you nothing further."

So delighted was the Admiralty with all that Mr Norrell had accomplished that Lord Mulgrave and Mr Horrocks soon looked about them to see what other tasks they could find for the

---

[1] Four years later during the Peninsular War Mr Norrell's pupil, Jonathan Strange, had similar criticisms to make about this form of magic.

magician. His Majesty's Navy had recently captured a French ship of the line with a very fine figurehead in the shape of a mermaid with bright blue eyes, coral-pink lips, a great mass of sumptuous golden curls artistically strewn with wooden representations of starfish and crabs, and a tail that was covered all over with silver-gilt as if it might be made of gingerbread inside. It was known that before it had been captured, the ship had been at Toulon, Cherbourg, Antwerp, Rotterdam and Genoa, and so the mermaid had seen a great deal of enemy defences and of the Emperor Napoleon Buonaparte's great scheme of ship-building which was going forward at that time. Mr Horrocks asked Mr Norrell to put a spell on her so that she might tell all she knew. This Mr Norrell did. But though the mermaid could be made to speak she could not at first be brought to answer any questions. She considered herself the implacable enemy of the British and was highly delighted to be given powers of speech so that she could express her hatred of them. Having passed all her existence among sailors she knew a great many insults and bestowed them very readily on anyone who came near her in a voice that sounded like the creaking of masts and timbers in a high wind. Nor did she confine herself to abusing Englishmen with words. There were three seamen that had work to do about the ship, but the moment that they got within reach of the mermaid's wooden arms she picked them up in her great wooden hands and threw them in the water.

Mr Horrocks who had gone down to Portsmouth to talk to her, grew tired of her and told her that he would have her chopped up and made a bonfire of. But, though French, she was also very brave and said she would like to see the man that would try to burn her. And she lashed her tail and waved her arms menacingly; and all the wooden starfish and crabs in her hair bristled.

The situation was resolved when the handsome young Captain who had captured her ship was sent to reason with her. He was able to explain to her in clear, comprehensible French the rightness of the British cause and the terrible wrongness of the French one, and whether it were the persuasiveness of his words or the handsomeness of his face that convinced her I do not know, but she told Mr Horrocks all he wished to know.

Mr Norrell rose every day to new heights of public greatness and an enterprising printmaker called Holland who had a print-shop in St Paul's Churchyard was inspired to commission an engraving of him to be sold in the shop. The engraving shewed Mr Norrell in the company of a young lady, scantily dressed in a loose smock. A great quantity of stiff, dark material swirled and coiled about the young lady's body without ever actually touching it and, for the further embellishment of her person, she wore a crescent moon tucked in among the tumbling locks of her hair. She had taken Mr Norrell (who appeared entirely astonished by the proceedings) by the arm and was energetically pulling him up a flight of stairs and pointing in most emphatic manner towards a lady of mature years who sat at the top. The lady of mature years was attired like the young lady in smock and draperies, with the handsome addition of a Roman helmet on her head; she appeared to be weeping in the most uninhibited fashion, while an elderly lion, her only companion, lay at her feet with a gloomy expression upon his countenance. This engraving, entitled *The Spirit of English Magic urges Mr Norrell to the Aid of Britannia*, was an immense success and Mr Holland sold almost seven hundred copies in a month.

Mr Norrell did not go out so much as formerly; instead he stayed at home and received respectful visits from all sorts of great people. It was not uncommon for five or six coronet-coaches to stop at his house in Hanover-square in the space of one morning. He was the still same silent, nervous little man he had always been and, had it not been for Mr Drawlight and Mr Lascelles, the occupants of those carriages must have found their visits dull indeed. Upon such occasions Mr Drawlight and Mr Lascelles supplied all the conversation. Indeed Mr Norrell's dependence upon these two gentlemen increased daily. Childermass had once said that it would be an odd sort of magician that would employ Drawlight, yet Mr Norrell now employed him constantly; Drawlight was forever being driven about in Mr Norrell's carriage upon Mr Norrell's business. Every day he came early to Hanover-square to tell Mr Norrell what was being said about the Town, who was rising, who falling, who was in debt, who in love, until Mr Norrell, sitting alone in his library, began to know as much of the Town's business as any City matron.

More surprizing, perhaps, was Mr Lascelles's devotion to the cause of English magic. The explanation, however, was quite simple. Mr Lascelles was one of that uncomfortable breed of men who despise steady employment of any sort. Though perfectly conscious of his own superior understanding, he had never troubled to acquire any particular skills or knowledge, and had arrived at the age of thirty-nine entirely unfitted for any office or occupation. He had looked about him and seen men, who had worked diligently all the years of their youth, risen to positions of power and influence; and there is no doubt that he envied them. Consequently it was highly agreeable to Mr Lascelles to become counsellor-in-chief to the greatest magician of the Age, and have respectful questions put to him by the King's Ministers. Naturally, he made a great shew of being the same careless, indifferent gentleman as before, but in truth he was extremely jealous of his new-found importance. He and Drawlight had come to an understanding one night in the Bedford over a bottle of port. Two friends, they had agreed, were quite sufficient for a quiet gentleman such as Mr Norrell, and they had formed an alliance to guard each other's interest and to prevent any other person from gaining any influence over the magician.

It was Mr Lascelles who first encouraged Mr Norrell to think of publication. Poor Mr Norrell was constantly affronted by people's misconceptions concerning magic and was forever lamenting the general ignorance upon the subject. "They ask me to shew them fairy-spirits," he complained, "and unicorns and manticores and things of that sort. The *utility* of the magic I have done is entirely lost on them. It is only the most frivolous sorts of magic that excite their interest."

Mr Lascelles said, "Feats of magic will make your *name* known everywhere, sir, but they will never make your *opinions* understood. For that you must publish."

"Yes, indeed," cried Mr Norrell, eagerly, "and I have every intention of writing a book – just as you advise – only I fear it will be many years before I have leisure enough to undertake it."

"Oh! I quite agree – a book would mean a world of work," said Mr Lascelles, languidly, "but I had no notion of a book. Two or three articles was what I had in mind. I dare say there is not an editor in London or Edinburgh who would not be delighted to publish any little thing you cared to send him – you may make your choice of the periodicals, but if you take my advice, sir, you will chuse *The Edinburgh Review*. There is scarcely a household in the kingdom with any pretensions to gentility that does not take it. There is no quicker way of making your views more widely understood."

Mr Lascelles was so persuasive upon the subject and conjured up such visions of Mr Norrell's articles upon every library-table and Mr Norrell's opinions discussed in every drawing-room that, had it not been for the great dislike that Mr Norrell had to *The Edinburgh Review*, he would have sat down there and then to begin writing. Unfortunately, *The Edinburgh Review* was a publication renowned chiefly for radical opinions, criticism of the Government and opposition to the war with France – none of which Mr Norrell could approve.

"Besides," said Mr Norrell, "I really have no desire to write reviews of other people's books. Modern publications upon magic are the most pernicious things in the world, full of misinformation and wrong opinions."

"Then sir, you may say so. The ruder you are, the more the editors will be delighted."

"But it is my own opinions which I wish to make better known, not other people's."

"Ah, but, sir," said Lascelles, "it is precisely by passing judgements upon other people's work and pointing out their errors that readers can be made to understand your own opinions better. It is the easiest thing in the world to turn a review to one's own ends. One only need mention the book once or twice and for the rest of the article one may develop one's theme just as one chuses. It is, I assure you, what every body else does."

"Hmm," said Mr Norrell thoughtfully, "you may be right. But, no. It would seem as if I were lending support to what ought never to have been published in the first place."

And upon this point Mr Norrell proved unpersuadable.

Lascelles was disappointed; *The Edinburgh Review* far surpassed its rivals in brilliance and wit. Its articles were devoured by everyone in the kingdom from the meanest curate to the Prime Minister. Other publications were very dull in comparison.

He was inclined to abandon the notion altogether and had almost forgotten all about it when he happened to receive a letter from a young bookseller named Murray. Mr Murray respectfully requested that Mr Lascelles and Mr Drawlight would do him the honour of permitting him to wait upon them at any hour and upon any day to suit them. He had, he said, a proposal to put before them, a proposal which concerned Mr Norrell.

Lascelles and Drawlight met the bookseller at Mr Lascelles's house in Bruton-street a few days later. His manner was energetic and businesslike and he laid his proposal before them immediately.

"Like every other inhabitant of these isles, gentlemen, I have been amazed and delighted at the recent extraordinary revival of English magic. And I have been equally struck by the enthusiasm with which the British Public has greeted this reappearance of an art long thought dead. I am convinced that a periodical devoted to magic would achieve a wide circulation. Literature, politics, religion and travel are all very well – they will always be popular subjects for a periodical, but magic – real, practical magic like Mr Norrell's – has the advantage of complete novelty. I wonder, gentlemen, if you could tell me whether Mr Norrell would look favourably upon my proposal? I have heard that Mr Norrell has a great deal to say upon the subject. I have heard that Mr Norrell's opinions are quite surprizing! Of course we all learnt a little of the history and theory of magic in our schoolrooms, but it is so long since any magic was practised in these islands that I dare say what we have been taught is full of errors and misconceptions."

"Ah!" cried Mr Drawlight. "How perceptive of you, Mr Murray! How happy it would make Mr Norrell to hear you say so! Errors and misconceptions – exactly so! Whenever, my dear sir, you are privileged to enjoy Mr Norrell's conversation – as I have been upon many occasions – you will learn that such is the exact state of affairs!"

"It has long been the dearest wish of Mr Norrell's heart," said Lascelles, "to bring a more precise understanding of modern magic before a wider audience, but alas, sir, private wishes are often frustrated by public duties, and the Admiralty and the War Office keep him so busy."

Mr Murray replied politely that of course all other considerations must give way before the great consideration of the war and Mr Norrell was a National Treasure. "But I hope that some way might be found to arrange matters so that the chief burden did not fall upon Mr Norrell's shoulders. We would employ an editor to plan each issue, solicit articles and reviews, make changes – all under Mr Norrell's guidance, naturally."

"Ah, yes!" said Lascelles. "Quite. All under Mr Norrell's guidance. We would insist upon that."

The interview ended very cordially upon both sides with Lascelles and Drawlight promising to speak to Mr Norrell immediately.

Drawlight watched Mr Murray leave the room. "A Scotchman," he said as soon as the door was closed.

"Oh, quite!" agreed Lascelles. "But I do not mind that. The Scotch are often very able, very canny in business. I believe this might do very well."

"He seemed quite a respectable person – almost a gentleman in fact. Except that he has a queer trick of fixing his right eye upon one while his other eye travels the room. I found that a little disconcerting."

"He is blind in his right eye."

"Indeed?"

"Yes. Canning told me. One of his schoolmasters stuck a pen-knife in it when he was boy."

"Dear me! But, just imagine, my dear Lascelles! A whole periodical devoted to one person's opinions! I would never have believed it possible! The magician will be astonished when we tell him."

Mr Lascelles laughed. "He will consider it the most natural thing in the world. His vanity is beyond any thing."

As Lascelles had predicted, Mr Norrell found nothing extraordinary in the proposal, but straightaway he began to make difficulties. "It is an excellent plan," he said, "but unfortunately completely impracticable. I have no time to edit a periodical and I could scarcely entrust so important a task to any one else."

"I was quite of the same mind, sir," said Mr Lascelles, "until I thought of Portishead."

"Portishead? Who is Portishead?" asked Mr Norrell.

"Well," said Lascelles, "He *was* a theoretical magician, but . . ."

"A theoretical magician?" interrupted Mr Norrell in alarm. "You know what I think of that!"

"Ah, but you have not heard what follows," said Lascelles. "So great is his admiration of *you*, sir, that on being told you did not approve of theoretical magicians he immediately gave up his studies."

"Did he indeed?" said Mr Norrell, somewhat placated by this information.

"He has published one or two books. I forget what exactly – a history of sixteenth-century magic for children or something of that sort.[2] I really feel that you might safely entrust the periodical to Lord Portishead, sir. There is no danger of him publishing any thing of which you disapprove; he is known as one of most honourable men in the kingdom. His first wish will be to please you, I am quite certain."[3]

Somewhat reluctantly Mr Norrell agreed to meet Lord Portishead and Mr Drawlight wrote a letter summoning him to Hanover-square.

Lord Portishead was about thirty-eight years of age. He was very tall and thin with long, thin hands and feet. He habitually wore a whitish coat and light-coloured breeches. He was a gentle soul whom everything made uncomfortable: his excessive height made him uncomfortable; his status as a former theoretical magician made him uncomfortable (being an intelligent man he knew that Mr Norrell disapproved of him); meeting such polished men of the world as Drawlight and Lascelles made him uncomfortable and meeting Mr Norrell – who was his great hero – made him most uncomfortable of all. At one point he became so agitated that he began to sway backwards and forwards – which, taken in conjunction with his height and whitish clothes, gave him the appearance of a silver-birch tree in a high wind.

---

[2] In this speech Mr Lascelles has managed to combine all Lord Portishead's books into one. By the time Lord Portishead gave up the study of magic in early 1808 he had published three books: *The Life of Jacques Belasis*, pub. Longman, London, 1801, *The Life of Nicholas Goubert*, pub. Longman, London, 1805, and *A Child's History of the Raven King*, pub. Longman, London, 1807, engravings by Thomas Bewick. The first two were scholarly discussions of two sixteenth-century magicians. Mr Norrell had no great opinion of them, but he had a particular dislike of *A Child's History*. Jonathan Strange, on the other hand, thought this an excellent little book.

[3] "It was odd that so wealthy a man – for Lord Portishead counted large portions of England among his possessions – should have been so very self-effacing, but such was the case. He was besides a devoted husband and the father of ten children. Mr Strange told me that to see Lord Portishead play with his children was the most delightful thing in the world. And indeed he was a little like a child himself. For all his great learning he could no more recognize evil than he could spontaneously understand Chinese. He was the gentlest lord in all of the British aristocracy."

The Life of Jonathan Strange by John Segundus, pub. John Murray, London, 1820.

Despite his nervousness he managed to convey his great sense of the honour done to him in being summoned to meet Mr Norrell. Indeed so gratified was Mr Norrell by Lord Portishead's extreme deference towards him that he graciously gave his permission for Lord Portishead to study magic again.

Naturally Lord Portishead was delighted, but when he heard that Mr Norrell desired him to sit for long periods of time in a corner of Mr Norrell's own drawing-room, soaking up Mr Norrell's opinions upon modern magic, and then to edit, under Mr Norrell's direction, Mr Murray's new periodical, it seemed that he could conceive of no greater happiness.

The new periodical was named *The Friends of English Magic*, the title being taken from Mr Segundus's letter to *The Times* in the previous spring. Curiously none of the articles which appeared in *The Friends of English Magic* were written by Mr Norrell, who was found to be entirely incapable of finishing a piece of writing; he was never satisfied with what he had written. He could never be sure that he had not said too much or too little.[4]

---

[4] *The Friends of English Magic* was first published in February 1808 and was an immediate success. By 1812 Norrell and Lascelles were boasting of a circulation in excess of 13,000, though how reliable this figure may be is uncertain.

From 1808 until 1810 the editor was nominally Lord Portishead but there is little doubt that both Mr Norrell and Lascelles interfered a great deal. There was a certain amount of disagreement between Norrell and Lascelles as to the general aims of the periodical. Mr Norrell wished *The Friends of English Magic* first to impress upon the British Public the great importance of English modern magic, secondly to correct erroneous views of magical history and thirdly to vilify those magicians and classes of magicians whom he hated. He did not desire to explain the procedures of English magic within its pages – in other words he had no intention of making it in the least informative. Lord Portishead, whose admiration of Mr Norrell knew no bounds, considered it his first duty as editor to follow Norrell's numerous instructions. As a result the early issues of *The Friends of English Magic* are rather dull and often puzzling – full of odd omissions, contradictions and evasions. Lascelles, on the other hand, understood very well how the periodical might be used to gain support for the revival of English magic and he was anxious to make it lighter in tone. He grew more and more irritated at Portishead's cautious approach. He manoeuvred and from 1810 he and Lord Portishead were joint editors.

John Murray was the publisher of *The Friends of English Magic* until early

146

There is not much to interest the serious student of magic in the early issues and the only entertainment to be got from them is contained in several articles in which Portishead attacks on Mr Norrell's behalf: gentleman-magicians; lady-magicians; street-magicians; vagabond-magicians; child-prodigy-magicians; the Learned Society of York Magicians; the Learned Society of Manchester Magicians; learned societies of magicians in general; any other magicians whatsoever.

---

[4] *cont'd*   1815 when he and Norrell quarrelled. Deprived of Norrell's support, Murray was obliged to sell the periodical to Thomas Norton Longman, another publisher. In 1816 Murray and Strange planned to set up a rival periodical to *The Friends of English Magic*, entitled *The Famulus*, but only one issue was ever published.

13

The magician of Threadneedle-street

December 1807

THE MOST FAMOUS street-magician in London was undoubtedly Vinculus. His magician's booth stood before the church of St Christopher Le Stocks in Threadneedle-street opposite the Bank of England, and it would have been difficult to say whether the bank or the booth were the more famous.

Yet the reason for Vinculus's celebrity – or notoriety – was a little mysterious. He was no better a magician than any of the other charlatans with lank hair and a dirty yellow curtain. His spells did not work, his prophecies did not come true and his trances had been proven false beyond a doubt.

For many years he was much addicted to holding deep and weighty conference with the Spirit of the River Thames. He would fall into a trance and ask the Spirit questions and the voice of the Spirit would issue forth from his mouth in accents deep, watery and windy. On a winter's day in 1805 a woman paid him a shilling to ask the Spirit to tell her where she might find her runaway husband. The Spirit provided a great deal of quite surprising information and a crowd began to gather around the booth to listen to it. Some of the bystanders believed in Vinculus's ability and were duly impressed by the Spirit's oration, but others began to taunt the magician and his client. One such jeerer (a most ingenious fellow) actually managed to set Vinculus's shoes on fire while Vinculus was speaking. Vinculus came out of his trance immediately: he leapt about, howling and attempting to pull off his shoes and stamp out the fire at one and the same time. He was throwing himself about and the crowd were all enjoying the sight immensely, when something popt out of his mouth. Two men picked it up and examined it: it was a little metal contraption not more than an inch and a half long. It was something like a mouth-organ and when one of the men placed it in his own mouth he too was able to produce the voice of the Spirit of the River Thames.

Despite such public humiliations Vinculus retained a certain authority, a certain native dignity which meant that he, among all the street-magicians of London, was treated with a measure of respect. Mr Norrell's friends and admirers were continually urging him to pay a visit to Vinculus and were surprised that he shewed no inclination to do it.

On a day in late December when storm clouds made Alpine landscapes in the sky above London, when the wind played such havoc in the heavens that the city was one moment plunged in gloom and the next illuminated by sunlight, when rain rattled upon the windowpane, Mr Norrell was seated comfortably in his library before a cheerful fire. The tea table spread with a quantity of good things stood before him and in his hand was Thomas Lanchester's *The Language of Birds*. He was turning the pages in search of a favourite passage when he was nearly frightened out of his wits by a voice suddenly saying very loudly and contemptu-ously, "Magician! You think that you have amazed everyone by your deeds!"

Mr Norrell looked up and was astonished to find that there was someone else in the room, a person he had never seen before, a thin, shabby, ragged hawk of a man. His face was the colour of three-day-old milk; his hair was the colour of a coal-smoke-and-ashes London sky; and his clothes were the colour of the Thames at dirty Wapping. Nothing about him – face, hair, clothes – was particularly clean, but in all other points he corresponded to the common notion of what a magician should look like (which Mr Norrell most certainly did not). He stood very erect and the expression of his fierce grey eyes was naturally imperious.

"Oh, yes!" continued this person, glaring furiously at Mr Norrell. "You think yourself a very fine fellow! Well, know this, Magician! Your coming was foretold long ago. I have been expecting you these past twenty years! Where have you been hiding yourself?"

Mr Norrell sat in amazed silence, staring at his accuser with open mouth. It was as if this man had reached into his breast, plucked out his secret thought and held it up to the light. Ever since his arrival in the capital Mr Norrell had realized that he had indeed been ready long ago; he could have been doing magic for England's benefit years before; the French might have been defeated and English magic raised to that lofty position in the Nation's regard which Mr Norrell believed it ought to occupy. He was tormented with the idea that he had betrayed English magic by his dilatoriness. Now it was as if his own conscience had taken concrete form and started to reproach him. This put him some-what at a disadvantage in dealing with the mysterious stranger. He stammered out an inquiry as to who the person might be.

"I am Vinculus, magician of Threadneedle-street!"

"Oh!" cried Mr Norrell, relieved to find that at least he was no supernatural apparition. "And you have come here to beg I suppose? Well, you may take yourself off again! I do not recognize you as a brother-magician and I shall not give you any thing! Not money. Not promises of help. Not recommendations to other people. Indeed I may tell you that I intend . . ."

"Wrong again, Magician! I want nothing for myself. I have come to explain your destiny to you, as I was born to do."

"Destiny? Oh, it's prophecies, is it?" cried Mr Norrell contemptuously. He rose from his chair and tugged violently at the bell pull, but no servant appeared. "Well, now I really have nothing to say to people who pretend to do prophecies. *Lucas!* Prophecies are without a doubt one of the most villainous tricks which rascals like you play upon honest men. Magic cannot see into the future and magicians who claimed otherwise were liars. *Lucas!*"

Vinculus looked round. "I hear you have all the books that were ever written upon magic," he said, "and it is commonly reported that you have even got back the ones that were lost when the library of Alexandria burnt – and know them all by heart, I dare say!"

"Books and papers are the basis of good scholarship and sound knowledge," declared Mr Norrell primly. "Magic is to be put on the same footing as the other disciplines."

Vinculus leaned suddenly forward and bent over Mr Norrell with a look of the most intense, burning concentration. Without quite meaning to, Mr Norrell fell silent and he leaned towards Vinculus to hear whatever Vinculus was about to confide to him.

"*I reached out my hand,*" whispered Vinculus, "*England's rivers turned and flowed the other way . . .*"

"I beg your pardon?"

"*I reached out my hand,*" said Vinculus, a little louder, "*my enemies's blood stopt in their veins . . .*" He straightened himself, opened wide his arms and closed his eyes as if in a religious ecstasy of some sort. In a strong, clear voice full of passion he continued:

"*I reached out my hand; thought and memory flew out of my enemies'*
heads like a flock of starlings;
My enemies crumpled like empty sacks.
I came to them out of mists and rain;
I came to them in dreams at midnight;
I came to them in a flock of ravens that filled a northern sky at dawn;
When they thought themselves safe I came to them in a cry that broke the
silence of a winter wood . . ."

"Yes, yes!" interrupted Mr Norrell. "Do you really suppose that this sort of nonsense is new to me? Every madman on every street-corner screams out the same threadbare gibberish and every vagabond with a yellow curtain tries to make himself mysterious by reciting something of the sort. It is in every third-rate book on magic published in the last two hundred years! 'I came to them in a flock of ravens!' What does that *mean*, I should like to know? Who came to whom in a flock of ravens? *Lucas!*"

Vinculus ignored him. His strong voice overpowered Mr Norrell's weak, shrill one.

"The rain made a door for me and I went through it;
The stones made a throne for me and I sat upon it;
Three kingdoms were given to me to be mine forever;
England was given to me to be mine forever.
The nameless slave wore a silver crown;
The nameless slave was a king in a strange country . . ."

"Three kingdoms!" exclaimed Mr Norrell. "Ha! Now I understand what this nonsense pretends to be! A prophecy of the Raven King! Well, I am sorry to tell you that if you hope to impress me by recounting tales of that gentleman you will be disappointed. Oh, yes, you are entirely mistaken! There is no magician whom I detest more!"[1]

"The weapons that my enemies raised against me are venerated in Hell as holy relics;
Plans that my enemies made against me are preserved as holy texts;
Blood that I shed upon ancient battlefields is scraped from the stained earth by Hell's sacristans and placed in a vessel of silver and ivory.
I gave magic to England, a valuable inheritance

---

[1] The Raven King was traditionally held to have possessed three kingdoms: one in England, one in Faerie and one, a strange country on the far side of Hell.

But Englishmen have despised my gift
Magic shall be written upon the sky by the rain but they shall not be able to
read it;
Magic shall be written on the faces of the stony hills but their minds shall
not be able to contain it;
In winter the barren trees shall be a black writing but they shall not
understand it . . ."

"It is every Englishman's birthright to be served by competent and well-educated magicians," interrupted Mr Norrell. "What do you offer them instead? Mystical ramblings about stones and rain and trees! This is like Godbless who told us that we should learn magic from wild beasts in the forest. Why not pigs in the sty? Or stray dogs, I wonder? This is not the sort of magic which civilized men wish to see practised in England nowadays!" He glared furiously at Vinculus and, as he did so, something caught his eye.

Vinculus had dressed himself with no particular care. His dirty neckcloth had been negligently wound about his neck and a little gap of unclean skin shewed between neckcloth and shirt. In that space was a curious curving mark of a vivid blue, not unlike the upward stroke of a pen. It might have been a scar – the relic of a street brawl perhaps – but what it most resembled was that barbaric painting of the skin which is practised by the natives of the South Sea islands. Curiously Vinculus, who was able to stand entirely at his ease in another man's house railing at him, seemed embarrassed by this mark and when he saw that Mr Norrell had observed it he put his hand to his throat and plucked at the cloth to hide it.

"Two magicians shall appear in England . . ."

A sort of exclamation broke from Mr Norrell, an exclamation that began as a cry and ended as a soft, unhappy sigh.

"The first shall fear me; the second shall long to behold me;
The first shall be governed by thieves and murderers; the second shall
conspire at his own destruction;

The first shall bury his heart in a dark wood beneath the snow, yet still feel its ache;
The second shall see his dearest possession in his enemy's hand . . ."

"Oh! Now I know that you have come here with no other aim but to wound me! False Magician, you are jealous of my success! You cannot destroy my magic and so you are determined to blacken my name and destroy my peace . . ."

"The first shall pass his life alone; he shall be his own gaoler;
The second shall tread lonely roads, the storm above his head, seeking a dark tower upon a high hillside . . ."

Just then the door opened and two men ran in.

"Lucas! Davey!" screeched Mr Norrell, hysterically. "Where have you been?"

Lucas began to explain something about the bell-cord.

"What? Seize hold of him! Quickly!"

Davey, Mr Norrell's coachman, was built on the same generous scale as others of his profession and had the strength that comes from daily opposing his will to that of four high-bred coach-horses in the prime of life. He took hold of Vinculus around his body and his throat. Vinculus struggled energetically. He did not neglect in the meantime to continue berating Mr Norrell:

"I sit upon a black throne in the shadows but they shall not see me.
The rain shall make a door for me and I shall pass through it;
The stones shall make a throne for me and I shall sit upon it . . ."

Davey and Vinculus careered against a little table upsetting a pile of books that stood upon it.

"Aaaah! Be careful!" exclaimed Mr Norrell, "For God's sake be careful! He will knock over that ink pot! He will damage my books!"

Lucas joined Davey in endeavouring to pinion Vinculus's wild, windmilling arms, while Mr Norrell scampered round the library a great deal faster than any one had seen him move for many years, gathering up books and putting them out of harm's way.

"*The nameless slave shall wear a silver crown,*" gasped Vinculus – Davey's arm tightening about his throat rendered his oration decidedly less impressive than before. Vinculus made one last effort and pulled the upper part of his body free of Davey's grasp and shouted, "*The nameless slave shall be a king in a strange country . . .*" Then Lucas and Davey half-pulled, half-carried him out of the room.

Mr Norrell went and sat down in the chair by the fire. He picked up his book again but he found that he was a great deal too agitated to return to his reading. He fidgeted about, bit his fingernails, walked about the room, returned constantly to those volumes which had been displaced in the struggle and examined them for signs of damage (there were none), but most of all he went to the windows and peered out anxiously to see if any one was watching the house. At three o'clock the room began to grow dusky. Lucas returned to light the candles and mend the fire and just behind him was Childermass.

"Ah!" cried Mr Norrell. "At last! Have you heard what happened? I am betrayed on all sides! Other magicians keep watch upon me and plot my downfall! My idle servants forget their duties. It is a matter of complete indifference to them whether my throat is cut or not! And as for you, you villain, you are the very worst of all! I tell you this man appeared so suddenly in the room – *as if by magic!* And when I rang the bell and cried out *no one came!* You must put aside all your other work. Your only task now is to discover what spells this man employed to gain entry to the house! Where did he learn his magic? What does he know?"

Childermass gave his master an ironical look. "Well, if that is my only task, it is done already. There was no magic. One of the kitchenmaids left the pantry window open and the sorcerer climbed in and crept about the house until he found you. That is all. No one came because he had cut the bell-cord and Lucas and the others did not hear you shout. They heard nothing until he started to rant and then they came immediately. Is that not so, Lucas?"

Lucas, kneeling at the hearth with the poker in his hand, agreed that that was exactly how it had been. "And so I tried to tell you, sir. Only you would not listen."

But Mr Norrell had worked himself up into such a frenzy of anxiety over Vinculus's supposed magical powers that this explanation had at first little power to soothe him. "Oh!" he said. "But still I am certain he means me harm. Indeed he has done me great harm already."

"Yes," agreed Childermass, "very great harm! For while he was in the pantry he ate three meat-pies."

"And two cream cheeses," added Lucas.

Mr Norrell was forced to admit to himself that this did not seem much like the actions of a great magician, but still he could not be entirely easy until he had vented his anger upon someone. Childermass and Lucas being most conveniently to hand, he began with them and treated them to a long speech, full of invective against Vinculus as the greatest villain who ever lived and ending with several strong hints about the bad ends that impudent and neglectful servants came to.

Childermass and Lucas, who had been obliged to listen to something of this sort practically every week since they had entered Mr Norrell's service, felt no particular alarm, but merely waited until their master had talked out his displeasure, whereupon Childermass said: "Leaving aside the pies and cheeses, he has put himself to a great deal of trouble and risked a hanging to pay you this visit. What did he want?"

"Oh! To deliver a prophecy of the Raven King's. Hardly an original idea. It was quite as impenetrable as such ramblings generally are. There was something about a battlefield and something about a throne and something about a silver crown, but the chief burden of what he had to say was to boast of another magician – by which I suppose he meant himself."

Now that Mr Norrell was reassured that Vinculus was not a terrible rival he began to regret that he had ever been led on to argue with him. It would have been far better, he thought, to maintain a lofty and magisterial silence. He comforted himself with the reflection that Vinculus had looked a great deal less imposing when Lucas and Davey were dragging him from the room. Gradually this thought and the consciousness of his own infinitely superior education and abilities began to make him feel comfortable again. But alas! such comfort was short-lived. For, on taking up *The Language of Birds* again, he came upon the following passage:

> . . . *There is nothing else in magic but the wild thought of the bird as it casts itself into the void. There is no creature upon the earth with such potential for magic. Even the least of them may fly straight out of this world and come by chance to the Other Lands. Where does the wind come from that blows upon your face, that fans the pages of your book? Where the harum-scarum magic of small wild creatures meets the magic of Man, where the language of the wind and the rain and the trees can be understood, there we will find the Raven King . . .*[2]

The next time that Mr Norrell saw Lord Portishead (which happened two days later) he immediately went up to his lordship and addressed him with the following words: "I hope, my lord, that you will have some very sharp things to say about Thomas Lanchester in the periodical. For years I have admired *The Language of Birds* as a valiant attempt to place before the reader a clear and comprehensive description of the magic of the *Aureate* magicians, but upon closer examination I find his writing is tainted with their worst characteristics . . . He is mystical, my lord! He is mystical!"

---

[2] Thomas Lanchester, *Treatise concerning the Language of Birds*, Chapter 6.

14

Heart-break Farm

January 1808

SOME THIRTY YEARS before Mr Norrell arrived in London
with a plan to astonish the world by restoring English magic,
a gentleman named Laurence Strange came into his inheritance. This comprised a house in an almost ruinous state, some
barren lands and a mountain of debts and mortgages. These were
grave ills indeed, but, thought Laurence Strange, they were nothing
that the acquisition of a large sum of money might not cure; and so
like many other gentlemen before and after him, he made it his
business to be particularly agreeable to heiresses whenever he met
with any, and, being a handsome man with elegant manners and a
clever way of talking, in no time at all he had captivated a Miss
Erquistoune, a young Scottish lady with £900 a year.

With the money Miss Erquistoune brought him, Laurence
Strange repaired his house, improved his lands and repaid his
debts. Soon he began to make money instead of owing it. He
extended his estate and lent out money at fifteen per cent. In these
and other similar pursuits he found occupation for every waking
hour. He could no longer be at the trouble of shewing his bride
much attention. Indeed he made it quite plain that her society and
conversation were irksome to him; and she, poor thing, had a very
hard time of it. Laurence Strange's estate was in Shropshire, in a
retired part of the country near the Welsh border. Mrs Strange

knew no one there. She was accustomed to city life, to Edinburgh balls and Edinburgh shops and the clever conversation of her Edinburgh friends; the sight of the high, gloomy hills forever shrouded in Welsh rain was very dispiriting. She bore with this lonely existence for five years, before dying of a chill she had caught while taking a solitary walk on those same hills in a storm.

Mr and Mrs Strange had one child who was, at the time of his mother's death, about four years of age. Mrs Strange had not been buried more than a few days when this child became the subject of a violent quarrel between Laurence Strange and his late wife's family. The Erquistounes maintained that in accordance with the terms of the marriage settlement a large part of Mrs Strange's fortune must now be put aside for her son for him to inherit at his majority. Laurence Strange – to no one's very great surprize – claimed that every penny of his wife's money was his to do with as he liked. Both parties consulted lawyers and two separate lawsuits were started, one in the Doctors Commons in London and one in the Scottish courts. The two lawsuits, Strange *versus* Erquistoune and Erquistoune *versus* Strange, went on for years and years and during this time the very sight of his son became displeasing to Laurence Strange. It seemed to him that the boy was like a boggy field or a copse full of diseased trees – worth money on paper but failing to yield a good annual return. If English law had entitled Laurence Strange to sell his son and buy a better one, he probably would have done it.[1]

Meanwhile the Erquistounes realized that Laurence Strange had it in his power to make his son every bit as unhappy as his wife had been, so Mrs Strange's brother wrote urgently to Laurence Strange suggesting that the boy spend some part of every year at his own house in Edinburgh. To Mr Erquistoune's great surprize, Mr Strange made no objection.[2]

---

[1] Eventually, both lawsuits were decided in favour of Laurence Strange's son.
[2] Upon the contrary Laurence Strange congratulated himself on avoiding paying for the boy's food and clothes for months at a time. So may a love of money make an intelligent man small-minded and ridiculous.

So it was that Jonathan Strange spent half of every year of his childhood at Mr Erquistoune's house in Charlotte-square in Edinburgh, where, it is to be presumed, he learnt to hold no very high opinion of his father. There he received his early education in the company of his three cousins, Margaret, Maria and Georgiana Erquistoune.[3] Edinburgh is certainly one of the most civilized cities in the world and the inhabitants are full as clever and as fond of pleasure as those of London. Whenever he was with them Mr and Mrs Erquistoune did everything they could to make him happy, hoping in this way to make up for the neglect and coldness he met with at his father's house. And so it is not to be wondered at if he grew up a little spoilt, a little fond of his own way and a little inclined to think well of himself.

Laurence Strange grew older and richer, but no better.

A few days before Mr Norrell's interview with Vinculus, a new manservant came to work at Laurence Strange's house. The other servants were very ready with help and advice: they told the new manservant that Laurence Strange was proud and full of malice, that everybody hated him, that he loved money beyond any thing, and that he and his son had barely spoken to each other for years and years. They also said that he had a temper like the devil and that upon no account whatsoever must the new manservant do any thing to offend him, or things would go the worse for him.

The new manservant thanked them for the information and promised to remember what they had said. But what the other servants did not know was that the new manservant had a temper to rival Mr Strange's own; that he was sometimes sarcastic, often rude, and that he had a very high opinion of his own abilities and a correspondingly low one of other people's. The new manservant did not mention his failings to the other servants for the simple

---

[3] Strange's biographer, John Segundus, observed on several occasions how Strange preferred the society of clever women to that of men. *Life of Jonathan Strange*, pub. John Murray, London, 1820.

reason that he knew nothing of them. Though he often found himself quarrelling with his friends and neighbours, he was always puzzled to discover the reason and always supposed that it must be their fault. But in case you should imagine that this chapter will treat of none but disagreeable persons, it ought to be stated at once that, whereas malice was the beginning and end of Laurence Strange's character, the new manservant was a more natural blend of light and shade. He possessed a great deal of good sense and was as energetic in defending others from real injury as he was in revenging imaginary insults to himself.

Laurence Strange was old and rarely slept much. Indeed it would often happen that he found himself more lively at night than during the day and he would sit up at his desk, writing letters and conducting his business. Naturally one of the servants always sat up as well, and a few days after he had first entered the household, this duty fell to the new manservant.

All went well until a little after two o'clock in the morning when Mr Strange summoned the new manservant and asked him to fetch a small glass of sherry-wine. Unremarkable as this request was, the new manservant did not find it at all easy to accomplish. Having searched for the sherry-wine in the usual places, he was obliged to wake first the maid, and ask her where the butler's bedroom might be, and next the butler and ask him where the sherry-wine was kept. Even then the new manservant had to wait some moments more while the butler talked out his surprize that Mr Strange should ask for sherry-wine, a thing he hardly ever took. Mr Strange's son, Mr Jonathan Strange – added the butler for the new manservant's better understanding of the household – was very fond of sherry-wine and generally kept a bottle or two in his dressing-room.

In accordance with the butler's instructions the new manservant fetched the sherry-wine from the cellars – a task which involved much lighting of candles, much walking down long stretches of dark, cold passage-ways, much brushing dirty old cobwebs from his clothes, much knocking of his head against rusty old implements hanging from musty old ceilings, and much wiping of blood and dirt from his face afterwards. He brought the glass to Mr Strange who drank it straight down and asked for another.

The new manservant felt that he had seen enough of the cellars for one night and so, remembering what the butler had said, he went upstairs to the dressing-room of Mr Jonathan Strange. Entering cautiously he found the room apparently unoccupied, but with candles still burning. This did not particularly surprize the new manservant who knew that conspicuous among the many vices peculiar to rich, unmarried gentlemen is wastefulness of candles. He began to open drawers and cupboards, pick up chamber-pots and look into them, look under tables and chairs, and peer into flower-vases. (And if you are at all surprized by all the places into which the new manservant looked, then all I can say is that he had more experience of rich, unmarried gentlemen than you do, and knew that their management of household affairs is often characterized by a certain eccentricity.) He found the bottle of sherry-wine, much as he had expected, performing the office of a boot-jack inside one of its owner's boots.

As the new manservant poured the wine into the glass, he happened to glance into a mirror that was hanging on the wall and discovered that the room was was not, after all, empty. Jonathan Strange was seated in a high-backed, high-shouldered chair watching every thing that the new manservant did with a look of great astonishment upon his face. The new manservant said not a word in explanation – for what explanation could he have given that a gentleman would have listened to? A servant would have understood him in an instant. The new manservant left the room.

Since his arrival in the house the new manservant had entertained certain hopes of rising to a position of authority over the other servants. It seemed to him that his superior intellects and greater experience of the world made him a natural lieutenant for the two Mr Stranges in any difficult business they might have; in his fancy they already said to him such things as: "As you know, Jeremy, these are serious matters, and I dare not trust any one but you with their execution." It would be going too far to say that he immediately abandoned these hopes, but he could not disguise from himself that Jonathan Strange had not seemed greatly pleased to discover someone in his private apartment pouring wine from his private supply.

Thus the new manservant entered Laurence Strange's writing-room with fledgling ambition frustrated and spirits dangerously irritated. Mr Strange drank the second glass of sherry straight down and remarked that he thought he would have another. At this the new manservant gave a sort of strangled shout, pulled his own hair and cried out, "Then why in God's name, you old fool, did you not say so in the first place? I could have brought you the bottle!"

Mr Strange looked at him in surprize and said mildly that of course there was no need to bring another glass if it was such a world of trouble to him.

The new manservant went back to the kitchen (wondering as he did so, if in fact he had been a little curt). A few minutes later the bell sounded again. Mr Strange was sitting at his desk with a letter in his hand, looking out through the window at the pitch-black, rainy night. "There is a man that lives up on the hill opposite," he said, "and this letter, Jeremy, must be delivered to him before break of day."

Ah! thought the new manservant, how quickly it begins! An urgent piece of business that must be conducted under the cover of night! What can it mean? – except that already he has begun to prefer *my* assistance to that of the others. Greatly flattered he declared eagerly that he would go straightaway and took the letter which bore only the enigmatic legend, "Wyvern". He inquired if the house had a name, so that he might ask someone if he missed his way.

Mr Strange began to say that the house had no name, but then he stopt himself and laughed. "You must ask for Wyvern of Heart-break Farm," he said. He told the new manservant that he must leave the high-road by a broken wicket that stood opposite Blackstock's ale-house; behind the wicket he would find a path that would take him straight to Heart-break Farm.

So the new manservant fetched a horse and a stout lantern and rode out on to the high-road. It was a dismal night. The air was a great confusion of noisy wind and bitter, driving rain which got into all the gaps in his clothing so that he was very soon chilled to death.

The path that began opposite Blackstock's ale-house and wound up the hill was fearfully overgrown. Indeed it scarcely deserved the name of "path", for young saplings grew in the middle of it, which the strong wind took and turned into rods to lash the new manservant as he struggled past. By the time he had travelled half a mile he felt as if he had fought several strong men one after the other (and being a hot-headed sort of person who was always getting into quarrels in public places it was a sensation perfectly familiar to him). He cursed Wyvern for a negligent, idle fellow who could not even keep his hedges in order. It was only after an hour or so that he reached a place which might have been a field once, but which was now a wilderness of briars and brambles and he began to regret that he had not brought an axe with him. He left the horse tied to a tree and tried to push his way through. The thorns were large, sharp and plentiful; several times he found himself pinned into the briar-bushes in so many places and in such an elaborate fashion (an arm up here, a leg twisted behind him) that he began to despair of ever getting out again. It seemed odd that any one could live behind such a high hedge of thorns, and he began to think that it would be no great surprize to discover that Mr Wyvern had been asleep for a hundred years or so. Well, I shall not mind *that* so much, he thought, so long as I am not expected to kiss him.

As a sad, grey dawn broke over the hillside he came upon a

ruined cottage which did not so much seem to have broken its heart, as its neck. The chimney wall sagged outwards in a great bow and the chimney tottered above it. A landslide of stone tiles from the roof had left holes where the timbers shewed like ribs. Elder-trees and thorn-bushes filled the interior and, in the vigour of their growth, had broken all the windows and pushed the doors out of the door-frames.

The new manservant stood in the rain for some time contemplating this dismal sight. On looking up he saw someone striding down the hillside towards him; a fairy-tale figure with a large and curious hat upon his head and a staff in his hand. As the figure drew closer it proved to be a yeoman-farmer, a sensible-looking man whose fantastic appearance was entirely due to his having folded a piece of canvas about his head to keep the rain off.

He greeted the new manservant thus: "Man! What have you done to yourself? You are all over blood and your good clothes are in tatters!"

The new manservant looked down at himself and discovered this was true. He explained that the path was overgrown and full of thorns.

The farmer looked at him in amazement. "But there is a good road," he cried, "not a quarter of a mile to the west that you could have walked in half the time! Who in the world directed you to come by that old path?"

The new manservant did not answer but instead asked if the farmer knew where Mr Wyvern of Heart-break Farm might be found?

"That is Wyvern's cottage, but he has been dead five years. Heart-break Farm, you say? Who told you it was called that? Someone has been playing tricks upon you. Old paths, Heart-break Farm indeed! But then I dare say it is as good a name as any; Wyvern did indeed break his heart here. He had the misfortune, poor fellow, to own some land which a gentleman in the valley took a fancy to and when Wyvern would not sell it, the gentleman sent ruffians in the middle of the night to dig up all the beans and carrots and cabbages that Wyvern had planted and when that did not work he put lawsuits upon him – poor Wyvern knew nothing of the law and could not make head or tail of it."

The new manservant thought about this for a moment. "And I fancy," he said at last, "that I could tell you the name of that gentleman."

"Oh!" said the farmer. "Anyone could do that." He looked a little closer at the new manservant. "Man," he said, "you are white as a milk pudding and shivering fit to break yourself in pieces!"

"I am cold," said the new manservant.

Then the farmer (who said his name was Bullbridge) was very pressing with the new manservant to return with him to his own fireside where he could warm himself and take something to eat and drink, and perhaps lie down a spell. The new manservant thanked him but said he was cold, that was all.

So Bullbridge led the new manservant back to his horse (by a way which avoided the thorns) and shewed him the proper way to the road and then the new manservant went back to Mr Strange's house.

A bleak, white sun rose in a bleak, white sky like an allegorical picture of despair and, as he rode, it seemed to the new manservant that the sun was poor Wyvern and that the sky was Hell, and that Wyvern had been put there by Mr Strange to be tormented for ever.

Upon his return the other servants gathered about him. "Ah, lad!" cried the butler in his concern. "What a sight you are! Was it the sherry-wine, Jeremy? Did you make him angry over the sherry-wine?"

The new manservant toppled off the horse on to the ground. He grasped the butler's coat and begged the butler to bring him a fishing-rod, explaining that he needed it to fish poor Wyvern out of Hell.

From this and other such coherent speeches the other servants quickly deduced that he had taken a cold and was feverish. They put him to bed and sent a man for the physician. But Laurence Strange got to hear about it and he sent a second messenger after the first to tell the physician he was not wanted. Next Laurence Strange said that he thought he would take some gruel and told the butler that he wanted the new manservant to bring it to him. This prompted the butler to go in search of Mr Jonathan Strange, to beg him to do something, but Jonathan Strange had, it seemed, got up early to ride to Shrewsbury and was not expected back until the following day. So the servants were obliged to get the new manservant out of bed, dress him, put the tray of gruel into his unresisting hand, and push him through the door. All day long Mr Strange maintained a steady succession of minor requests, each of which – and Mr Strange was most particular about this – was for the new manservant to carry out.

By nightfall the new manservant was as hot to the touch as a iron kettle and talked wildly of oyster-barrels. But Mr Strange declared his intention of sitting up another night and said that the new manservant should wait upon him in the writing-room.

The butler pleaded bravely with his master to let him sit up instead.

"Ah! but you cannot conceive what a fancy I have taken to this fellow," said Mr Strange, his eyes all bright with dislike, "and how I wish to have him always near me. You think he does not look well? In *my* opinion he only wants fresh air." And so saying he unfastened the window above his writing-table. Instantly the room became bitter-cold and a handful of snow flakes blew in from outside.

The butler sighed, and propped the new manservant (who had begun to fall down again) more securely against the wall, and secretly put hand-warmers in his pockets.

At midnight the maid went in to take Mr Strange some gruel. When she returned to the kitchen she reported that Mr Strange had found the hand-warmers and taken them out and put them on the table. The servants went sorrowfully to bed, convinced that the new manservant would be dead by morning.

Morning came. The door to Mr Strange's writing-room was closed. Seven o'clock came and no one rang the bell for the servant; no one appeared. Eight o'clock came. Nine o'clock. Ten. The servants wrung their hands in despair.

But what they had forgot – what, indeed, Laurence Strange had forgot – was that the new manservant was a young, strong man, whereas Laurence Strange was an old one – and some of what the new manservant had been made to suffer that night, Laurence Strange had been forced to share. At seven minutes past ten the butler and the coachman ventured in together and found the new manservant upon the floor fast asleep, his fever gone. On the other side of the room, seated at his writing-table was Laurence Strange, frozen to death.

When the events of those two nights became more generally known there was a great curiosity to see the new manservant, such as there might be to see a dragonslayer or a man who had toppled a giant. Of course the new manservant was glad to be thought remarkable, and as he told and re-told the story he discovered that what he had *actually* said to Mr Strange when he asked for the third glass of sherry-wine was: "Oh! it may suit you very well now, you wicked old sinner, to abuse honest men and drive them into their graves, but a day is coming – and not far off either – when you shall have to answer for every sigh you have forced from an honest man's breast, every tear you have wrung from a widow's eye!" Likewise it was soon well known in the neighbourhood that when Mr Strange had opened the window with the kind intention of starving the new manservant to death with cold the new manservant had cried out, "Cold at first, Laurence Strange, but hot at last! Cold at first, hot at last!" – a prophetic reference to Mr Strange's present situation.

15

"How is Lady Pole?"

January 1808

"How is Lady Pole?"

In every part of the Town and among all stations and degrees of citizen the question was to be heard. In Covent-garden at break of dawn, costermongers asked flower-girls, "How is Lady Pole?". In Ackermann's in the Strand, Mr Ackermann himself inquired of his customers (members of the nobility and persons of distinction) whether they had any news of Lady Pole. In the House of Commons during dull speeches, Members of Parliament whispered the question to their neighbours (each regarding Sir Walter out of the corner of his eye as he did so). In Mayfair dressing-rooms in the early hours of the morning, maids begged their mistresses' pardons, ". . . but was Lady Pole at the party tonight? And how is her ladyship?"

And so the question went round and round; "How is Lady Pole?"

And, "Oh!" (came back the reply), "her ladyship is very well, exceedingly well."

Which demonstrates the sad poverty of the English language, for her ladyship was a great deal more than well. Next to her ladyship every other person in the world looked pale, tired, half-dead. The extraordinary energy she had exhibited the morning after her resurrection had never left her; when she took her walk people stared to see a lady get on so fast. And as for the footman who was meant to attend her, he, poor fellow, was generally many yards in the rear, red-faced and breathless. The Secretary of War, coming out of Drummond's in Charing Cross one morning, was brought into sudden and unexpected conjunction with her lady-ship walking rapidly along the street and was quite overturned. She helped him to his feet, said she hoped she had not hurt him and was gone before he could think of a reply.

Like every other young lady of nineteen Lady Pole was wild for dancing. She would dance every dance at a ball without ever once losing her breath and was dismayed that everyone went away so soon. "It is ridiculous to call such a half-hearted affair a ball!" she told Sir Walter. "We have had scarcely three hours dancing!" And she marvelled too at the frailty of the other dancers. "Poor things! I pity them."

Her health was drunk by the Army, the Navy and the Church. Sir Walter Pole was regularly named as the most fortunate man in the Kingdom and Sir Walter himself was quite of the same opinion. Miss Wintertowne – poor, pale, sick Miss Wintertowne – had excited his compassion, but Lady Pole, in a constant glow of extraordinary good health and happy spirits, was the object of his admiration. When she accidentally knocked the Secretary of War to the ground he thought it the best joke in the world and spoke of it to everyone he met. He privately confided to Lady Winsell, his particular friend, that her ladyship was exactly the wife to suit him – so clever, so lively, so everything he could have wished for. He was particularly struck by her independent opinions.

"She advised me last week that the Government ought not to send money and troops to the King of Sweden – which is what we have decided – but instead to lend our support to the Governments of Portugal and Spain and make these countries the bases of our operations against Buonaparte. At nineteen, to have thought so deeply upon all manner of things and to have come to so many conclusions about them! At nineteen, to contradict all the Gov-

171

ernment so boldly! Of course I told her that she ought to be in Parliament!"

Lady Pole united in one person all the different fascinations of Beauty, Politics, Wealth and *Magic*. The fashionable world had no doubt but that she was destined to become one of its most brilliant leaders. She had been married almost three months now; it was time to embark upon the course that Destiny and the fashionable world had marked out for her. Cards were sent out for a magnificent dinner-party to be held in the second week of January.

The first dinner-party of a bride's career is a momentous occasion, entailing a world of small anxieties. The accomplishments which have won her acclaim in the three years since she left the schoolroom are no longer enough. It is no longer enough to dress exquisitely, to chuse jewels exactly appropriate to the occasion, to converse in French, to play the pianoforte and sing. Now she must turn her attention to French cooking and French wines. Though other people may advise her upon these important matters, her own taste and inclinations must guide her. She is sure to despise her mother's style of entertaining and wish to do things differently. In London fashionable people dine out four, five times a week. However will a new bride – nineteen years old and scarcely ever in a kitchen before – think of a meal to astonish and delight such jaded palates?

Then there are the servants. In the new bride's new house the footmen are all new to their business. If something is needed quickly – candles, a different sort of fork, a heavy cloth in which to carry a hot soup tureen – will they be able to find it? In the case of Lady Pole's establishment at no. 9 Harley-street the problems were multiplied threefold. Half of the servants were from Northamptonshire – from her ladyship's estate at Great Hitherden – and half were newly hired in London; and as everybody knows there is a world of difference between country servants and London servants. It is not a matter of duties exactly. Servants must cook and clean and fetch and carry in Northamptonshire just as in

London. No, the distinction lies more in the manner in which those duties are carried out. Say a country squire in Northamptonshire visits his neighbour. The visit over, the footman fetches the squire's greatcoat and helps the squire on with it. While he is doing so it is only natural for the footman to inquire respectfully after the squire's wife. The squire is not in the least offended and responds with some inquiries of his own. Perhaps the squire has heard that the footman's grandmother fell over and hurt herself while cutting cabbages in her garden and he wishes to know if she is recovered. The squire and the footman inhabit a very small world and have known each other from childhood. But in London this will never do. A London footman must not address his master's guests. He must look as if he did not know there were such things as grand-mothers and cabbages in the world.

At no. 9 Harley-street Lady Pole's country servants were continually ill at ease, afraid of going wrong and never sure of what was right. Even their speech was found fault with and mocked. Their Northamptonshire accent was not always intelli-gible to the London servants (who, it must be said, made no very great efforts to understand them) and they used words like goosegogs, sparrow-grass, betty-cat and battle-twigs, when they should have said gooseberries, asparagus, she-cat and earwigs.

The London servants delighted in playing tricks on the country servants. They gave Alfred, a young footman, plates of nasty, dirty water and told him it was French soup and bade him serve it up to the other servants at dinner. Often they gave the country servants messages to pass on to the butcher's boy, the baker and the lamplighter. The messages were full of London slang and the country servants could make neither head nor tail of them, but to the butcher's boy, the baker and the lamplighter, who understood them very well, they were both vulgar and insulting. The butch-er's boy punched Alfred in the eye on account of what was said to him, while the London servants hid in the larder, to listen and laugh.

Naturally, the country servants complained vigorously to Lady Pole (whom they had known all their lives) about the manner in which they were persecuted and Lady Pole was shocked to find that all her old friends were unhappy in their new home. But she was inexperienced and uncertain how to proceed. She did not doubt the truth of what the country servants said for a moment, but she feared making matters worse.

"What ought I to do, Sir Walter?" she asked.

"Do?" said Sir Walter in surprize. "Do nothing. Leave it all to Stephen Black. By the time Stephen has finished with them they will all be as meek as lambs and as harmonious as blackbirds."

Before his marriage Sir Walter had had only one servant, Stephen Black, and Sir Walter's confidence in this person knew scarcely any bounds. At no. 9 Harley-street he was called "butler", but his duties and responsibilities extended far beyond the range of any ordinary butler: he dealt with bankers and lawyers on Sir Walter's behalf; he studied the accounts of Lady Pole's estates and reported to Sir Walter upon what he found there; he hired servants and workmen without reference to any one else; he directed their work and paid bills and wages.

Of course in many households there is a servant who by virtue of his exceptional intelligence and abilities is given authority beyond what is customary. But in Stephen's case it was all the more extraordinary since Stephen was a negro. I say "extraordinary", for is it not generally the case that a negro servant is the least-regarded person in a household? No matter how hardworking he or she may be? No matter how clever? Yet somehow Stephen Black had found a way to thwart this universal principle. He had, it is true, certain natural advantages: a handsome face and a tall, well-made figure. It certainly did him no harm that his master was a politician who was pleased to advertise his liberal principles to the world by entrusting the management of his house and business to a black servant.

The other servants were a little surprized to find they were put under a black man – a sort of person that many of them had never even seen before. Some were inclined to be indignant at first and told each other that if he dared to give them an order they would return him a very rude answer. But whatever their intentions, they discovered that when they were actually in Stephen's presence they did nothing of the sort. His grave looks, air of authority and reasonable instructions made it very natural to do whatever he told them.

The butcher's boy, the baker, the lamplighter and other similar new acquaintances of the Harley-street servants shewed great interest in Stephen from the first. They asked the Harley-street servants questions about Stephen's mode of life. What did he eat and drink? Who were his friends? Where did he like to go whenever he should happen to be at liberty to go anywhere? When the Harley-street servants replied that Stephen had had three boiled eggs for breakfast, the Secretary at War's Welsh valet was a great friend of his and that he had attended a servants' ball in Wapping the night before, the butcher's boy, the baker and the lamplighter were most grateful for the information. The Harley-street servants asked them why they wished to know. The butcher's boy, the baker and the lamplighter were entirely astonished. Did the Harley-street servants really not know? The Harley-street servants really did not. The butcher's boy, the baker and the lamplighter explained that a rumour had been circulating London for years to the effect that Stephen Black was not really a butler at all. Secretly he was an African prince, the heir to a vast kingdom, and it was well known that as soon as he grew tired of being a butler he would return there and marry a princess as black as himself.

After this revelation the Harley-street servants watched Stephen out of the corners of their eyes and agreed among themselves that nothing was more likely. In fact, was not their own obedience to Stephen the best proof of it? For it was hardly likely that such independent, proud-spirited Englishmen and women would have submitted to the authority of a *black man*, had they not instinctively felt that respect and reverence which a commoner feels for a king!

Meanwhile Stephen Black knew nothing of these curious speculations. He performed his duties diligently as he had always done. He continued to polish silver, train the footmen in the duties of *service à la française*, admonish the cooks, order flowers, linen, knives and forks and do all the thousand and one things necessary to prepare house and servants for the important evening of the magnificent dinner-party. When it finally came, everything was as splendid as his ingenuity could make it. Vases of hot-house roses filled the drawing-room and dining-room and lined the staircase. The dining-table was laid with a heavy white damask cloth and shone with all the separate glitters that silver, glass and candlelight can provide. Two great Venetian mirrors hung upon the wall and on Stephen's instructions these had been made to face each other, so that the reflections doubled and tripled and twice-tripled the silver and the glasses and the candles, and when the guests finally sat down to dinner they appeared to be gently dissolving in a dazzling, golden light like a company of the blessed in glory.

Chief among the guests was Mr Norrell. What a contrast now with that period when he had first arrived in London! Then he had been disregarded – a Nobody. Now he sat among the highest in the land and was courted by them! The other guests continually directed remarks and questions to him and seemed quite delighted by his short, ungracious replies: "I do not know whom you mean," or "I have not the pleasure of that gentleman's acquaintance," or "I have never been to the place you mention."

Some of Mr Norrell's conversation – the more entertaining part – was supplied by Mr Drawlight and Mr Lascelles. They sat upon either side of him, busily conveying his opinions upon modern magic about the table. Magic was a favourite subject that evening. Finding themselves at one and the same time in the presence of England's only magician and of the most famous subject of his magic, the guests could neither think nor talk of any thing else.

Very soon they fell to discussing the numerous claims of successful spells which had sprung up all over the country following Lady Pole's resurrection.

"Every provincial newspaper seems to have two or three reports," agreed Lord Castlereagh. "In the *Bath Chronicle* the other day I read about a man called Gibbons in Milsom-street who awoke in the night because he heard thieves breaking into his house. It seems that this man has a large library of magical books. He tried a spell he knew and turned the housebreakers into mice."

"Really?" said Mr Canning. "And what happened to the mice?"

"They all ran away into holes in the wainscotting."

"Ha!" said Mr Lascelles. "Believe me, my lord, there was no magic. Gibbons heard a noise, feared a housebreaker, said a spell, opened a door and found – not housebreakers, but mice. The truth is, it was mice all along. All of these stories prove false in the end. There is an unmarried clergyman and his sister in Lincoln called Malpas who have made it their business to look into supposed instances of magical occurrences and they have found no truth in any of them."

"They are such admirers of Mr Norrell, this clergyman and his sister!" added Mr Drawlight, enthusiastically. "They are so delighted that such a man has arisen to restore the noble art of English magic! They cannot bear that other people should tell falsehoods and claim to imitate his great deeds! They hate it that other people should make themselves seem important at Mr Norrell's expense! They feel it as a personal affront! Mr Norrell has been so kind as to supply them with certain infallible means of establishing beyond a doubt the falsity of all such claims and Mr Malpas and Miss Malpas drive about the country in their phaeton confounding these imposters!"

"I believe you are too generous to Gibbons, Mr Lascelles," said Mr Norrell in his pedantic fashion. "It is not at all certain that he did not have some malicious purpose in making his false claim. At the very least he lied about his library. I sent Childermass to see it and Childermass says there is not a book earlier than 1760. Worthless! Quite worthless!"

"Yet we must hope," said Lady Pole to Mr Norrell, "that the clergyman and his sister will soon uncover a magician of genuine ability – someone to help you, sir."

"Oh! But there is no one!" exclaimed Drawlight. "No one at all! You see, in order to accomplish his extraordinary deeds Mr Norrell shut himself away for years and years reading books. Alas, such devotion to the interests of one's country is very rare! I assure you there is no one else!"

"But the clergyman and his sister must not give up their search," urged her ladyship. "I know from my own example how much labour is involved in one solitary act of magic. Think how desirable it would be if Mr Norrell were provided with an assistant."

"Desirable yet hardly likely," said Mr Lascelles. "The Malpases have found nothing to suggest that any such person is in existence."

"But by your own account, Mr Lascelles, they have not been looking!" said Lady Pole. "Their object has been to expose false magic, not find new magicians. It would be very easy for them, as they drive about in their phaeton, to make some inquiries as to who does magic and who has a library. I am certain they will not mind the extra trouble. They will be glad to do what they can to help you, sir." (This to Mr Norrell.) "And we shall all hope that they soon succeed, because I think you must feel a little lonely."

In due course a suitable proportion of the fifty or so dishes was deemed to have been eaten and the footmen took away what was left. The ladies withdrew and the gentlemen were left to their wine. But the gentlemen found they had less pleasure in each other's society than usual. They had got to the end of all they had to say about magic. They had no relish for gossiping about their acquaintance and even politics seemed a little dull. In short they felt that they should like to have the pleasure of looking at Lady Pole again, and so they told Sir Walter – rather than asked him – that he missed his wife. He replied that he did not. But this was not allowed to be possible; it was well known that newly married gentlemen were never happy apart from their wives; the briefest of absences could depress a new husband's spirits and interfere with his digestion. Sir Walter's guests asked each other if they thought he looked bilious and they agreed that he did. He denied it. Ah, he was putting a brave face on it, was he? Very good. But clearly it was a desperate case. They would have mercy on him and go and join the ladies.

In the corner by the sideboard Stephen Black watched the gentlemen leave. Three footmen – Alfred, Geoffrey and Robert – remained in the room.

"Are we to go and serve the tea, Mr Black?" inquired Alfred, innocently.

Stephen Black raised one thin finger as a sign they were to stay where they were and he frowned slightly to shew they were to be silent. He waited until he was sure the gentlemen were out of hearing and then he exlaimed, "What in the world was the matter with everyone tonight? Alfred! I know that you have not often been in such company as we have tonight, but that is no reason to forget all your training! I was astonished at your stupidity!"

Alfred mumbled his apologies.

"Lord Castlereagh asked you to bring him *partridges with truffles*. I heard him most distinctly! Yet you brought him a *strawberry jelly*! What were you thinking of?"

Alfred said something rather indistinct in which only the word "fright" was distinguishable.

"You had a fright? What fright?"

"I thought I saw a queer figure standing behind her ladyship's chair."

"Alfred, what are you talking about?"

"A tall person with a head of shining silver hair and a green

179

coat. He was leaning down to look at her ladyship. But the next moment there was no one at all."

"Alfred, look to that end of the room."

"Yes, Mr Black."

"What do you see?"

"A curtain, Mr Black."

"And what else?"

"A chandelier."

"A green velvet curtain and a chandelier ablaze with candles. That is your green-coated, silver-headed person, Alfred. Now go and help Cissie put away the china and do not be so foolish in future." Stephen Black turned to the next footman. "Geoffrey! Your behaviour was every bit as bad as Alfred's. I swear your thoughts were somewhere else entirely. What have you to say for yourself?"

Poor Geoffrey did not answer immediately. He was blinking his eyes and pressing his lips together and generally doing all those things that a man will do when he is trying not to cry. "I am sorry, Mr Black, but it was the music that distracted me."

"What music?" asked Stephen. "There was no music. There! Listen! That is the string quartet just starting up in the drawing-room. They have not played until now."

"Oh, no, Mr Black! I mean the pipe and fiddle that were playing in the next room all the time the ladies and gentlemen were at dinner. Oh, Mr Black! It was the saddest music that I ever heard. I thought it would break my heart!"

Stephen stared at him in perplexity. "I do not understand you," he said. "There was no pipe and fiddle." He turned to the last footman, a solid-looking, dark-haired man of forty or so. "And Robert! I scarcely know what to say to you! Did we not talk yesterday?"

"We did, Mr Black."

"Did I not tell you how much I relied upon you to set an example to the others?"

"Yes, Mr Black."

"Yet half a dozen times this evening you went to the window! What were you thinking of? Lady Winsell was looking round for someone to bring her a clean glass. Your business was at the table, attending to her ladyship's guests, not at the window."

"I am sorry, Mr Black, but I heard a knocking at the window."

"A knocking? What knocking?"

"Branches beating against the glass, Mr Black."

Stephen Black made a little gesture of impatience. "But, Robert, there is no tree near the house! You know very well there is not."

"I thought a wood had grown up around the house," said Robert.

"What?" cried Stephen.

16

Lost-hope

January 1808

THE SERVANTS IN Harley-street continued to believe that they were haunted by eerie sights and mournful sounds. The cook, John Longridge, and the kitchenmaids were troubled by a sad bell. The effect of the bell, explained John Longridge to Stephen Black, was to bring vividly to mind everyone they had ever known who had died, all the good things they had ever lost and every bad thing which had ever happened to them. Consequently, they had become dejected and low and their lives were not worth living.

Geoffrey and Alfred, the two youngest footmen, were tormented by the sound of the fife and violin which Geoffrey had first heard on the night of the dinner-party. The music always appeared to come from the next room. Stephen had taken them all over the house and proved that nowhere was any one playing any such instruments, but it did no good; they continued afraid and unhappy.

Most bewildering of all, in Stephen's opinion, was the behaviour of Robert, the eldest footman. Robert had struck Stephen from the first as a sensible man, conscientious, reliable – in short the last person in the world to fall prey to imaginary fears. Yet Robert still insisted that he could hear an invisible wood growing up around the house. Whenever he paused in his work, he heard ghostly branches scraping at the walls and tapping upon the windows, and tree-roots slyly extending themselves beneath the foundations and prising apart the bricks. The wood was old, said Robert, and full of malice. A traveller in the wood would have as much to fear from the trees as from another person hiding there.

But, argued Stephen, the nearest wood of any size was four miles away upon Hampstead Heath and even there the trees were quite domesticated. They did not crowd around people's houses and try to destroy them. Stephen could say what he liked; Robert only shook his head and shivered.

Stephen's only consolation was that this peculiar mania had erased all the servants' other differences. The London servants no longer cared that the country servants were slow of speech and had old-fashioned manners. The country servants no longer complained to Stephen that the London servants played tricks upon them and sent them on imaginary errands. All the servants were united by the belief that the house was haunted. They sat in the kitchen after their work was done and told stories of all the other houses that they had ever heard of where there were ghosts and horrors, and of the horrible fates that had befallen the people who lived there.

One evening, about a fortnight after Lady Pole's dinner-party, they were gathered about the kitchen fire, engaged in this favourite occupation. Stephen soon grew tired of listening to them and retired to his own little room to read a newspaper. He had not been there more than a few minutes when he heard a bell ringing. So he put down his newspaper, put on his black coat and went to see where he was wanted.

In the little passage-way that connected the kitchen to the butler's room was a little row of bells and beneath the bells the names of various rooms were neatly inscribed in brown paint: *The Venetian Drawing-room*; *The Yellow Drawing-room*; *The Dining-room*; *Lady Pole's Sitting-room*; *Lady Pole's Bed-chamber*; *Lady Pole's Dressing-room*; *Sir Walter's Study*; *Sir Walter's Bed-chamber*; *Sir Walter's Dressing-room*; *Lost-hope*.

"Lost-hope?" thought Stephen. "What in the world is that?"

He had paid the carpenter that very morning for the work in putting up the bells and he had entered the amount in his account-book: *To Amos Judd, for putting up 9 bells in the kitchen passageway and painting the names of the rooms beneath, 4 shillings*. But now there were ten bells. And the bell for Lost-hope was ringing violently.

"Perhaps," thought Stephen, "Judd means it as a joke. Well, he shall be fetched back tomorrow and made to put it right."

Not knowing quite what else to do, Stephen went up to the ground floor and looked in every room; all were empty. And so he climbed the staircase to the first floor.

At the top of the staircase was a door which he had never seen before.

"Who's there?" whispered a voice from behind the door. It was not a voice Stephen knew and, though it was only a whisper, it was curiously penetrating. It seemed to get into Stephen's head by some other means than his ears.

"There is someone upon stairs!" insisted the whispering voice. "Is it the servant? Come here, if you please! I need you!"

Stephen knocked and went in.

The room was every bit as mysterious as the door. If anyone had asked Stephen to describe it, he would have said it was decorated in the Gothic style – this being the only explanation he could think of to account for its extraordinary appearance. But it had none of the usual Gothic embellishments such as one might see depicted in the pages of Mr Ackermann's *Repository of the Arts*. There were no pointed mediaeval arches, no intricately carved wood, no ecclesiastical motifs. The walls and floor of the room were of plain grey stone, very worn and uneven in places. The ceiling was of vaulted stone. One small window looked out upon a starlit sky. The window had not so much as a scrap of glass in it and the winter wind blew into the room.

A pale gentleman with an extraordinary quantity of silvery, thistle-down hair was looking at his reflection in an old cracked mirror with an air of deep dissatisfaction. "Oh, there you are!" he said, glancing sourly at Stephen. "A person may call and call in this house, but no one comes!"

"I am very sorry, sir," said Stephen, "but no one told me you were here." He supposed the gentleman must be a guest of Sir Walter's or Lady Pole's – which explained the gentleman, but not the room. Gentlemen are often invited to stay in other people's houses. Rooms hardly ever are.

"In what way may I serve you, sir?" asked Stephen.

"How stupid you are!" cried the gentleman with the thistle-down hair. "Don't you know that Lady Pole is to attend a ball tonight at my house? My own servant has run off and hidden himself somewhere. How can I appear by the side of the beautiful Lady Pole in this condition?"

The gentleman had cause for complaint: his face was unshaven, his curious hair was a mass of tangles and he was not dressed, but only wrapped in an old-fashioned powdering gown.

"I shall be with you in an instant, sir," Stephen assured him. "But first I must find the means to shave you. You do not happen to know what your servant has done with the razor, I suppose?"

The gentleman shrugged.

There was no dressing-table in the room. Indeed there was very little furniture of any description. There was the mirror, an old three-legged milking stool and a queer carved chair that appeared to be made of bones. Stephen did not quite believe that they were human bones, although they did look remarkably like it.

Atop the milking stool, next to a pretty little box, Stephen found a delicate silver razor. A battered pewter basin full of water stood upon the floor.

Curiously there was no fireplace in the room, but only a rusting iron brazier full of hot coals, that spilt its dirty ashes on the floor. So Stephen heated the basin of water on the brazier and then he shaved the gentleman. When he had finished, the gentleman inspected his face and pronounced himself excessively pleased.

He removed his gown and stood patiently in his dressing-trousers while Stephen massaged his skin with a bristle-brush. Stephen could not help but observe that, whereas other gentlemen grow red as lobsters under such treatment, this gentleman remained as pale as ever and the only difference was that his skin took on a whitish glow as of moonlight or mother-of-pearl.

His clothes were the finest Stephen had ever seen; his shirt was exquisitely laundered and his boots shone like black mirrors. But best of all were a dozen or so white muslin neckcloths, each as thin as a cobweb and as stiff as music paper.

It took two hours to complete the gentleman's toilet, for he was, Stephen found, extremely vain. During this time the gentleman became more and more delighted with Stephen. "I tell you that my own ignorant fellow has not got half your skill at dressing hair," he declared, "and when it comes to the delicate art of tying a muslin neckcloth, why! he cannot be made to understand it at all!"

"Well, sir, it is exactly the sort of task I like," said Stephen. "I wish I could persuade Sir Walter to take more care of his clothes, but political gentlemen have no leisure for thinking of such things."

Stephen helped the gentleman on with his leaf-green coat (which was of the very best quality and most fashionable cut), then the gentleman went over to the milking stool and picked up the little box that lay there. It was made of porcelain and silver, and was about the size of a snuff box but a little longer than snuff boxes generally are. Stephen made some admiring remark about the colour which was not exactly pale blue and not exactly grey, not precisely lavender and not precisely lilac.

"Yes, indeed! It is beautiful," agreed the gentleman enthusiastically. "And very hard to make. The pigment must be mixed with the tears of spinsters of good family, who must live long lives of impeccable virtue and die without ever having had a day of true happiness!"

"Poor ladies!" said Stephen. "I am glad it is so rare."

"Oh! It is not the tears that make it rare – I have bottles full of those – it is the skill to mix the colour."

The gentleman had by now become so affable, so willing to talk that Stephen had no hesitation in asking him, "And what do you keep in such a pretty little box, sir? Snuff?"

"Oh, no! It is a great treasure of mine that I wish Lady Pole to wear at my ball tonight!" He opened the box and shewed Stephen a small, white finger.

At first this struck Stephen as a little unusual, but his surprize faded in a moment and if any one had questioned him about it just then, he would have replied that gentlemen often carried fingers about with them in little boxes and that this was just one of many examples he had seen.

"Has it been in your family long, sir?" he asked, politely.

"No, not long."

The gentleman snapped shut the box and put it in his pocket.

Together, he and Stephen admired his reflection in the mirror. Stephen could not help but notice how they perfectly complemented each other: gleaming black skin next to opalescent white skin, each a perfect example of a particular type of masculine beauty. Exactly the same thought seemed to strike the gentleman.

"How handsome we are!" he said in a wondering tone. "But I see now that I have made a horrible blunder! I took you for a servant in this house! But that is quite impossible! Your dignity and handsomeness proclaim you to be of noble, perhaps kingly birth! You are a visitor here, I suppose, as I am. I must beg your pardon for imposing upon you and thank you for the great service you have done me in making me ready to meet the beautiful Lady Pole."

Stephen smiled. "No, sir. I am a servant. I am Sir Walter's servant."

The gentleman with the thistle-down hair raised his eye-brow in astonishment. "A man as talented and handsome as yourself ought not be a servant!" he said in a shocked tone. "He ought to be the ruler of a vast estate! What is beauty for, I should like to know, if not to stand as a visible sign of one's superiority to everyone else? But I see how it is! Your enemies have conspired together to deprive you of all your possessions and to cast you down among the ignorant and lowly!"

"No, sir. You are mistaken. I have always been a servant."

"Well, I do not understand it," declared the gentleman with the thistle-down hair, with a puzzled shake of his head. "There is some mystery here and I shall certainly look into it just as soon as I am at liberty. But, in the meantime, as a reward for dressing my hair so well and all the other services you have done me, you shall attend my ball tonight."

This was such a very extraordinary proposal that for a moment Stephen did not know quite what to say. "Either he is mad," he thought, "or else he is some sort of radical politician who wishes to destroy all distinctions of rank."

Aloud he said, "I am very sensible of the honour you do me, sir, but only consider. Your other guests will come to your house expecting to meet ladies and gentlemen of their own rank. When they discover that they are consorting with a servant I am sure they will feel the insult very keenly. I thank you for your kindness, but I should not wish to embarrass you or offend your friends."

This seemed to astonish the gentleman with the thistle-down hair even more. "What nobility of feeling!" he cried. "To sacrifice your own pleasure to preserve the comfort of others! Well, it is a thing, I confess, that would never occur to me. And it only increases my determination to make you my friend and do everything in my power to aid you. But you do not quite understand. These guests of mine on whose account you are so scrupulous, they are all my vassals and subjects. There is not one of them who would dare to criticize *me* or any one I chose to call my friend. And if they did, why! we could always kill them! But really," he added as if he were suddenly growing bored of this conversation, "there is very little use debating the point since you are already here!"

With that the gentleman walked away and Stephen found that he was standing in a great hall where a crowd of people were dancing to sad music.

Once again he was a little surprized but, as before, he grew accustomed to the idea in a moment and began to look about him. Despite all that the gentleman with the thistle-down hair had said upon the point, he was a little apprehensive at first that he would be recognized. A few glances about the room were enough to reassure him that there were no friends of Sir Walter present – indeed there was no one Stephen had ever seen before and in his neat black clothes and clean white linen he believed he might very easily pass for a gentleman. He was glad that Sir Walter had never required him to wear livery or a powdered wig, which would have marked him out as a servant in an instant.

Everyone was dressed in the very height of fashion. The ladies wore gowns of the most exquisite colours (though, to own the truth, very few of them were colours that Stephen could remember having seen before). The gentlemen wore knee breeches and white stockings and coats of brown, green, blue and black, their linen was a sparkling, shining white and their kid gloves had not so much as a stain or mark upon them.

But in spite of all the fine clothes and gaiety of the guests, there were signs that the house was not so prosperous as once it had been. The room was dimly lit by an insufficient number of tallow candles, and there was just one viol and one fife to provide the music.

"That must be the music that Geoffrey and Alfred spoke of," thought Stephen. "How odd that I could not hear it before! It is every bit as melancholy as they said."

He made his way to a narrow unglazed window and looked out upon a dark, tangled wood under starlight. "And this must be the wood which Robert talks about. How malevolent it looks! And is there a bell, I wonder?"

"Oh, yes!" said a lady who was standing close by. She wore a

190

gown the colour of storms, shadows and rain and a necklace of broken promises and regrets. He was surprized to find himself addressed by her since he was quite certain that he had not spoken his thoughts out loud.

"There is indeed a bell!" she told him, "It is high up in one of the towers."

She was smiling and regarding him with such frank admiration that Stephen thought it only polite to say something.

"This is certainly a most elegant assembly, madam. I do not know when I last saw so many handsome faces and graceful figures gathered together in one place. And every one of them in the utmost bloom of youth. I confess that I am surprized to see no older people in the room. Have these ladies and gentlemen no mothers and fathers? No aunts or uncles?"

"What an odd remark!" she replied, laughing. "Why should the Master of Lost-hope House invite aged and unsightly persons to his ball? Who would want to look at them? Besides we are not so young as you suppose. England was nothing but dreary wood and barren moor when last we saw our sires and dams. But wait! See! There is Lady Pole!"

Between the dancers Stephen caught a glimpse of her ladyship. She was wearing a blue velvet gown and the gentleman with the thistle-down hair was leading her to the top of the dance.

Then the lady in the gown the colour of storms, shadows and rain inquired if he would like to dance with her.

"Gladly," he said.

When the other ladies saw how well Stephen danced, he found he could have any partner he wished for. After the lady in the gown the colour of storms, shadows and rain he danced with a young woman who had no hair, but who wore a wig of shining beetles that swarmed and seethed upon her head. His third partner complained bitterly whenever Stephen's hand happened to brush against her gown; she said it put her gown off its singing; and, when Stephen looked down, he saw that her gown was indeed covered with tiny mouths which opened and sang a little tune in a series of high, eerie notes.

Although in general the dancers followed the usual custom and changed partners at the end of two dances, Stephen observed that the gentleman with the thistle-down hair danced with Lady Pole the whole night long and that he scarcely spoke to any other person in the room. But he had not forgotten Stephen. Whenever Stephen chanced to catch his eye, the gentleman with the thistle-down hair smiled and bowed his head and gave every sign of wishing to convey that, of all the delightful circumstances of the ball, what pleased him most was to see Stephen Black there.

17

The unaccountable appearance of twenty-five guineas

January 1808

THE BEST GROCER'S in Town is Brandy's in St James's-street. I am not alone in that opinion; Sir Walter Pole's grandfather, Sir William Pole, declined to purchase coffee, chocolate or tea from any other establishment, declaring that in comparison with Mr Brandy's Superfine High Roasted Turkey Coffee, all other coffees had a mealy flavour. It must be said, however, that Sir William Pole's patronage was a somewhat mixed blessing. Though liberal in his praise and always courteous and condescending to the shop-people, he was scarcely ever known to pay a bill and when he died, the amount of money owing to Brandy's was considerable. Mr Brandy, a short-tempered, pinched-faced, cross little old man, was beside himself with rage about it. He died shortly afterwards, and was presumed by many people to have done so on purpose and to have gone in pursuit of his noble debtor.

At Mr Brandy's death, the business came into the possession of his widow. Mr Brandy had married rather late in life and my readers will not be much surprised, I dare say, to learn that Mrs Brandy had not been entirely happy in her marriage. She had quickly discovered that Mr Brandy loved to look at guineas and shillings more than he had ever loved to look at her – though *I* say it must have been a strange sort of man that did not love to look at her, for she was everything that was delightful and amiable, all soft brown curls, light blue eyes and a sweet expression. It would seem to me that an old man, such as Mr Brandy, with nothing to recommend him but his money, ought to have treasured a young, pretty wife, and studied hard to please her in everything he could; but he did not. He had even denied her a house of her own to live in – which was something he could have afforded very easily. So loath had he been to part with a sixpence that he declared they should live in the little room above the shop in St. James's Street, and for the twelve years of her marriage this apartment served Mrs Brandy as parlour, bedroom, dining-parlour and kitchen. But Mr Brandy had not been dead three weeks when she bought a house in Islington, near the Angel, and acquired three maids, whose names were Sukey, Dafney and Delphina.

She also employed two men to attend the customers in the shop. John Upchurch was a steady soul, hard-working and capable. Toby Smith was a red-haired, nervous man whose behaviour often puzzled Mrs Brandy. Sometimes he would be silent and unhappy and at other times he would be suddenly cheerful and full of unexpected confidences. From certain discrepancies in the accounts (such as may occur in any business) and from the circumstances of Toby looking miserable and ill at ease whenever she questioned him about it, Mrs Brandy had begun to fear that he might be pocketing the difference. One January evening her dilemma took a strange turn. She was sitting in her little parlour above the shop when there was a knock upon the door and Toby Smith came shuffling in, quite unable to meet her eye.

"What's the matter, Toby?"

"If you please, ma'am," said Toby looking this way and that, "the money won't come right. John and me have counted it out again and again, ma'am, and cast up the sums a dozen times or more, but we cannot make head or tail of it."

Mrs Brandy tutted and sighed and asked by how much they were out.

"Twenty-five guineas, ma'am."

"Twenty-five guineas!" cried Mrs Brandy in horror. "Twenty-five guineas! How could we possibly have lost so much? Oh! I hope you are mistaken, Toby. Twenty-five guineas! I would not have supposed there to be so much money in the shop! Oh, Toby!" she cried, as another thought struck her. "We must have been robbed!"

"No, ma'am," said Toby. "Beg your pardon, ma'am, but you mistake. I did not mean to say we are twenty-five guineas short. We are over, ma'am. By that amount."

Mrs Brandy stared at him.

"Which you may see for yourself, ma'am," said Toby, "if you will just come down to the shop," and he held the door open for her with an anxious, pleading expression upon his face. So Mrs Brandy ran downstairs into the shop and Toby followed after her.

It was about nine o'clock on a moonless night. The shutters were all put up and John and Toby had extinguished the lamps. The shop ought to have been as dark as the inside of a tea-caddy, but instead it was filled with a soft, golden light which appeared to emanate from something golden which lay upon the counter-top.

A heap of shining guineas was lying there. Mrs Brandy picked up one of the coins and examined it. It was as if she held a ball of soft yellow light with a coin at the bottom of it. The light was odd. It made Mrs Brandy, John and Toby look quite unlike themselves: Mrs Brandy appeared proud and haughty, John looked sly and deceitful and Toby wore an expression of great ferocity. Needless to say, all of these were qualities quite foreign to their characters. But stranger still was the transformation that the light worked upon the dozens of small mahogany drawers that formed one wall of the shop. Upon other evenings the gilt lettering upon the drawers proclaimed the contents to be such things as: *Mace (Blades), Mustard (Unhusked), Nutmegs, Ground Fennel, Bay Leaves,*

Pepper of Jamaica, *Essence of Ginger*, *Caraway*, *Peppercorns* and *Vinegar* and all the other stock of a fashionable and prosperous grocery business. But now the words appeared to read: *Mercy (Deserved)*, *Mercy (Undeserved)*, *Nightmares*, *Good Fortune*, *Bad Fortune*, *Persecution by Families*, *Ingratitude of Children*, *Confusion*, *Perspicacity* and *Veracity*. It was as well that none of them noticed this odd change. Mrs Brandy would have been most distressed by it had she known. She would not have had the least notion what to charge for these new commodities.

"Well," said Mrs Brandy, "they must have come from somewhere. Has any one sent today to pay their bill?"

John shook his head. So did Toby. "And, besides," added Toby, "no one owes so much, excepting, of course, the Duchess of Worksop and frankly, ma'am, in that case . . ."

"Yes, yes, Toby, that will do," interrupted Mrs Brandy. She thought for a moment. "Perhaps," she said, "some gentleman, wishing to wipe the rain from his face, pulled out his handkerchief, and so caused the money to tumble out of his pocket on to the floor."

"But we did not find it upon the floor," said John, "it was here in the cash-box with all the rest."

"Well," said Mrs Brandy, "I do not know what to say. Did anyone pay with a guinea today?"

No, said Toby and John, no one had paid today with a guinea, let alone twenty-five such guineas or twenty-five such persons.

"And such yellow guineas, ma'am," remarked John, "each one the very twin of all the others, without a spot of tarnish upon any of them."

"Should I run and fetch Mr Black, ma'am?" asked Toby.

"Oh, yes!" said Mrs Brandy, eagerly. "But then again, perhaps no. We ought not to trouble Mr Black unless there is any thing very wrong. And nothing is wrong, is it, Toby? Or perhaps it is. I cannot tell."

The sudden and unaccountable arrival of large sums of money is such a very rare thing in our Modern Age that neither Toby nor John was able to help their mistress decide whether it were a wrong thing or a right.

"But, then," continued Mrs Brandy, "Mr Black is so clever. I dare say he will understand this puzzle in an instant. Go to Harley-street, Toby. Present my compliments to Mr Black and say that if he is at liberty I should be glad of a few moments' conversation with him. No, wait! Do not say that, it sounds so presumptuous. You must apologize for disturbing him and say that whenever he should happen to be at liberty I should be grateful – no, honoured – no, grateful – I should be grateful for a few moments' conversation with him."

Mrs Brandy's acquaintance with Stephen Black had begun when Sir Walter had inherited his grandfather's debts and Mrs Brandy had inherited her husband's business. Every week or so Stephen had come with a guinea or two to help pay off the debt. Yet, curiously, Mrs Brandy was often reluctant to accept the money. "Oh! Mr Black!" she would say, "Pray put the money away again! I am certain that Sir Walter has greater need of it than I. We did such excellent business last week! We have got some carracca chocolate in the shop just at present, which people have been kind enough to say is the best to be had any where in London – infinitely superior to other chocolate in both flavour and texture! – and they have been sending for it from all over Town. Will not you take a cup, Mr Black?"

Then Mrs Brandy would bring the chocolate in a pretty blue-and-white china chocolate-pot, and pour Stephen a cup, and anxiously inquire how he liked it; for it seemed that, even though people had been sending for it from all over Town, Mrs Brandy could not feel quite convinced of its virtues until she knew Stephen's opinion. Nor did her care of him end with making him chocolate. She was solicitous for his health. If it happened to be a cold day, she would be concerned that he was not warm enough; if it were raining she would worry that he might catch a cold; if it were a hot, dry day she would insist that he sit by a window overlooking a little green garden to refresh himself.

When it was time for him to go, she would revive the question of the guinea. "But as to next week, Mr Black, I cannot say. Next week I may need a guinea very badly – people do not always pay their bills – and so I will be so bold as to ask you to bring it again on Wednesday. Wednesday at about three o'clock. I shall be quite disengaged at three o'clock and I shall be sure to have a pot of chocolate ready, as you are so kind as to say you like it very much."

The gentlemen among my readers will smile to themselves and say that women never did understand business, but the ladies may agree with me that Mrs Brandy understood her business very well, for the chief business of Mrs Brandy's life was to make Stephen Black as much in love with her as she was with him.

In due course Toby returned, not with a message from Stephen Black, but with Stephen himself and Mrs Brandy's anxiety about the coins was swept away by a new and altogether more pleasant agitation. "Oh, Mr Black! We did not expect to see you so soon! I did not imagine you would be at liberty!"

Stephen stood in the darkness outside the radiance cast by the strange coins. "It does not matter where I am tonight," he said in a dull tone quite unlike his usual voice. "The house is all at sixes and sevens. Her ladyship is not well."

Mrs Brandy, John and Toby were shocked to hear this. Like every other citizen of London they took a close interest in every-thing that concerned her ladyship. They prided themselves upon their connexion with all sorts of aristocratic persons, but it was the patronage of Lady Pole which gave them the greatest satisfaction. Nothing pleased them so much as being able to assure people that when Lady Pole sat down to breakfast, her ladyship's roll was spread with Mrs Brandy's preserves and her coffee cup was filled with coffee made with Mrs Brandy's beans.

Mrs Brandy was suddenly struck with a most unpleasant idea.

"I hope her ladyship did not eat something which disagreed with her?" she asked.

"No," said Stephen with a sigh, "it is nothing of that sort. She complains of aches in all her limbs, odd dreams and feeling cold. But mostly she is silent and out of spirits. Her skin is icy to the touch."

Stephen stepped into the queer light.

The strange alterations which it had made to the appearance of Toby, John and Mrs Brandy were nothing to the changes it worked upon Stephen: his native handsomeness increased five-, seven-, tenfold; he acquired an expression of almost supernatural nobility; and, most extraordinary of all, the light somehow seemed to concentrate in a band around his brow so that he appeared to have been crowned with a diadem. Yet, just as before, none of those present noticed anything out of the common.

He turned the coins over in his thin black fingers. "Where were they, John?"

"Here in the cash-box with all the rest of the money. Where in the world can they have come from, Mr Black?"

"I am as puzzled as you are. I have no explanation to offer." Stephen turned to Mrs Brandy. "My chief concern, ma'am, is that you should protect yourself from any suspicion that you have come by the money dishonestly. I think you must give the money to a lawyer. Instruct him to advertise in *The Times* and *The Morning Chronicle* to discover if any one lost twenty-five guineas in Mrs Brandy's shop."

"A lawyer, Mr Black!" cried Mrs Brandy, horrified. "Oh, but that will cost a world of money!"

"Lawyers always do, ma'am."

At that moment a gentleman in St. James's-street passed Mrs Brandy's shop and, discerning a golden radiance shining out of the chinks in the shutters, realized that someone was within. He happened to be in need of tea and sugar and so he knocked upon the door.

"Customer, Toby!" cried Mrs Brandy.

Toby hurried to open the door and John put the money away. The instant that he closed the lid of the cash-box, the room became dark and for the first time they realized that they had been seeing each other by the light of the eerie coins. So John ran around, re-lighting the lamps and making the place look cheerful and Toby weighed out the things which the customer wanted.

Stephen Black sank into a chair and passed his hand across his forehead. He looked grey-faced and tired to death.

Mrs Brandy sat down in the chair next to his and touched his hand very gently. "You are not well, my dear Mr Black."

"It is just that I ache all over – as a man does who has been dancing all night." He sighed again and rested his head upon his hand.

Mrs Brandy withdrew her hand. "I did not know there was a ball last night," she said. There was a tinge of jealousy to her words. "I hope you had a most delightful time. Who were your partners?"

"No, no. There was no ball. I seem to have all the pains of dancing, without having had any of the pleasure." He raised his head suddenly. "Do you hear that?" he asked.

"What, Mr Black?"

"That bell. Tolling for the dead."

She listened a moment. "No, I do not hear any thing. I hope you will stay to supper, my dear Mr Black? It would do us so much honour. I fear it will not be a very elegant meal. There is very little. Hardly anything at all. Just some steamed oysters and a pigeon-pie and a harrico of mutton. But an old friend like you will make allowances, I am sure. Toby can fetch some . . ."

"Are you certain you do not hear it?"

"No."

"I cannot stay." He looked as if he meant to say something more – indeed he opened his mouth to say it, but the bell seemed to intrude itself upon his attention again and he was silent. "Good evening to you!" He rose and, with a rapid half-bow, he walked out.

In St James's-street the bell continued to toll. He walked like a man in a fog. He had just reached Piccadilly when an aproned porter carrying a basket full of fish came very suddenly out of a little alleyway. In trying to get out of the porter's way, Stephen collided with a stout gentleman in a blue coat and a Bedford hat who was standing on the corner of Albemarle-street.

The stout gentleman turned and saw Stephen. Instantly he was all alarm; he saw a black face close to his own face and black hands near his pockets and valuables. He paid no attention to Stephen's expensive clothes and respectable air but, immediately concluding that he was about to be robbed or knocked down, he raised his umbrella to strike a blow in his own defence.

It was the moment that Stephen had dreaded all his life. He supposed that constables would be called and he would be dragged before the magistrates and it was probable that even the patronage and friendship of Sir Walter Pole would not save him. Would an English jury be able to conceive of a black man who did not steal and lie? A black man who was a respectable person? It did not seem very likely. Yet now that his fate had come upon him, Stephen found he did not care very much about it and he watched events unfold as though he were watching a play through thick glass or a scene at the bottom of a pond.

The stout gentleman opened his eyes wide in fright, anger and indignation. He opened his mouth wide to begin accusing Stephen but in that moment he began to change. His body became the trunk of a tree; he suddenly sprouted arms in all directions and all the arms became branches; his face became a bole and he shot up twenty feet; where his hat and umbrella had been there was a thick crown of ivy.

"An oak tree in Piccadilly," thought Stephen, not much interested. "That is unusual."

Piccadilly was changing too. A carriage happened to be passing.

It clearly belonged to someone of importance for as well as the coachman upon his box, two footmen rode behind; there was a coat of arms upon the door and it was drawn by four matched greys. As Stephen watched the horses grew taller and thinner until they seemed about to disappear entirely and at that point they were suddenly transformed into a grove of delicate silver birches. The carriage became a holly bush and the coachman and the footmen became an owl and two nightingales which promptly flew away. A lady and gentleman walking along together suddenly sprouted twigs in every direction and became an elder-bush, a dog became a shaggy clump of dry bracken. The gas lamps that hung above the street were sucked up into the sky and became stars in a fretwork of winter trees and Piccadilly itself dwindled to a barely discernible path through a dark winter wood.

But just as in a dream where the most extraordinary events arrive complete with their own explanation and become reasonable in an instant, Stephen found nothing to be surprised at. Rather, it seemed to him that he had always known that Piccadilly stood in close proximity to a magical wood.

He began to walk along the path.

The wood was very dark and quiet. Above his head the stars were the brightest he had ever seen and the trees were nothing more than black shapes, mere absences of stars.

The thick grey misery and stupidity which had enveloped his mind and spirit all day disappeared and he began to muse upon the curious dream he had the night before about meeting a strange green-coated person with thistle-down hair who had taken him to a house where he had danced all night with the queerest people.

The sad bell sounded much clearer in the wood than it had in London and Stephen followed the sound along the path. In a very short while he came to an immense stone house with a thousand windows. A feeble light shone out of some of these openings. A high wall surrounded the house. Stephen passed through (though he did not quite understand how, for he saw no sign of a gate) and found himself in a wide and dreary courtyard where skulls, broken bones, and rusting weapons were scattered about, as if they had lain there for centuries. Despite the size and grandeur of the house its only entrance was a mean little door and Stephen had to bend low to pass through. Immediately he beheld a vast crowd of people all dressed in the finest clothes.

Two gentlemen stood just inside the door. They wore fine dark coats, spotless white stockings and gloves and dancing pumps. They were talking together, but the moment Stephen appeared, one turned and smiled.

"Ah, Stephen Black!" he said. "We have been waiting for you!"

At that moment the viol and pipe started up again.

18

Sir Walter consults
gentlemen in several professions

February 1808

L ADY POLE SAT by the window, pale and unsmiling. She
said very little and whenever she did say any thing her
remarks were odd and not at all to the point. When her
husband and friends anxiously inquired what the matter was, she
replied that she was sick of dancing and wished to dance no more.
As for music, it was the most detestable thing in the world – she
wondered that she had never realized it before.

Sir Walter regarded this lapse into silence and indifference as
highly alarming. It was altogether too like that illness which had
caused her ladyship so much suffering before her marriage and
ended so tragically in her early death. Had she not been pale
before? Well, she was pale now. Had she not been cold before? She
was so again.

During her ladyship's previous illness no doctor had ever
attended her and naturally doctors everywhere resented this as
an insult to their profession. "Oh!" they cried whenever Lady
Pole's name was mentioned, "the magic which brought her back
to life was no doubt very wonderful, but if only the proper
medicines had been administered in time then there would have
been no need for the magic in the first place."

Mr Lascelles had been right when he declared the fault to be entirely Mrs Wintertowne's. She detested doctors and had never allowed one to come near her daughter. Sir Walter, however, was hindered by no such prejudice; he sent immediately for Mr Baillie.

Mr Baillie was a Scottish gentleman who had long been considered the foremost practitioner of his profession in London. He had written a great many books with important-sounding titles and he was Physician Extraordinary to the King. He had a sensible face and carried a gold-topped stick as a symbol of his pre-eminence. He answered Sir Walter's summons swiftly, eager to prove the superiority of medicine to magic. The examination done, he came out again. Her ladyship was in excellent health, he said. She had not got so much as a cold.

Sir Walter explained again how different she was today from what she had been only a few days ago.

Mr Baillie regarded Sir Walter thoughtfully. He said he believed he understood the problem. Sir Walter and her ladyship had not been married long, had they? Well, Sir Walter must forgive him, but doctors were often obliged to say things which other people would not. Sir Walter was not accustomed to married life. He would soon discover that married people often quarrelled. It was nothing to be ashamed of – even the most devoted couples disagreed sometimes, and when they did it was not uncommon for one partner to pretend an indisposition. Nor was it always the lady that did so. Was there perhaps something that Lady Pole had set her heart upon? Well, if it were a small thing, like a new gown or a bonnet, why not let her have it since she wanted it so much? If it were a large thing like a house or a visit to Scotland, then perhaps it would be best to talk to her about it. Mr Baillie was sure that her ladyship was not an unreasonable person.

There was a pause during which Sir Walter stared at Mr Baillie down his long nose. "Her ladyship and I have not quarrelled," he said at last.

Ah, said Mr Baillie in a kindly fashion. It might well appear to Sir Walter that there had been no quarrel. It was often the case that gentlemen did not observe the signs. Mr Baillie advised Sir Walter to think carefully. Might he not have said something to vex her ladyship? Mr Baillie did not speak of blame. It was all part of the little accommodations that married people must make in beginning their life together.

"But it is not Lady Pole's character to behave like a spoilt child!"

No doubt, no doubt, said Mr Baillie. But her ladyship was very young and young persons ought always be permitted some licence for folly. Old heads did not sit upon young shoulders. Sir Walter ought not to expect it. Mr Baillie was rather warming to his subject. He had examples to hand (drawn from history and literature) of sober-minded, clever men and women who had all done foolish things in their youth, however a glance at Sir Walter's face persuaded him that he should press the point no further.

Sir Walter was in a similar situation. He too had several things to say and a great mind to say some of them, but he felt himself on uncertain ground. A man who marries for the first time at the age of forty-two knows only too well that almost all his acquaintance are better qualified to manage his domestic affairs than him. So Sir Walter contented himself with frowning at Mr Baillie and then, since it was almost eleven o'clock, he called for his carriage and his secretary and drove to Burlington House where he had an appointment to meet the other Ministers.

At Burlington House he walked through pillared courtyards and gilded ante-rooms. He mounted great marble staircases that were overhung by painted ceilings in which impossible numbers of painted gods, goddesses, heroes and nymphs tumbled out of blue skies or reclined on fluffy white clouds. He was bowed at by a whole host of powdered, liveried footmen until he came to the room where the Ministers were looking at papers and arguing with one another.

"But why do you not send for Mr Norrell, Sir Walter?" asked

Mr Canning, the moment he heard what the matter was. "I am astonished that you have not already done so. I am sure that her ladyship's indisposition will prove to be nothing more than some slight irregularity in the magic which brought her back to life. Mr Norrell can make some small adjustment to a spell and her ladyship will be well again."

"Oh, quite!" agreed Lord Castlereagh. "It seems to me that Lady Pole has gone beyond physicians. You and I, Sir Walter, are set upon this earth by the Grace of God, but her ladyship is here by the grace of Mr Norrell. Her hold upon life is different from the rest of us – theologically and, I dare say, medically as well."

"Whenever Mrs Perceval is unwell," interjected Mr Perceval, a small, precise lawyer of unremarkable aspect and manners who held the exalted position of Chancellor of the Exchequer, "the first person I apply to is her maid. After all, who knows a lady's state of health better than her maid? What does Lady Pole's maid say?"

Sir Walter shook his head. "Pampisford is as mystified as I am. She agreed with me that her ladyship was in excellent health two days ago and now she is cold, pale, listless and unhappy. That is the beginning and end of Pampisford's information. That and a great deal of nonsense about the house being haunted. I do not know what is the matter with the servants just now. They are all in an odd, nervous condition. One of the footmen came to me this morning with a tale of meeting someone upon the stairs at midnight. A person with a green coat and a great quantity of pale, silvery hair."

"What? A ghost? An apparition?" asked Lord Hawkesbury.

"I believe that is what he meant, yes."

"How very extraordinary! Did it speak?" asked Mr Canning.

"No. Geoffrey said it gave him a cold, disdainful look and passed on."

"Oh! Your footman was dreaming, Sir Walter. He was certainly dreaming," said Mr Perceval.

"Or drunk," offered Mr Canning.

"Yes, that occurred to me too. So naturally I asked Stephen Black," said Sir Walter, "but Stephen is as foolish as the rest of them. I can scarcely get him to speak to me."

"Well," said Mr Canning, "you will not, I think, attempt to deny that there is something here that suggests magic? And is it not Mr Norrell's business to explain what other people cannot? Send for Mr Norrell, Sir Walter!"

This was so reasonable that Sir Walter began to wonder why he had not thought of it himself. He had the highest opinion of his own abilities and did not think he would generally miss so obvious a connection. The truth was, he realized, that he did not really *like* magic. He had never liked it – not at the beginning when he had supposed it to be false and not now that it had proved to be real. But he could hardly explain this to the other Ministers – he who had persuaded them to employ a magician for the first time in two hundred years!

At half-past three he returned to Harley-street. It was the eeriest part of a winter day. Twilight was turning all the buildings and people to blurred, black nothingnesses while, above, the sky remained a dizzying silver-blue and was full of cold light. A winter sunset was painting a swathe of rose-colour and blood-colour at the end of all the streets – pleasing to the eyes but somehow chilling to the heart. As Sir Walter gazed from his carriage-window, he thought it fortunate that he was not in any way a fanciful person. Someone else might have been quite unsettled by the combination of the disagreeable task of consulting a magician and this queer, black-and-bloody dissolution of the London streets.

Geoffrey opened the door of no. 9 Harley-street and Sir Walter rapidly mounted the stairs. On the first floor he passed the Venetian drawing-room where her ladyship had been sitting that morning. A sort of presentiment made him look inside. At first it did not seem as though any body could be there. The fire was low in the grate, creating a sort of second twilight within the room. No body had lit a lamp or candle yet. And then he saw her.

She was sitting very upright in a chair by the window. Her back was towards him. Everything about her – chair, posture, even the folds of her gown and shawl – was precisely the same as when he had left her that morning.

The moment he reached his study, he sat down and wrote an urgent message to Mr Norrell.

Mr Norrell did not come immediately. An hour or two passed. At last he arrived with an expression of fixed calm upon his face. Sir Walter met him in the hall and described what had happened. He then proposed that they go upstairs to the Venetian drawing-room.

"Oh!" said Mr Norrell, quickly. "From what you tell me, Sir Walter, I am quite certain there is no need to trouble Lady Pole because, you see, I fear I can do nothing for her. Much as it pains me to say this to you, my dear Sir Walter – for as you know I should always wish to serve you when I can – but whatever it is that has distressed her ladyship I do not believe that it is in the power of magic to remedy."

Sir Walter sighed. He ran his hand through his hair and looked unhappy. "Mr Baillie found nothing wrong and so I thought . . . ."

"Oh! But it is precisely that circumstance which makes me so certain that I cannot help you. Magic and medicine are not always so distinct from one another as you seem to imagine. Their spheres often overlap. An illness may have both a medical cure and a magical one. If her ladyship were truly ill or if, God forbid!, she were to die again, then certainly there is magic to cure or restore her. But forgive me, Sir Walter, what you have described seems more a spiritual ailment than a physical one and as such belongs neither to magic nor medicine. I am no expert in these matters but perhaps a clergyman might be found to answer better?"

"But Lord Castlereagh thought – I do not know if it is true – Lord Castlereagh thought that since Lady Pole owes her life to magic – I confess that I did not understand him very well, but I believe he meant to say that since her ladyship's life is founded upon magic, she would only be susceptible to cure by magic."

"Indeed? Lord Castlereagh said that? Oh! He is quite mistaken, but I am most intrigued that he should have thought of it. That is what used to be called the Meraudian Heresy.[1] A twelfth-century abbot of Rievaulx dedicated himself to its destruction and was later made a saint. Of course the theology of magic has never been a favourite subject of mine, but I believe I am correct in saying that in the sixty-ninth chapter of William Pantler's *Three Perfectible States of Being . . .*"[2]

Mr Norrell seemed about to embark upon one of his long, dull speeches upon the history of English magic, full of references to books no one had ever heard of. Sir Walter interrupted him with, "Yes, yes! But do you have any notion who the person with the green coat and the silver hair might be?"

"Oh!" said Mr Norrell. "You think there was somebody then? But that seems to me most unlikely. Might it not be something more in the nature of a dressing gown left hanging on a hook by a negligent servant? Just where one does not expect to see it? I myself have often been badly startled by this wig which you see now upon my head. Lucas ought to put it away each night – he knows he ought – but several times now he has left it on its wig stand on the mantelpiece where it is reflected in the mirror above the fireplace

---

[1] This theory was first expounded by a Cornish magician called Meraud in the twelfth century and there were many variants. In its most extreme form it involves the belief that any one who has been cured, saved or raised to life by magic is no longer subject to God and His Church, though they may owe all sorts of allegiance to the magician or fairy who has helped them.

Meraud was arrested and brought before Stephen, King of Southern England, and his bishops at a Council in Winchester. Meraud was branded, beaten and stripped half-naked. Then he was cast out. The bishops ordered that no one should help him. Meraud tried to walk from Winchester to Newcastle, where the Raven King's castle was. He died on the way.

The Northern English belief that certain sorts of murderers belong not to God or to the Devil but to the Raven King is another form of the Meraudian Heresy.

[2] *Three Perfectible States of Being* by William Pantler, pub. Henry Lintot, London, 1735. The three perfectible beings are angels, men and fairies.

and resembles nothing so much in the world as two gentlemen with their heads together, whispering about me."

Mr Norrell blinked his small eyes rapidly at Sir Walter. Then, having declared that he could do nothing, he wished Sir Walter good evening and left the house.

Mr Norrell went straight home. As soon as he arrived at his house in Hanover-square he immediately went up to a little study upon the second floor. This was a quiet room at the back of the house, overlooking the garden. The servants never entered when he was working in this room and even Childermass needed some unusually pressing reason to disturb him there. Though Mr Norrell rarely gave warning of when he intended to use this little study, it was one of the rules of the household that it was always kept in readiness for him. Just now a fire was burning brightly in the grate and all the lamps were lit, but someone had neglected to draw the curtains and consequently the window had become a black mirror, in which the room was reflected.

Mr Norrell sat down at the desk which faced the window. He opened a large volume, one of many upon the desk, and began to murmur a spell to himself.

A coal falling from the grate, a shadow moving in the room, caused him to look up. He saw his own alarmed reflection in the dark window and he saw someone standing behind him – a pale, silvery face with a mass of shining hair around it.

Mr Norrell did not turn but instead addressed the reflection in the window in a bitter, angry tone. "When you said that you would take half the young lady's life, I thought you would permit her to remain with her friends and family for half seventy-five years. I thought it would appear as if she had simply died!"

"I never said so."

"You cheated me! You have not helped me at all! You risk undoing everything by your tricks!" cried Mr Norrell.

The person in the window made a sound of disapproval. "I had hoped that I would find you more reasonable at our second meeting. Instead you are full of arrogance and unreasonable anger against me! *I* have kept to the terms of our agreement! I have done what you asked and taken nothing that was not mine to take! If you were truly concerned for the happiness of Lady Pole, you would rejoice that she is now placed among friends who truly admire and esteem her!"

"Oh! As to that," said Mr Norrell, scornfully, "I do not care one way or the other. What is the fate of one young woman compared to the success of English magic? No, it is her husband that concerns me – the man for whom I did all this! He is brought quite low by your treachery. Supposing he should not recover! Supposing he were to resign from Government! I might never find another ally so willing to help me.[3] I shall certainly never again have a Minister so much in my debt!"

"Her husband, is it? Well, then I shall raise him up to some lofty position! I shall make him much greater than any thing he could achieve by his own efforts. He shall be Prime Minister. Or Emperor of Great Britain perhaps? Will that suit you?"

"No, no!" cried Mr Norrell. "You do not understand! I merely want him to be pleased with me and to talk to the other Ministers and to persuade them of the great good that my magic can do the country!"

"It is entirely mysterious to me," declared the person in the window, haughtily, "why you should prefer the help of this person to mine! What does he know of magic? Nothing! *I* can teach you to raise up mountains and crush your enemies beneath them! I can make the clouds sing at your approach. I can make it spring when you arrive and winter when you leave. I can . . ."

"Oh, yes! And all you want in return is to shackle English magic to your whims! You will steal Englishmen and women away from

---

[3] It is clear from this remark that Mr Norrell did not yet comprehend how highly the Ministers in general regarded him nor how eager they were to make use of him in the war.

their homes and make England a place fit only for your degenerate race! The price of your help is too high for me!"

The person in the window did not reply directly to these accusations. Instead a candlestick suddenly leapt from its place on a little table and flew across the room, shattering a mirror on the opposite wall and a little china bust of Thomas Lanchester.

Then all was quiet.

Mr Norrell sat in a state of fright and trembling. He looked down at the books spread out upon his desk, but if he read, then it was in a fashion known only to magicians, for his eye did not travel over the page. After an interval of several minutes he looked up again. The person reflected in the window was gone.

Everyone's plans concerning Lady Pole came to nothing. The marriage – which for a few short weeks had seemed to promise so much to both partners – lapsed into indifference and silence upon her part and into anxiety and misery upon his. Far from becoming a leader of the fashionable world, she declined to go any where. No one visited her and the fashionable world very soon forgot her.

The servants at Harley-street grew reluctant to enter the room where she sat, though none of them could have said why. The truth was that there hung about her the faintest echo of a bell. A chill wind seemed to blow upon her from far away and caused any one who came near her to shiver. So she sat, hour after hour, wrapped in her shawl, neither moving nor speaking, and bad dreams and shadows gathered about her.

19

The Peep-O'Day-Boys

February 1808

CURIOUSLY, NO ONE noticed that the strange malady that afflicted her ladyship was to a precision the same as that which afflicted Stephen Black. He too complained of feeling tired and cold, and on the rare occasions that either of them said any thing, they both spoke in a low, exhausted manner.

But perhaps it was not so curious. The different styles of life of a lady and a butler tend to obscure any similarities in their situations. A butler has his work and must do it. Unlike Lady Pole, Stephen was not suffered to sit idly by the window, hour after hour, without speaking. Symptoms that were raised to the dignity of an illness in Lady Pole were dismissed as mere low spirits in Stephen.

John Longridge, the cook at Harley-street, had suffered from low spirits for more than thirty years, and he was quick to welcome Stephen as a newcomer to the freemasonry of melancholy. He seemed glad, poor fellow, of a companion in woe. In the evenings when Stephen would sit at the kitchen table with his head buried in his hands, John Longridge would come and sit down on the other side of the table, and begin commiserating with him.

"I condole with you, sir, indeed I do. Low spirits, Mr Black, are the very worst torment that a man can be afflicted with. Sometimes it seems to me that all of London resembles nothing so much as cold pease porridge, both in colour and consistency. I see people with cold-pease-porridge faces and cold-pease-porridge hands walking down cold-pease-porridge streets. Ah, me! How bad I feel then! The very sun up in the sky is cold and grey and porridge-y, and has no power to warm me. Do you often feel chilled, sir?" John Longridge would lay his hand upon Stephen's hand. "Ah, Mr Black, sir," he would say, "you are cold as the tomb."

Stephen felt he was like a person sleepwalking. He did not live any more; he only dreamed. He dreamed of the house in Harley-street and of the other servants. He dreamed of his work and his friends and of Mrs Brandy. Sometimes he dreamed of things that were very strange – things that he knew, in some small, chilly, far-off part of himself, ought not to be. He might be walking along a hallway or up the stairs in the house in Harley-street and he would turn and see other hallways and staircases leading off into the distance – hallways and staircases which did not belong there. It would be as if the house in Harley-street had accidentally got lodged inside a much larger and more ancient edifice. The passageways would be stone-vaulted and full of dust and shadows. The stairs and floors would be so worn and uneven that they would more resemble stones found in nature than architecture. But the strangest thing of all about these ghostly halls was that they would be quite familiar to Stephen. He did not understand why or how, but he would catch himself thinking, "Yes, just beyond that corner is the Eastern Armoury." Or, "Those stairs lead to the Disemboweller's Tower."

Whenever he saw these passageways or, as he sometimes did, sensed their presence without actually perceiving them, then he would feel a little more lively, a little more like his old self. Whatever part of him it was that had frozen up (his soul? his heart?) unfroze itself the merest hair's breadth and thought, curiosity and feeling began to pulse again within him. But for the rest nothing amused him; nothing satisfied him. All was shadows, emptiness, echoes and dust.

Sometimes his restless spirit would cause him to go on long, solitary wanders through the dark winter streets around Mayfair and Piccadilly. On one such evening in late February he found himself outside Mr Wharton's coffee-house in Oxford-street. It was a place he knew well. The upper-room was home to the Peep-O'Day-Boys, a club for the grander sort of male servants in London's grand houses. Lord Castlereagh's valet was a notable member; the Duke of Portland's coachman was another and so was Stephen. The Peep-O'Day-Boys met upon the third Tuesday of every month and enjoyed the same pleasures as the members of any other London club – they drank and ate, gambled, talked politics and gossiped about their mistresses. On other evenings of the month it was the habit of Peep-O'Day-Boys who happened to find themselves disengaged to repair to the upper-room of Mr Wharton's coffee-house, there to refresh their spirits with the society of their fellows. Stephen went inside and mounted the stairs to the upper-room.

This apartment was much like the corresponding part of any similar establishment in the city. It was as full of tobacco smoke as such resorts of the masculine half of society usually are. It was panelled in dark wood. Partitions of the same wood divided off the room into boxes so that customers were able to enjoy being in a little wooden world all their own. The bare floor was kept pleasant with fresh sawdust everyday. White cloths covered the tables and oil-lamps were kept clean and their wicks trimmed. Stephen sat down in one of the boxes and ordered a glass of port which he then proceeded to stare at gloomily.

Whenever one of the Peep-O'Day-Boys passed Stephen's box, they would stop for a word with Stephen and he would raise a hand to them in half-hearted salutation, but tonight he did not trouble himself to answer them. This had happened, Oh!, two or three times, when suddenly Stephen heard someone say in a vivid whisper, "You are quite right to pay them no attention! For, when all is said and done, what are they but servants and drudges? And when, with my assistance, you are elevated to your rightful place at the very pinnacle of nobility and greatness, it will be a great comfort to you to remember that you spurned their friendship!" It was only a whisper, yet Stephen heard it most distinctly above the voices and laughter of the Peep-O'Days and other gentlemen. He had the odd idea that, though only a whisper, it could have passed through stone or iron or brass. It could have spoken to you from a thousand feet beneath the earth and you would have still heard it. It could have shattered precious stones and brought on madness.

This was so very extraordinary that for a moment he was roused from his lethargy. A lively curiosity to discover who had spoken took hold of him and he looked around the room but saw no one he did not know. So he stuck his head round the partition and looked into the next box. It contained one person of very striking appearance. He appeared very much at his ease. His arms were resting on the tops of the partition and his booted feet were resting on the table. He had several remarkable features, but the chief among them was a mass of silvery hair, as bright and soft and shining as thistle-down. He winked at Stephen. Then he rose from his own box and came and sat in Stephen's.

"I may as well tell you," he said, speaking in a highly confidential manner, "that this city has not the hundredth part of its former splendour! I have been gravely disappointed since my return. Once upon a time, to look upon London was to look upon a forest of towers and pinnacles and spires. The many-coloured flags and banners that flew from each and every one dazzled the eye! Upon every side one saw stone carvings as delicate as fingerbones and as intricate as flowing water! There were houses ornamented with stone dragons, griffins and lions, symbolizing the wisdom, courage and ferocity of the occupants, while in the gardens of those same houses might be found flesh-and-blood dragons, griffins and lions, locked in strong cages. Their roars, which could be clearly heard in the street, terrified the faint-of-heart. In every church a blessed saint lay, performing miracles hourly at the behest of the populace. Each saint was confined within an ivory casket, which was secreted in a jewel-studded coffin, which in turn was displayed in a magnificent shrine of gold and silver that shone night and day with the light of a thousand wax candles! Every day there was a splendid procession to celebrate one or other of these blessed saints, and London's fame passed from world to world! Of course in those days the citizens of London were wont to come to *me* for advice about the construction of their churches, the arrangement of their gardens, the decoration of their houses. If they were properly respectful in their petitions I would generally give them good counsel. Oh, yes! When London owed its appearance to *me* it was beautiful, noble, peerless. But now . . ."

He made an eloquent gesture, as if he had crumpled London into a ball in his hand and thrown it away. "But how stupid you look when you stare at me so! I have put myself to any amount of trouble to pay you this visit – and you sit there silent and sullen, with your mouth hanging open! You are surprized to see me, I dare say, but that is no reason to forget all your good manners. Of course," he remarked in the manner of someone making a great concession, "Englishmen are often all amazement in my presence – *that* is the most natural thing in the world – but you and I are such friends that I think I have deserved a better welcome than this!"

"Have we met before, sir?" asked Stephen in astonishment. "I have certainly dreamt of you. I dreamt that you and I were together in an immense mansion with endless, dusty corridors!"

" 'Have we met before, sir?' " mocked the gentleman with the thistle-down hair. "Why! What nonsense you talk! As if we had not attended the same feasts and balls and parties every night for weeks and weeks!"

"Certainly in my dreams . . ."

"I had not thought you could be so dull-witted!" cried the gentleman. "Lost-hope is not a *dream*! It is the oldest and most beautiful of my mansions – which are numerous – and it is quite as real as Carlton House.[1] In fact it is a great deal more so! Much of

---

[1] The London home of the Prince of Wales in Pall Mall.

the future is known to me and I tell you that Carlton House will be levelled to the ground in twenty years' time and the city of London itself will endure, oh!, scarcely another two thousand years, whereas Lost-hope will stand until the next age of the World!" He looked ridiculously pleased with this thought, and indeed it must be said that his natural manner seemed to be one of extreme self-congratulation. "No, it is no dream. You are merely under an enchantment which brings you each night to Lost-hope to join our fairy revels!"

Stephen stared at the gentleman uncomprehendingly. Then, remembering that he must speak or lay himself open to accusations of sullenness and bad manners, he gathered his wits and stammered out, "And . . . And is the enchantment yours, sir?"

"But of course!"

It was clear from the pleased air with which he spoke that the gentleman with the thistle-down hair considered that he had bestowed the greatest of favours upon Stephen by enchanting him. Stephen thanked him politely for it. ". . . although," he added, "I cannot imagine what I have done to deserve such kindness from you. Indeed, I am sure I have done nothing at all."

"Ah!" cried the gentleman, delighted. "Yours are excellent manners, Stephen Black! You could teach the proud English a thing or two about the proper respect that is due to persons of quality. *Your* manners will bring you good luck in the end!"

"And those golden guineas in Mrs Brandy's cash box," said Stephen, "were they yours too?"

"Oh! Have you only just guessed it? But only observe how clever I have been! Remembering all that you told me about how you are surrounded night and day by enemies who wish you harm, I conveyed the money to a friend of yours. Then when you and she marry, the money will be yours."

"How did . . ." began Stephen and stopt. Clearly there was no part of his life that the gentleman did not know about and nothing with which the gentleman did not feel entitled to interfere. "But you are mistaken about my enemies, sir," he said, "I do not have any."

"My dear Stephen!" cried the gentleman, greatly amused, "*Of course* you have enemies! And the chief among them is that wicked man who is your master and Lady Pole's husband! He forces you to be his servant and do his bidding night and day. He sets tasks before you that are entirely unsuited to a person of your beauty and nobility. And why does he do these things?"

"I suppose because . . ." began Stephen.

"Precisely!" declared the gentleman triumphantly. "Because in the fulsomeness of his wickedness he has captured you and girded you with chains and now he triumphs over you, dancing about and howling with wicked laughter to see you in such straits!"

Stephen opened his mouth to protest that Sir Walter Pole had never done any of those things; that he had always treated Stephen with great kindness and affection; that when Sir Walter was younger he had paid money he could ill afford so that Stephen could go to school; and that later, when Sir Walter was poorer still, they had often eaten the same food and shared the same fire. As for triumphing over his enemies, Stephen had often seen Sir Walter wear a very self-satisfied smirk when he believed he had scored a point against his political opponents, but he had never seen him dance about or howl with wicked laughter. Stephen was about to say these things, when the mention of the word "chains" seemed to send a sort of silent thunderbolt through him. Suddenly in his fancy he saw a dark place – a terrible place – a place full of horror – a hot, rank, closed-in place. There were shadows in the darkness and the slither and clank of heavy iron chains. What this image meant or where it had come from he had not the least idea. He did not think it could be a memory. Surely he had never been in such a place?

". . . If he ever were to discover that every night you and she escape from him to be happy in my house, why! he would be thrown instantly into fits of jealousy and would, I dare say, try to kill you both. But fear not, my dear, dear Stephen! I will take good care he never finds out. Oh! How I detest such selfish people! *I* know what it is to be scorned and slighted by the proud English and put to perform tasks that are beneath one's dignity. I cannot bear to see the same fate befall you!" The gentleman paused to caress Stephen's cheek and brow with his icy white fingers, which produced a queer tingling sensation in Stephen's skin. "You cannot conceive what a warm interest I feel in you and how anxious I am to do you some lasting service! – which is why I have conceived a plan to make you the king of some fairy kingdom!"

"I . . . I beg your pardon, sir. I was thinking of something else. A king, you say? No, sir. I could not be a king. It is only your great kindness to me that makes you think it possible. Besides I am very much afraid that fairyland does not quite agree with me. Ever since I first visited your house I have been stupid and heavy. I am tired morning, noon and night and my life is a burden to me. I dare say the fault is all mine, but perhaps mortals are not formed for fairy bliss?"

"Oh! That is simply the sadness you feel at the dreariness of England compared to the delightful life you lead at my house where there is always dancing and feasting and everyone is dressed in their finest clothes!"

"I dare say you are right, sir, yet if you were to find it in your heart to release me from this enchantment, I should be very grateful to you."

"Oh! But that is impossible!" declared the gentleman. "Do you not know that my beautiful sisters and cousins – for each of whom, I may say, kings have killed each other and great empires fallen into decay – all quarrel over who will be your next dancing-partner? And what would they say if I told them you would come to Lost-hope no more? For amongst my many other virtues I am a most attentive brother and cousin and always try to please the females in my household when I can. And as for declining to become a king, there is nothing, I assure you, more agreeable than having everyone bow before one and call one by all sorts of noble titles."

He resumed his extravagant praises of Stephen's beauty, dignified countenance and elegant dancing – all of which he seemed to consider the chief qualifications for the ruler of a vast kingdom in Faerie – and he began to speculate upon which kingdom would suit Stephen best. "Untold-Blessings is a fine place, with dark, impenetrable forests, lonely mountains and uncrossable seas. It has the advantage of being without a ruler at present – but then it has the disadvantage that there are twenty-six other claimants already and you would be plunged straightaway into the middle of a bloody civil war – which perhaps you would not care for? Then there is the Dukedom of Pity-Me. The present Duke has no friends to speak of. Oh, but I could not bear to see any friend of mine ruler of such a miserable little place as Pity-Me!"

20

The unlikely milliner

February 1808

T HOSE PEOPLE WHO had expected the war to be over now that the magician had appeared upon the scene were soon disappointed. "Magic!" said Mr Canning, the Foreign Secretary. "Do not speak to me of magic! It is just like everything else, full of setbacks and disappointments."

There was some justice in this, and Mr Norrell was always happy to give long, difficult explanations of why something was not possible. Once, in making one of these explanations, he said something which he later regretted. It was at Burlington House and Mr Norrell was explaining to Lord Hawkesbury, the Home Secretary,[1] that something or other could not be attempted since it would take, oh!, at least a dozen magicians working day and night. He made a long, tedious speech about the pitiful state of English magic, ending, "I would it were otherwise but, as your lordship is aware, our talented young men look to the Army, the Navy and the Church for their careers. My own poor profession is sadly neglected." And he gave a great sigh.

Mr Norrell meant nothing much by this, except perhaps to draw attention to his own extraordinary talent, but unfortunately Lord Hawkesbury took up quite another idea.

---

[1] Robert Banks Jenkinson, Lord Hawkesbury (1770–1828). On the death of his father in December 1808 he became the Earl of Liverpool. For the next nine years he would prove to be one of Mr Norrell's most steady supporters.

"Oh!" he cried. "You mean we need more magicians? Oh, yes! I quite see that. Quite. A school perhaps? Or a Royal Society under His Majesty's patronage? Well, Mr Norrell, I really think we will leave the details to you. If you will be so good as to draw up a memorandum upon the subject I shall be glad to read it and submit its proposals to the other Ministers. We all know your skill at drawing up such things, so clear and so detailed and your handwriting so good. I dare say, sir, we shall find you a little money from somewhere. When you have time, sir. There is no hurry. I know how busy you are."

Poor Mr Norrell! Nothing could be less to his taste than the creation of other magicians. He comforted himself with the thought that Lord Hawkesbury was an exemplary Minister, devoted to business, with a thousand and one things to think about. Doubtless he would soon forget all about it.

But the very next time that Mr Norrell was at Burlington House Lord Hawkesbury came hurrying up to him, crying out, "Ah! Mr Norrell! I have spoken to the King about your plan for making new magicians. His Majesty was very pleased, thought the idea an excellent one and asked me to tell you that he will be glad to extend his patronage to the scheme."

It was fortunate that before Mr Norrell could reply, the sudden arrival of the Swedish Ambassador in the room obliged his lordship to hurry away again.

But a week or so later Mr Norrell met Lord Hawkesbury again, this time at a special dinner given by the Prince of Wales in honour of Mr Norrell at Carlton House. "Ah! Mr Norrell, there you are! I don't suppose that you have the recommendations for the Magicians School about you? Only I have just been speaking to the Duke of Devonshire and he is most interested – thinks he has a house in Leamington Spa which would be just the thing and has asked me questions about the curriculum and whether there would be prayers and where the magicians would sleep – all sorts of things I have not the least idea about. I wonder – would you be so kind as to speak to him? He is just over there by the mantelpiece – he has seen us – he is coming this way. Your Grace, here is Mr Norrell ready to tell you all about it!"

It was with some difficulty that Mr Norrell was able to convince Lord Hawkesbury and the Duke of Devonshire that a school would take up far too much time and moreover he had yet to see any young men with sufficient talent to make the attempt worthwhile. Reluctantly his Grace and his lordship were obliged to agree and Mr Norrell was able to turn his attention to a far more agreeable project: that of destroying the magicians already in existence.

The street-sorcerers of the City of London had long constituted a standing irritation of his spirits. While he was still unknown and unregarded, he had begun to petition members of the Government and other eminent gentlemen for the removal of these vagabond magicians. Naturally, the moment that he attained public eminence he doubled and tripled his efforts. His first idea was that magic ought to be regulated by the Government and magicians ought to be licensed (though naturally he had no idea of any one being licensed but himself). He proposed that a proper regulatory Board of Magic be established, but in this he was too ambitious.

As Lord Hawkesbury said to Sir Walter; "We have no wish to offend a man who has done the country such service, but in the middle of a long and difficult war to demand that a Board be set up with Privy Councillors and Secretaries and Lord knows what else! And for what? To listen to Mr Norrell talk and to pay Mr Norrell compliments! It is quite out of the question. My dear Sir Walter, persuade him to some other course, I beg you."

So the next time that Sir Walter and Mr Norrell met (which was at Mr Norrell's house in Hanover-square) Sir Walter addressed his friend with the following words.

"It is an admirable purpose, sir, and no one quarrels with it, but a Board is precisely the wrong way of going about it. Within the City of London – which is where the problem chiefly lies – the

Board would have no authority. I tell you what we shall do; tomorrow you and I shall go to the Mansion House to wait upon the Lord Mayor and one or two of the aldermen. I think we shall soon find some friends for our cause."

"But, my dear Sir Walter!" cried Mr Norrell. "It will not do. The problem is not confined to London. I have looked into it since I left Yorkshire . . ." (Here he delved about in a pile of papers upon a little table at his elbow to fetch out a list.) "There are twelve street-sorcerers in Norwich, two in Yarmouth, two in Gloucester, six in Winchester, *forty-two* in Penzance! Why! Only the other day, one – a dirty female – came to my house and would not be satisfied without seeing me, whereupon she demanded that I give her a paper – a certificate of competence, no less! – testifying to my belief that she could do magic. I was never more astonished in my life! I said to her, 'Woman . . .'"

"As to the other places that you mention," said Sir Walter, interrupting hastily. "I think you will find that once London rids itself of this nuisance then the others will be quick to follow. They none of them like to feel themselves left behind."

Mr Norrell soon found that it was just as Sir Walter had predicted. The Lord Mayor and the aldermen were eager to be part of the glorious revival of English magic. They persuaded the Court of Common Council to set up a Committee for Magical Acts and the Committee decreed that only Mr Norrell was permitted to do magic within the City boundaries and that other persons who "set up booths or shops, or otherwise molested the citizens of London with claims to do magic" were to be expelled forthwith.

The street-sorcerers packed up their little stalls, loaded their shabby possessions into handcarts and trudged out of the City. Some took the trouble to curse London as they left, but by and large they bore the change in their fortunes with admirable philosophy. Most had simply settled it in their own minds that henceforth they would give up magic and become instead beggars and thieves and, since they had indulged in beggary and thievery

226

in an amateur way for years, the wrench was not so great as you might imagine.

But one did not go. Vinculus, the magician of Threadneedle-street, stayed in his booth and continued to foretell unhappy futures and to sell petty revenges to slighted lovers and resentful apprentices. Naturally, Mr Norrell complained very vigorously to the Committee for Magical Acts about this state of affairs since Vinculus was the sorcerer whom he hated most. The Committee for Magical Acts dispatched beadles and constables to threaten Vinculus with the stocks but Vinculus paid them no attention, and he was so popular among London's citizens that the Committee feared a riot if he was removed by force.

On a bleak February day Vinculus was in his magician's booth beside the church of St Christopher Le Stocks. In case there are any readers who do not remember the magicians' booths of our child-hood, it ought to be stated that in shape the booth rather resembled a Punch and Judy theatre or a shopkeeper's stall at a fair and that it was built of wood and canvas. A yellow curtain, ornamented to half its height with a thick crust of dirt, served both as a door and as a sign to advertise the services that were offered within.

On this particular day Vinculus had no customers and very little hope of getting any. The City streets were practically deserted. A bitter grey fog that tasted of smoke and tar hung over London. The City shopkeepers had heaped coals upon their fires and lit every lamp they possessed in a vain attempt to dispel the dark and the cold, but today their bow windows cast no cheerful glow into the streets: the light could not penetrate the fog. Consequently no one was enticed into the shops to spend money and the shopmen in their long white aprons and powdered wigs stood about at their ease, chatting to each other or warming themselves at the fire. It was a day when any one with something to do indoors stayed indoors to do it, and any one who was obliged to go outside did so quickly and got back inside again as soon as he could.

Vinculus sat gloomily behind his curtain half frozen to death, turning over in his mind the names of the two or three ale-house-keepers who might be persuaded to sell him a glass or two of hot spiced wine on credit. He had almost made up his mind which of them to try first when the sounds of someone stamping their feet and blowing upon their fingers seemed to suggest that a customer stood without. Vinculus raised the curtain and stepped outside.

"Are you the magician?"

Vinculus agreed a little suspiciously that he was (the man had the air of a bailiff).

"Excellent. I have a commission for you."

"It is two shillings for the first consultation."

The man put his hand in his pocket, pulled out his purse and put two shillings into Vinculus's hand.

Then he began to describe the problem that he wished Vinculus to magic away. His explanation was very clear and he knew exactly what it was that he wished Vinculus to do. The only problem was that the more the man talked, the less Vinculus believed him. The man said that he had come from Windsor. That was perfectly possible. True, he spoke with a northern accent, but there was nothing odd in that; people often came down from the northern counties to make their fortunes. The man also said he was the owner of a successful millinery business – now that seemed a good deal less likely, for any one less like a milliner it was difficult to imagine. Vinculus knew little enough about milliners but he did know that they generally dress in the very height of fashion. This fellow wore an ancient black coat that had been patched and mended a dozen times. His linen, though clean and of a good quality, would have been old-fashioned twenty years ago. Vinculus did not know the names of the hundred and one little fancy articles that milliners make, but he knew that milliners know them. This man did not; he called them "fol-de-lols".

In the freezing weather the ground had become an unhappy compound of ice and frozen mud and as Vinculus was writing down the particulars in a greasy little book, he somehow missed his footing and fell against the unlikely milliner. He tried to stand but so treacherous was the icy ground that he was obliged to use the other man as a sort of ladder to climb up. The unlikely milliner looked rather appalled to have strong fumes of ale and cabbage breathed in his face and bony fingers grabbing him all over, but he said nothing.

"Beg pardon," muttered Vinculus, when at last he was in an upright position again.

"Granted," said the unlikely milliner politely, brushing from his coat the stale crumbs, gobbets of matted grease and dirt and other little signs of Vinculus having been there.

Vinculus too was adjusting his clothes which had got somewhat disarranged in his tumble.

The unlikely milliner continued with his tale.

"So, as I say, my business thrives and my bonnets are the most sought-after in all of Windsor and scarcely a week goes by but one of the Princesses up at the Castle comes to order a new bonnet or fol-de-lol. I have put a great golden plaster image of the Royal Arms above my door to advertise the royal patronage I enjoy. Yet still I cannot help but think that millinery is a great deal of work. Sitting up late at night sewing bonnets, counting my money and so forth. It seems to me that my life might be a great deal easier if one of the Princesses were to fall in love with me and marry me. Do you have such a spell, Magician?"

"A love spell? Certainly. But it will be expensive. I generally charge four shillings for a spell to catch a milkmaid, ten shillings for a seamstress and six guineas for a widow with her own business. A Princess . . . Hmm." Vinculus scratched his unshaven cheek with his dirty fingernails. "Forty guineas," he hazarded.

"Very well."

"And which is it?" asked Vinculus.

"Which what is what?" asked the unlikely milliner.

"Which Princess?"

229

"They are all pretty much the same, aren't they? Does the price vary with the Princess?"

"No, not really. I will give you the spell written upon a piece of paper. Tear the paper in two and sew half inside the breast of your coat. You need to place the other half in a secret place inside the garments of whichever Princess you decide upon."

The unlikely milliner looked astonished. "And how in the world can I do that?"

Vinculus looked at the man. "I thought you just said that you sewed their bonnets?"

The unlikely milliner laughed. "Oh yes! Of course."

Vinculus stared at the man suspiciously. "You are no more a milliner than I am a . . . a . . ."

"A magician?" suggested the unlikely milliner. "You must certainly admit that it is not your only profession. After all you just picked my pockets."

"Only because I wished to know what sort of villain you are," retorted Vinculus, and he shook his arm until the articles he had taken from the pockets of the unlikely milliner fell out of his sleeve. There were a handful of silver coins, two golden guineas and three or four folded sheets of paper. He picked up the papers.

The sheets were small and thick and of excellent quality. They were all covered in close lines of small, neat handwriting. At the top of the first sheet was written, *Two Spells to Make an Obstinate Man leave London and One Spell to Discover what My Enemy is doing Presently.*

"The magician of Hanover-square!" declared Vinculus.

Childermass (for it was he) nodded.

Vinculus read through the spells. The first was intended to make the subject believe that every London churchyard was haunted by the people who were buried there and that every bridge was haunted by the suicides who had thrown themselves from it. The subject would see the ghosts as they had appeared at their deaths with all the marks of violence, disease and extreme old age upon them. In this way he would become more and more terrified until he dared not pass either a bridge or a church – which in London is a serious inconvenience as the bridges are not more than a hundred yards apart and the churches considerably less. The second spell was intended to persuade the subject that he would find his one true love and all sorts of happiness in the country and the third spell – the one to discover what your enemy was doing – involved a mirror and had presumably been intended by Norrell to enable Childermass to spy upon Vinculus.

Vinculus sneered. "You may tell the Mayfair magician that his spells have no effect upon me!"

"Indeed?" said Childermass, sarcastically. "Well, that is probably because I have not cast them."

Vinculus flung the papers down upon the ground. "Cast them now!" He folded his arms in an attitude of defiance and made his eyes flash as he did whenever he conjured the Spirit of the River Thames.

"Thank you, but no."

"And why not?"

"Because, like you, I do not care to be told how to conduct my business. My master has ordered me to make sure that you leave London. But I intend to do it in my way, not his. Come, I think it will be best if you and I have a talk, Vinculus."

Vinculus thought about this. "And could this talk take place somewhere warmer? An ale-house perhaps?"

"Certainly if you wish."

The papers with Norrell's spells upon them were blowing about their feet. Vinculus stooped down, gathered them together and, paying no regard to the bits of straw and mud sticking to them, put them in the breast of his coat.

21

The cards of Marseilles

February 1808

T HE ALE-HOUSE WAS called the Pineapple and had once been the refuge and hiding-place of a notorious thief and murderer. This thief had had an enemy, a man as bad as himself. The thief and his enemy had been partners in some dreadful crime, but the thief had kept both shares of the spoils and sent a message to the magistrates telling them where his enemy might be found. As soon as the enemy had escaped from Newgate, he had come to the Pineapple in the dead of night with thirty men. He had set them to tear the slates off the roof and unpick the very bricks of walls until he could reach inside and pluck out the thief. No one had seen what happened next but many had heard the dreadful screams issuing from the pitch-black street. The landlord had discovered that the Pineapple's dark reputation was good for business and consequently he had never troubled to mend his house, other than by applying timber and pitch to the holes, which gave it the appearance of wearing bandages as if it had been fighting with its neighbours.

Three greasy steps led down from the street-door into a gloomy parlour. The Pineapple had its own particular perfume, compounded of ale, tobacco, the natural fragrance of the customers and the unholy stink of the Fleet River, which had been used as a sewer for countless years. The Fleet ran beneath the Pineapple's foundations and the Pineapple was generally supposed to be sinking into it. The walls of the parlour were ornamented with cheap engravings – portraits of famous criminals of the last century who had all been hanged and portraits of the King's dissolute sons who had not been hanged yet.

Childermass and Vinculus sat down at a table in a corner. A shadowy girl brought a cheap tallow candle and two pewter tankards of hot spiced ale. Childermass paid.

They drank in silence a while and then Vinculus looked up at Childermass. "What was all that nonsense about bonnets and princesses?"

Childermass laughed. "Oh, that was just a notion I had. Ever since the day you appeared in his library my master has been petitioning all his great friends to help him destroy you. He asked Lord Hawkesbury and Sir Walter Pole to complain to the King on his behalf. I believe he had an idea that His Majesty might send the Army to make war upon you, but Lord Hawkesbury and Sir Walter said that the King was unlikely to put himself to a great deal of trouble over one yellow-curtained, ragged-arsed sorcerer. But it occurred to me that if His Majesty were to learn that you had somehow threatened the virgin state of his daughters, he might take a different view of the matter."[1] Childermass took another draught of his spiced ale. "But tell me, Vinculus, don't you tire of fake spells and pretend oracles? Half your customers come to laugh at you. They no more believe in your magic than you do. Your day is over. There is a real magician in England now."

Vinculus gave a little snort of disgust. "The magician of Hanover-square! All the great men in London sit telling one another that they never saw a man so honest. But I know magicians and I

---

[1] The King was a most loving and devoted father to his six daughters, but his affection was such that it led him to act almost as if he were their jailer. He could not bear the thought that any of them might marry and leave him. They were required to lead lives of quite intolerable dullness with the ill-tempered Queen at Windsor Castle. Out of the six only one contrived to get married before she was forty.

know magic and I say this: all magicians lie and this one more than most."

Childermass shrugged as if he would not trouble to deny it.

Vinculus leaned forward across the table. "*Magic shall be written on the faces of the stony hills, but their minds shall not be able to contain it. In winter the barren trees shall be a black writing but they shall not understand it.*"

"Trees and hills, Vinculus? When did you last see a tree or a hill? Why don't you say that magic is written on the faces of the dirty houses or that the smoke writes magic in the sky?"

"It is not my prophecy!"

"Ah, yes. Of course. You claim it as a prophecy of the Raven King. Well there is nothing unusual in that. Every charlatan I ever met was the bearer of a message from the Raven King."

"*I sit upon a black throne in the shadows,*" muttered Vinculus, "*but they shall not see me. The rain shall make a door for me and I shall pass through it.*"

"Quite. So, since you did not write this prophecy yourself, where did you find it?"

For a moment Vinculus looked as if he would not answer, but then he said, "It is written in a book."

"A book? What book? My master's library is extensive. He knows of no such prophecy."

Vinculus said nothing.

"Is it your book?" asked Childermass.

"It is in my keeping."

"And where did *you* get a book? Where did you steal it?"

"I did not steal it. It is my inheritance. It is the greatest glory and the greatest burden that has been given to any man in this Age."

"If it is really valuable then you can sell it to Norrell. He has paid great prices for books before now."

"The magician of Hanover-square will never own this book. He will never even see it."

"And where do you keep such a great treasure?"

Vinculus laughed coldly as if to say it was not very likely that he would tell that to the servant of his enemy.

Childermass called to the girl to bring them some more ale. She brought it and they drank for a while longer in silence. Then Childermass took a pack of cards from the breast of his coat and shewed them to Vinculus. "The cards of Marseilles. Did you ever see their like before?"

"Often," said Vinculus, "but yours are different."

"They are copies of a set belonging to a sailor I met in Whitby. He bought them in Genoa with the intention of using them to discover the hiding places of pirates' gold, but when he came to look at them, he found that he could not understand them. He offered to sell them to me, but I was poor and could not pay the price he asked. So we struck a bargain: I would tell him his fortune and in return he would lend me the cards long enough to make copies. Unfortunately his ship set sail before I was able to complete the drawings and so half are done from memory."

"And what fortune did you tell him?"

"His true one. That he would be drowned dead before the year was out."

Vinculus laughed approvingly.

It seemed that when Childermass had made the bargain with the dead sailor he had been too poor even to afford paper and so the cards were drawn upon the backs of ale-house bills, laundry lists, letters, old accounts and playbills. At a later date he had pasted the papers on to coloured cardboard, but in several instances the printing or writing on the other side shewed through, giving them an odd look.

Childermass laid out nine cards in a line. He turned over the first card.

Beneath the picture was a number and a name: *VIIII. L'Ermite.* It shewed an old man in a monkish robe with a monkish hood. He carried a lantern and walked with a stick as if he had come near to losing the use of his limbs through too much sitting and studying. His face was pinched and suspicious. A dry atmosphere seemed to rise up and envelop the observer as if the card itself were peppery with dust.

"Hmm!" said Childermass . "For the present your actions are governed by a hermit. Well, we knew that already."

The next card was *Le Mat*, which is the only picture card to remain numberless, as if the character it depicts is in some sense outside the story. Childermass's card shewed a man walking along a road beneath a summer tree. He had a stick to lean upon and another stick over his shoulder with a handkerchief bundle hanging from it. A little dog skipped after him. The figure was intended to represent the fool or jester of ancient times. He had a bell in his hat and ribbons at his knees which Childermass had coloured red and green. It appeared that Childermass did not know quite how to interpret this card. He considered a while and then turned over the next two cards: *VIII. La Justice*, a crowned woman holding a sword and a pair of scales; and *The Two of Wands*. The wands were crossed and might among other things be thought to represent a crossroads.

Childermass let out a brief burst of laughter. "Well, well!" he said, crossing his arms and regarding Vinculus with some amusement. "This card here," he tapped *La Justice*, "tells me you have weighed your choices and come to a decision. And this one," he indicated *The Two of Wands*. "tells me what your decision is: you are going wandering. It seems I have wasted my time. You have already made up your mind to leave London. So many protestations, Vinculus, and yet you always intended to go!"

Vinculus shrugged, as if to say, what did Childermass expect?

The fifth card was the *Valet de Coupe*, the Page of Cups. One naturally thinks of a page as being a youthful person, but the picture shewed a mature man with bowed head. His hair was shaggy and his beard was thick. In his left hand he carried a heavy cup, yet it could not be that which gave such an odd, strained expression to his countenance – not unless it were the heaviest cup in the world. No, it must be some other burden, not immediately

236

apparent. Owing to the materials which Childermass had been compelled to use to construct his cards this picture had a most peculiar look. It had been drawn upon the back of a letter and the writing shewed through the paper. The man's clothes were a mass of scribble and even his face and hands bore parts of letters.

Vinculus laughed when he saw it as though he recognized it. He gave the card three taps in friendly greeting. Perhaps it was this that made Childermass less certain than he had been before. "You have a message to deliver to someone," he said in an uncertain tone.

Vinculus nodded. "And will the next card shew me this person?" he asked.

"Yes."

"Ah!" exclaimed Vinculus and turned over the sixth card himself.

The sixth card was the *Cavalier de Baton*. The Knight of Wands. A man in a broad-brimmed hat sat upon a horse of a pale colour. The countryside through which he rode was indicated by a few rocks and tufts of grass at his horse's hooves. His clothes were well-made and expensive-looking, but for some inexplicable reason he was carrying a heavy club. Even to call it a club was to make it sounder grander than it was. It was scarcely more than a thick branch torn from a tree or hedge; there were still twigs and leaves protruding from it.

Vinculus picked up the card and studied it carefully.

The seventh card was *The Two of Swords*. Childermass said nothing but immediately turned over the eighth card – *Le Pendv*, The Hanged Man. The ninth card was *Le Monde*, The World. It shewed a naked female figure dancing; in the four corners of the card were an angel, an eagle, a winged bull and a winged lion – the symbols of the evangelists.

"You may expect a meeting," said Childermass, "leading to an ordeal of some sort, perhaps even death. The cards do not say whether you survive or not, but whatever happens, this," he touched the last card, "says that you will achieve your purpose."

"And do you know what I am now?" asked Vinculus.

"Not exactly, but I know more of you than I did."

"You see that I am not like the others," said Vinculus.

"There is nothing here that says you are anything more than a charlatan," said Childermass and he began to collect his cards.

"Wait," said Vinculus, "I will tell your fortune."

Vinculus took the cards and laid out nine. Then he turned them over one by one: *XVIII La Lune, XVI La Maison Dieu* reversed, *The Nine of Swords, Valet de Baton, The Ten of Batons* reversed, *II La Papesse, X La Rove de Fortvne, The Two of Coins, The King of Cups.* Vinculus looked at them. He picked up *La Maison Dieu* and examined it, but he said nothing at all.

Childermass laughed. "You are right, Vinculus. You are not like the others. That is my life – there on the table. But you cannot read it. You are a strange creature – the very reverse of all the magicians of the last centuries. They were full of learning but had no talent. You have talent and no knowledge. You cannot profit by what you see."

Vinculus scratched his long, sallow cheek with his unclean fingernails.

Childermass began again to gather up his cards, but once again Vinculus prevented him and indicated that they should lay out the cards again.

"What?" asked Childermass in surprize. "I have told you your fortune. You have failed to tell me mine. What more is there?"

"I am going to tell his fortune."

"Whose? Norrell's? But you will not understand it."

"Shuffle the cards," said Vinculus, stubbornly.

So Childermass shuffled the cards and Vinculus took nine and laid them out. Then he turned over the first card. *IIII. L'Emperevr.* It shewed a king seated upon a throne in the open air with all the customary kingly accoutrements of crown and sceptre. Childermass leaned forward and examined it.

"What is it?" asked Vinculus.

"I do not seem to have copied this card very well. I never noticed before. The inking is badly done. The lines are thick and smudged so that the Emperor's hair and robe appear almost black. And someone has left a dirty thumbprint over the eagle. The Emperor should be an older man than this. I have drawn a young man. Are you going to hazard an interpretation?"

"No," said Vinculus and indicated by a contemptuous thrust of his chin that Childermass should turn the next card.

IIII. L'Emperevr.

There was a short silence.

"That is not possible," said Childermass. "There are not two Emperors in this pack. I know there are not."

If anything the king was younger and fiercer than before. His hair and robes were black and the crown upon his head had become a thin band of pale metal. There was no trace of the thumbprint upon the card, but the great bird in the corner was now decidedly black and it had cast off its eagle-like aspects and settled itself into a shape altogether more English: it had become a raven.

Childermass turned over the third card. *IIII. L'Emperevr.* And the fourth. *IIII. L'Emperevr.* By the fifth the number and name of the card had disappeared, but the picture remained the same: a young, dark-haired king at whose feet strutted a great, black bird. Childermass turned over each and every card. He even examined the remainder of the pack, but in his anxiety to see he fumbled and the cards somehow fell everywhere. Black Kings crowded about Childermass, spinning in the cold, grey air. Upon each card was the same figure with the same pale, unforgiving gaze.

"There!" said Vinculus softly. "That is what you may tell the magician of Hanover-square! That is his past and his present and his future!"

Needless to say when Childermass returned to Hanover-square and told Mr Norrell what had occurred, Mr Norrell was very angry. That Vinculus should continue to defy Mr Norrell was bad

enough; that he should claim to have a book and Mr Norrell not be able read it was considerably worse; but that he should pretend to tell Mr Norrell's fortune and threaten him with pictures of Black Kings was absolutely unbearable.

"He tricked you!" declared Mr Norrell, angrily. "He hid your own cards and supplanted them with a deck of his own. I am amazed you were so taken in!"

"Quite," agreed Mr Lascelles, regarding Childermass coldly.

"Oh, to be sure, Vinculus is nothing but conjuring tricks," agreed Drawlight. "But still I should have liked to have seen it. I am as fond as any thing of Vinculus. I wish you had told me, Mr Childermass, that you were going to see him. I would have come with you."

Childermass ignored Lascelles and Drawlight and addressed Mr Norrell. "Even supposing that he is an able enough conjuror to perform such a trick – which I am very far from allowing – how was he to know I possessed such a thing as a pack of Marseilles cards? How was he to know when you did not?"

"Aye, and it was as well for you that I did not know! Telling fortunes with picture cards – it is everything I despise! Oh, it has been a very ill-managed business from start to finish!"

"And what of this book that the sorcerer claims to have?" asked Lascelles.

"Yes, indeed," said Mr Norrell. "That odd prophecy. I dare say it is nothing, yet there were one or two expressions which suggested great antiquity. I believe it would be best if I examined that book."

"Well, Mr Childermass?" asked Lascelles.

"I do not know where he keeps it."

"Then we suggest you find out."

So Childermass set spies to follow Vinculus and the first and most surprizing discovery they made was that Vinculus was married. Indeed he was a great deal more married than most people. His wives were five in number and they were scattered throughout the various parishes of London and the surrounding towns and villages. The eldest was forty-five and the youngest fifteen and each was entirely ignorant of the existence of the other four. Childermass contrived to meet with each of them in turn. To two of them he appeared in the character of the unlikely milliner; to another he presented himself as a customs officer; for the benefit of the fourth he became a drunken, gambling rogue; and he told the fifth that, though he appeared to the world to be a servant of the great Mr Norrell of Hanover-square, he was in secret a magician himself. Two tried to rob him; one said she would tell him any thing he wanted to know as long as he paid for her gin; one tried to make him go with her to a Methodist prayer meeting; and the fifth, much to everyone's surprize, fell in love with him. But in the end all his playacting was for nothing because none of them were even aware that Vinculus possessed such a thing as a book, let alone where he kept it.

Mr Norrell refused to believe this and in his private study on the second floor he cast spells and peered into a silver dish of water, examining the lodgings of Vinculus's five wives, but nowhere was there any thing resembling a book.

Meanwhile on the floor above, in a little room set aside for his own particular use, Childermass laid out his cards. The cards had all returned to their original form, except for *The Emperevr* who had not shaken off his Raven-Kingish look. Certain cards appeared over and over again, among them *The Ace of Cups* – an ecclesiastical-looking chalice of such elaborate design that it more resembled a walled city on a stalk – and *II. La Papesse*. According to Childermass's way of thinking both these cards stood for something hidden. The suit of Wands also appeared with quite unwonted frequency, but they were always in the higher numbers, the Seven, the Eight, the Nine and Ten. The more Childermass gazed at these rows of wands the more they appeared to him to be lines of writing. Yet at the same time they were a barrier, an obstacle to understanding, and so Childermass came to believe that Vinculus's book, whatever it was, was in an unknown language.

22

The Knight of Wands

February 1808

J ONATHAN STRANGE WAS a very different sort of person from his father. He was not avaricious; he was not proud; he was not ill-tempered and disagreeable. But though he had no striking vices, his virtues were perhaps almost as hard to define. At the pleasure parties of Weymouth and in the drawing-rooms of Bath he was regularly declared to be "the most charming man in the world" by the fashionable people he met there, but all that they meant by this was that he talked well, danced well, and hunted and gambled as much as a gentleman should.

In person he was rather tall and his figure was considered good. Some people thought him handsome, but this was not by any means the universal opinion. His face had two faults: a long nose and an ironic expression. It is also true that his hair had a reddish tinge and, as everybody knows, no one with red hair can ever truly be said to be handsome.

At the time of his father's death he was much taken up with a scheme to persuade a certain young lady to marry him. When he arrived home from Shrewsbury on the day of his father's death and the servants told him the news, his first thoughts were to wonder how his suit would be affected. Was she more likely to say yes now? Or less?

This marriage ought to have been the easiest matter in the world to arrange. Their friends all approved the match and the lady's brother – her only relation – was scarcely less ardent in wishing for it than Jonathan Strange himself. True, Laurence Strange had objected strongly to the lady's poverty, but he had put it out of his power to make any serious difficulty when he froze himself to death.

But, though Jonathan Strange had been the acknowledged suitor of this young lady for some months, the engagement – hourly expected by all their acquaintance – did not follow. It was not that she did not love him; he was quite certain that she did, but sometimes it seemed as if she had fallen in love with him for the sole purpose of quarrelling with him. He was quite at a loss to account for it. He believed that he had done everything she wanted in the way of reforming his behaviour. His card-playing and other sorts of gambling had dwindled away almost to nothing and he drank very little now – scarcely more than a bottle a day. He had told her that he had no objection to going to church more if that would please her – as often, say, as once a week – twice, if she would like it better – but she said that she would leave such matters to his own conscience, that they were not the sort of thing that could be dictated by another person. He knew that she disliked his frequent visits to Bath, Brighton, Weymouth and Cheltenham and he assured her that she had nothing to fear from the women in those places – doubtless they were very charming, but they were nothing to him. She said that was not what concerned her. *That* had not even occurred to her. It was just that she wished he could find a better way to occupy his time. She did not mean to moralize and no one loved a holiday better than her, but perpetual holidays! Was that really what he wanted? Did that make him happy?

He told her that he quite agreed with her and in the past year he had continually been forming plans to take up this or that profession or regular train of study. The plans themselves were very good. He thought he might seek out a destitute poetic genius and become his patron; he thought he would study law; look for fossils on the beach at Lyme Regis; buy an ironworks; study iron-founding; ask a fellow he knew about new methods of agriculture; study theology; and finish reading a fascinating work on engineering which he was almost certain he had put down on a little table at the furthest corner of his father's library two or three years ago. But to each of these projected courses some formidable obstacle was found to exist. Destitute poetic geniuses were harder to come by than he had imagined;[1] lawbooks were dull; he could not remember the name of the fellow who knew about agriculture; and the day that he intended to start for Lyme Regis it was raining heavily.

And so on and so on. He told the young lady that he heartily wished that he had gone into the Navy years ago. Nothing in the world would have suited him so well! But his father would never have agreed to it and he was twenty-eight now. It was far too late to take up a naval career.

The name of this curiously dissatisfied young woman was Arabella Woodhope and she was the daughter of the late curate

---

[1] It appears that Strange did not abandon the notion of a poetical career easily. In *The Life of Jonathan Strange*, pub. John Murray, London, 1820, John Segundus describes how, having been disappointed in his search for a poet, Strange decided to write the poems himself. "Things went very well upon the first day; from breakfast to dinner he sat in his dressing gown at the little writing table in his dressing room and scribbled very fast upon several dozen sheets of quarto. He was very delighted with everything he wrote and so was his valet, who was a literary man himself and who gave advice upon the knotty questions of metaphor and rhetoric, and who ran about gathering up the papers as they flew about the room and putting them in order and then running downstairs to read the most exhilarating parts to his friend, the under-gardener. It really was astonishing how quickly Strange wrote; indeed the valet declared that when he put his hand close to Strange's head he could feel a heat coming off it because of the immense creative energies within. On the second day Strange sat down to write another fifty or so pages and immediately got into difficulties because he could not think of a rhyme for " 'let love suffice'. 'Sunk in vice' was not promising; 'a pair of mice' was nonsense, and 'what's the price?' merely vulgar. He struggled for an hour, could think of nothing, went for a ride to loosen his brains and never looked at his poem again."

of St Swithin's in Clunbury.[2] At the time of Laurence Strange's death she was paying an extended visit to some friends in the Gloucestershire village where her brother was a curate. Her letter of condolence reached Strange on the morning of the funeral. It expressed everything that was proper – sympathy for his loss tempered by an understanding of the elder Mr Strange's many failings as a parent. But there was something more besides. She was concerned about him. She regretted her absence from Shropshire. She did not like him being alone and friendless at such a time.

His mind was made up upon the instant. He could not imagine that he was ever likely to find himself in a more advantageous situation. She would never be more full of anxious tenderness than she was at this moment and he would never be richer. (He could not quite believe that she was as indifferent to his wealth as she claimed.) He supposed he ought to allow a proper interval between his father's funeral and his proposal of marriage. Three days seemed about right, so on the morning of the fourth day he ordered his valet to pack his clothes and his groom to make his horse ready and he set off for Gloucestershire.

He took with him the new manservant. He had spoken at length to this man and had found him to be energetic, resourceful and able. The new manservant was delighted to be chosen (though his vain spirit told him that this was the most natural thing in the world). But now that the new manservant has passed the giant-toppling stage of his career – now that he has, as it were, stepped out of myth and into the workaday world, it will perhaps be found more convenient to give him his name like an ordinary mortal. His name was Jeremy Johns.

Upon the first day they endured nothing but the commonplace adventures which befall any traveller: they quarrelled with a man who set his dog to bark at them for no reason and there was an

<hr>

[2] A village five or six miles from Strange's home.

alarm about Strange's horse which began to shew signs of being sickly and which then, upon further investigation, was discovered to be in perfect health. On the morning of the second day they were riding through a pretty landscape of gently sloping hills, winter woods and prosperous-looking, tidy farms. Jeremy Johns was occupied in practising the correct degree of haughtiness for the servant of a gentleman newly come into an extensive property and Jonathan Strange was thinking about Miss Woodhope.

Now that the day had arrived when he was to see her again he began to have some doubts of his reception. He was glad to think she was with her brother – dear, good Henry who saw nothing but good in the match and who, Strange was quite certain, never failed to encourage his sister to think favourably of it. But he had some doubts about the friends with whom she was staying. They were a clergyman and his wife. He knew nothing of them, but he had the natural distrust that a young, rich, self-indulgent man feels for members of the clergy. Who could say what notions of extra-ordinary virtue and unnecessary self-sacrifice they might be daily imparting to her?

The low sun cast immense shadows. Ice and frost sparkled upon the branches of the trees and in hollows of the fields. Catching sight of a man ploughing a field, he was reminded of the families who lived upon his land and whose welfare had always been cause for concern to Miss Woodhope. An ideal conversation began to develop in his head. *And what are your intentions regarding your tenants?* she would ask – *Intentions?* he would say – *Yes*, she would say. *How will you ease their burdens? Your father took every penny he could from them. He made their lives miserable – I know he did*, Strange would say, *I have never defended my father's actions – Have you lowered the rents yet?* she would say. *Have you talked to the parish council? Have you thought about almshouses for the old people and a school for the children?*

"It is really quite unreasonable for her to be talking of rents, almshouses and a school," thought Strange gloomily. "After all, my father only died last Tuesday."

"Well, that is odd!" remarked Jeremy Johns.

"Hmmm?" said Strange. He discovered that they had halted at a white gate. At the side of the road was a neat little white-painted cottage. It was newly built and had six sides and Gothic windows.

"Where is the toll-keeper?" asked Jeremy Johns.

"Hmmm?" said Strange.

"It is a tollhouse, sir. See, there is the board with the list of money to pay. But there is no one about. Shall I leave them sixpence?"

"Yes, yes. As you wish."

So Jeremy Johns left the toll upon the doorstep of the cottage and opened the gate so that Strange and he could pass through. A hundred yards further on they entered a village. There was an ancient stone church with winter's golden light upon it, an avenue of ancient, twisted hornbeams that led somewhere or other, and twenty or so neat stone cottages with smoke rising up from their chimneys. A stream ran by the side of the road. It was bordered by dry, yellow grasses with pendants of ice hanging from them.

"Where are all the people?" said Jeremy.

"What?" said Strange. He looked around and saw two little girls looking out of a cottage window. "There," he said.

"No, sir. Those are children. I meant grown-ups. I do not see any."

This was true; there were none to be seen. There were some chickens strutting about, a cat sitting on some straw in an ancient cart and some horses in a field, but no people. Yet as soon as Strange and Jeremy Johns left the village, the reason for this queer state of affairs became apparent. A hundred yards or so from the last house in the village a crowd was gathered round a winter hedge. They carried an assortment of weapons – billhooks, sickles, sticks and guns. It was a very odd picture, both sinister and a little ridiculous. Any one would have thought that the village had decided to make war upon hawthorn bushes and elder-trees. The low winter sun shone full upon the villagers, gilding their clothes and weapons and their strange, intent expressions. Long, blue shadows streamed behind them. They were completely silent and whenever one of them moved, he did so with great care as though afraid of making a noise.

As they rode by, Strange and Jeremy stood up in the stirrups and craned their necks to catch a glimpse of whatever it was that the villagers were looking at.

"Well, that is odd!" exclaimed Jeremy when they were past. "There was nothing there!"

"No," said Strange, "there was a man. I am not surprized you could not see him. At first I took him for a hedge-root, but it was definitely a man – a grey, gaunt, weather-worn man – a man remarkably like a hedge-root, but a man nevertheless."

The road led them into a dark winter wood. Jeremy John's curiosity had been excited and he wondered who the man could be and what the villagers were intending to do to him. Strange answered once or twice at random, but soon fell to thinking of Miss Woodhope.

"It will be best to avoid discussing the changes brought on by my father's death," he thought. "It is altogether too dangerous. I will begin with light, indifferent subjects – the adventures of this journey for example. Now, what has happened that will amuse her?" He looked up. Dark, dripping trees surrounded him. "There must have been something." He remembered a windmill he had seen near Hereford with a child's red cloak caught up on one of the sails. As the sails turned the cloak was one moment being dragged through the slush and the mud and the next flying through the air like a vivid scarlet flag. "Like an allegory of something or other. Then I can tell her about the empty village and the children at the window peeping out between the curtains, one with a doll in her hand and the other with a wooden horse. Next come the silent crowd with their weapons and the man beneath the hedge."

Oh! she was certain to say, *Poor man! What happened to him? – I do not know*, Strange would say. *But surely you stayed to help him*, she would say. *No*, Strange would say. *Oh!*, she would say . . .

"Wait!" cried Strange, reining in his horse. "This will not do at all! We must go back. I do not feel easy in my mind about the man under the hedge."

"Oh!" cried Jeremy Johns, in relief. "I am very glad to hear you say so, sir. Neither am I."

"I don't suppose you thought to bring a set of pistols, did you?" said Strange.

"No, sir."

"D——!" said Strange and then flinched a little, because Miss Woodhope did not approve of oaths. "What about a knife? Something of that sort?"

"No, nothing, sir. But do not fret." Jeremy jumped off his horse and went delving about in the undergrowth. "I can make us some clubs out of these branches which will do almost as well as pistols."

There were some stout branches which someone had cut from a coppice of trees and left lying on the ground. Jeremy picked one up and offered it to Strange. It was scarcely a club, more a branch with twigs growing out of it.

"Well," said Strange, doubtfully, "I suppose that it is better than nothing."

Jeremy equipped himself with another branch just the same, and, thus armed, they rode back to the village and the silent crowd of people.

"You there!" cried Strange, singling out a man dressed in a shepherd's smock with a number of knitted shawls tied over it and a wide-brimmed hat upon his head. He made a few flourishing gestures with his club in what he hoped was a threatening manner. "What . . . ?"

Upon the instant several of the crowd turned together and put their fingers to their lips.

Another man came up to Strange. He was dressed rather more respectably than the first in a coat of brown cord. He touched his fingers to his hat and said very softly, "Beg pardon, sir, but could

250

not you take the horses further off? They stamp their feet and breathe very loud."

"But . . ." began Strange.

"Hush, sir!" whispered the man, "Your voice. It is too loud. You will wake him up!"

"Wake him up? Who?"

"The man under the hedge, sir. He is a magician. Did you never hear that if you wake a magician before his time, you risk bringing his dreams out of his head into the world?"

"And who knows what horrors he is dreaming of!" agreed another man, in a whisper.

"But how . . ." began Strange. Once again several people among the crowd turned and frowned indignantly at him and made signs that he was to speak more softly.

"But how do you know he is a magician?" he whispered.

"Oh! He has been in Monk Gretton for the past two days, sir. He tells everyone he is a magician. On the first day he tricked some of our children into stealing pies and beer from their mothers' larders, saying that they were for the Queen of the Fairies. Yesterday he was found wandering in the grounds of Farwater Hall, which is our great house here, sir. Mrs Morrow – whose property it is – hired him to tell her fortune, but all he said was that her son, Captain Morrow, has been shot dead by the French – and now, poor lady, she has lain down upon her bed and says she will lie there until she dies. And so, sir, we have had enough of this man. We mean to make him go. And if he will not, we shall send him to the workhouse."

"Well, that seems most reasonable," whispered Strange. "But what I do not understand is . . ."

Just at that moment the man under the hedge opened his eyes. The crowd gave a sort of soft, communal gasp and several people took a step or two backwards.

The man extracted himself from the hedge. This was no easy task because various parts of it – hawthorn twigs, elder branches, strands of ivy, mistletoe and witches' broom – had insinuated

251

themselves among his clothes, limbs and hair during the night or glued themselves to him with ice. He sat up. He did not seem in the least surprized to find he had an audience; indeed one would almost have supposed from his behaviour that he had been expecting it. He looked at them all and gave several disparaging sniffs and snorts.

He ran his fingers through his hair, removing dead leaves, bits of twig and half a dozen earwigs. "I reached out my hand," he muttered to no one in particular. "England's rivers turned and flowed the other way." He loosened his neckcloth and fished out some spiders which had taken up residence inside his shirt. In doing so, he revealed that his neck and throat were ornamented with an odd pattern of blue lines, dots, crosses and circles. Then he wrapped his neckcloth back about his neck and, having thus completed his toilet to his satisfaction, he rose to his feet.

"My name is Vinculus," he declared. Considering that he had just spent a night under a hedge his voice was remarkably loud and clear. "For ten days I have been walking westwards in search of a man who is destined to be a great magician. Ten days ago I was shewn a picture of this man and now by certain mystic signs I see that it is you!"

Everyone looked around to see who he meant.

The man in the shepherd's smock and the knitted shawls came up to Strange and plucked at his coat. "It is you, sir," he said.

"Me?" said Strange.

Vinculus approached Strange.

"Two magicians shall appear in England," he said.
"The first shall fear me; the second shall long to behold me;
The first shall be governed by thieves and murderers; the second shall conspire at his own destruction;
The first shall bury his heart in a dark wood beneath the snow, yet still feel its ache;
The second shall see his dearest possession in his enemy's hand . . ."

"I see," interrupted Strange. "And which am I, the first or the second? No, do not tell me. It does not matter. Both sound entirely dreadful. For someone who is anxious that I should become a magician, I must say you do not make the life sound very appealing. I hope to be married soon and a life spent in dark woods surrounded by thieves and murderers would be inconvenient to say the least. I suggest you chuse someone else."

"I did not chuse you, Magician! You were chosen long ago."

"Well, whoever it was, they will be disappointed."

Vinculus ignored this remark and took a firm grasp of the bridle of Strange's horse as a precaution against his riding off. He then proceeded to recite in its entirety the prophecy which he had already performed for the benefit of Mr Norrell in the library at Hanover-square.

Strange received it with a similar degree of enthusiasm and when it was done, he leant down from his horse and said very slowly and distinctly, "I do not know any magic!"

Vinculus paused. He looked as if he was prepared to concede that this might be a legitimate obstacle to Strange's becoming a great magician. Happily the solution occurred to him immediately; he stuck his hand into the breast of his coat and pulled out some sheets of paper with bits of straw sticking to them. "Now," he said, looking even more mysterious and impressive than before, "I have here some spells which . . . No, no! I cannot *give* them to you!" (Strange had reached out to take them.) "They are precious objects. I endured years of torment and suffered great ordeals in order to possess them."

"How much?" said Strange.

"Seven shillings and sixpence," said Vinculus.

"Very well."

"Surely you do not intend to give him any money, sir?" asked Jeremy Johns.

"If it will stop him talking to me, then, yes, certainly."

Meanwhile the crowd was regarding Strange and Jeremy Johns

in no very friendly manner. Their appearance had coincided more or less with Vinculus's waking and the villagers were starting to wonder if they might not be two apparitions from Vinculus's dreams. The villagers began to accuse one another of having woken Vinculus up. They were just starting to quarrel about it when an official-looking person in an important-looking hat arrived and informed Vinculus that he must go to the workhouse as a pauper. Vinculus retorted that he would do no such thing as he was not a pauper any longer – he had seven shillings and sixpence! And he dangled the money in the man's face in a very impertinent fashion. Just as a fight seemed certain to ensue from one cause or another, peace was suddenly restored to the village of Monk Gretton by the simple expedient of Vinculus turning and walking off one way and Strange and Jeremy Johns riding off another.

Towards five o'clock they arrived at an inn in the village of S— near Gloucester. So little hope had Strange that his meeting with Miss Woodhope would be productive of any thing but misery to them both that he thought he would put it off until the following morning. He ordered a good dinner and went and sat down by the fire in a comfortable chair with a newspaper. But he soon discovered that comfort and tranquillity were poor substitutes for Miss Woodhope's company and so he cancelled the dinner and went immediately to the house of Mr and Mrs Redmond in order to begin being unhappy as soon as possible. He found only the ladies at home, Mrs Redmond and Miss Woodhope.

Lovers are rarely the most rational beings in creation and so it will come as no surprize to my readers to discover that Strange's musings concerning Miss Woodhope had produced a most inexact portrait of her. Though his imaginary conversations might be said to describe her *opinions*, they were no guide at all to her *disposition* and *manners*. It was *not* her habit to harass recently bereaved persons with demands that they build schools and almshouses. Nor did she find fault with everything they said. She was not so unnatural.

She greeted him in a very different manner from the cross, scolding young lady of his imaginings. Far from demanding that he immediately undo every wrong his father had ever done, she behaved with particular kindness towards him and seemed altogether delighted to see him.

She was about twenty-two years of age. In repose her looks were only moderately pretty. There was very little about her face and figure that was in any way remarkable, but it was the sort of face which, when animated by conversation or laughter, is completely transformed. She had a lively disposition, a quick mind and a fondness for the comical. She was always very ready to smile and, since a smile is the most becoming ornament that any lady can wear, she had been known upon occasion to outshine women who were acknowledged beauties in three counties.

Her friend, Mrs Redmond, was a kindly, placid creature of forty-five. She was not rich, widely travelled or particularly clever. Under other circumstances she would have been puzzled to know what to say to a man of the world like Jonathan Strange, but happily his father had just died and that provided a subject.

"I dare say you are a great deal occupied just now, Mr Strange," she said. "I remember when my own father died, there was a world of things to do. He left so many bequests. There were some china jugs that used to stand upon the kitchen mantelpiece at home. My father wished a jug to be given to each of our old servants. But the descriptions of the jugs in his will were most confusing and no one could tell which jug was meant for which person. And then the servants quarrelled and they all desired to be given the yellow jug with pink roses. Oh! I thought I would never be done with those bequests. Did your father leave many bequests, Mr Strange?"

"No, madam. None. He hated everybody."

"Ah! That is fortunate, is it not? And what shall you do now?"

"Do?" echoed Strange.

"Miss Woodhope says your poor, dear father bought and sold things. Shall you do the same?"

"No, madam. If I have my way – and I believe I shall – my father's business will all be wound up as soon as possible."

"Oh! But then I dare say you will be a good deal taken up with farming? Miss Woodhope says your estate is a large one."

"It is, madam. But I have tried farming and I find it does not suit me."

"Ah!" said Mrs Redmond, wisely.

There was a silence. Mrs Redmond's clock ticked and the coals shifted in the grate. Mrs Redmond began to pull about some embroidery silks that lay in her lap and had got into a fearful knot. Then her black cat mistook this activity for a game and stalked along the sopha and tried to catch at the silks. Arabella laughed and caught up the cat and started to play with it. This was exactly the sort of tranquil domestic scene that Strange had set his heart upon (though he did not want Mrs Redmond and was undecided about the cat) and it was all the more desirable in his eyes since he had never met with anything other than coldness and disagreeableness in his childhood home. The question was: how to persuade Arabella that it was what she wanted too? A sort of inspiration came over him and he suddenly addressed Mrs Redmond again. "In short, madam, I do not think that I shall have the time. I am going to study magic."

"Magic!" exclaimed Arabella, looking at him in surprize.

She seemed about to question him further, but at this highly interesting moment Mr Redmond was heard in the hall. He was accompanied by his curate, Henry Woodhope – the same Henry Woodhope who was both brother to Arabella and childhood friend to Jonathan Strange. Naturally there were introductions and explanations to get through (Henry Woodhope had not known Strange was coming) and for the moment Strange's unexpected announcement was forgotten.

The gentlemen were just come from a parish meeting and as soon as everyone was seated again in the drawing-room, Mr Redmond and Henry imparted various items of parish news to

Mrs Redmond and Arabella. Then they inquired about Strange's journey, the state of the roads and how the farmers got on in Shropshire, Herefordshire and Gloucestershire (these being the counties Strange had travelled through). At seven o'clock the tea things were brought in. In the silence that followed, while they were all eating and drinking, Mrs Redmond remarked to her husband, "Mr Strange is going to be a magician, my love." She spoke as if it were the most natural thing in the world, because to her it was.

"A magician?" said Henry, quite astonished. "Why should you want to do that?"

Strange paused. He did not wish to tell his real reason – which was to impress Arabella with his determination to do something sober and scholarly – and so he fell back upon the only other explanation he could think of. "I met a man under a hedge at Monk Gretton who told me that I was a magician."

Mr Redmond laughed, approving the joke. "Excellent!" he said.

"Did you, indeed?" said Mrs Redmond.

"I do not understand," said Henry Woodhope.

"You do not believe me, I suppose?" said Strange to Arabella.

"Oh, on the contrary, Mr Strange!" said Arabella with an amused smile. "It is all of a piece with your usual way of doing things. It is quite as strong a foundation for a career as I should expect from you."

Henry said, "But if you are going to take up a profession – and I cannot see why you should want one at all, now that you have come into your property – surely you can chuse something better than magic! It has no practical application."

"Oh, but I think you are wrong!" said Mr Redmond. "There is that gentleman in London who confounds the French by sending them illusions! I forget his name. What is it that he calls his theory? Modern magic?"

"But how is that different from the old-fashioned sort?" wondered Mrs Redmond. "And which will you do, Mr Strange?"

"Yes, do tell us, Mr Strange," said Arabella, with an arch look. "Which will you do?"

"A little of both, Miss Woodhope. A little of both!" Turning to Mrs Redmond, he said, "I purchased three spells from the man under the hedge. Should you like to see one, madam?"

"Oh, yes, indeed!"

"Miss Woodhope?" asked Strange.

"What are they for?"

"I do not know. I have not read them yet." Jonathan Strange took the three spells Vinculus had given him out of his breast pocket and gave them to her to look at.

"They are very dirty," said Arabella.

"Oh! We magicians do not regard a little dirt. Besides I dare say they are very old. Ancient, mysterious spells such as these are often . . ."

"The date is written at the top of them. 2nd February 1808. That is two weeks ago."

"Indeed? I had not observed."

"*Two Spells to Make an Obstinate Man leave London*," read Arabella. "I wonder why the magician would want to make people leave London?"

"I do not know. There are certainly too many people in London, but it seems a great deal of work to make them leave one at a time."

"But these are horrible! Full of ghosts and horrors! Making them think that they are about to meet their one true love, when in truth the spell does nothing of the sort!"

"Let me see!" Strange snatched back the offending spells. He examined them rapidly and said, "I promise you I knew nothing of their content when I purchased them – nothing whatsoever. The truth is that the man I bought them from was a vagabond and quite destitute. With the money I gave him he was able to escape the workhouse."

"Well, I am glad of that. But his spells are still horrible and I hope you will not use them."

"But what of the last spell? *One Spell to Discover what My Enemy is doing Presently*. I think you can have no objection to that? Let me do the last spell."

"But will it work? You do not have any enemies, do you?"

"None that I know of. And so there can be no harm in attempting it, can there?"

The instructions called for a mirror and some dead flowers,[3] so Strange and Henry lifted a mirror off the wall and laid it upon the table. The flowers were more difficult; it was February and the only flowers Mrs Redmond possessed were some dried lavender, roses and thyme.

"Will these do?" she asked Strange.

He shrugged. "Who knows? Now . . ." He studied the instructions again. "The flowers must be placed around, like so. And then I draw a circle upon the mirror with my finger like this. And quarter the circle. Strike the mirror thrice and say these words . . ."

"Strange," said Henry Woodhope, "where did you get this nonsense?"

"From the man under the hedge. Henry, you do not listen."

"And he seemed honest, did he?"

"Honest? No, not particularly. He seemed, I would say, cold. Yes, 'cold' is a good word to describe him and 'hungry' another."

"And how much did you pay for these spells?"

"Henry!" said his sister. "Did you not just hear Mr Strange say that he bought them as an act of charity?"

Strange was absent-mindedly drawing circles upon the surface of the mirror and quartering them. Arabella, who was sitting next to him, gave a sudden start of surprize. Strange looked down.

"Good God!" he cried.

---

[3] Mr Norrell appears to have adapted it from a description of a Lancashire spell in Peter Watershippe's *Death's Library* (1448).

In the mirror was the image of a room, but it was not Mrs Redmond's drawing-room. It was a small room, furnished not extravagantly but very well. The ceiling – which was high – gave the idea of its being a small apartment within a large and perhaps rather grand house. There were bookcases full of books and other books lay about on tables. There was a good fire in the fireplace and candles on the desk. A man worked at a desk. He was perhaps fifty and was dressed very plainly in a grey coat. He was a quiet, unremarkable sort of man in an old-fashioned wig. Several books lay open on his desk and he read a little in some and wrote a little in others.

"Mrs Redmond! Henry!" cried Arabella. "Come quickly! See what Mr Strange has done!"

"But who in the world is he?" asked Strange, mystified. He lifted the mirror and looked under it, apparently with the idea that he might discover there a tiny gentleman in a grey coat, ready to be questioned. When the mirror was replaced upon the table the vision of the other room and the other man was still there. They could hear no sounds from the other room but the flames of the fire danced in the grate and the man, with his glinting spectacles on his nose, turned his head from one book to another.

"Why is he your enemy?" asked Arabella.

"I have not the least idea."

"Do you owe him money, perhaps?" asked Mr Redmond.

"I do not *think* so."

"He could be a banker. It looks a little like a counting house," suggested Arabella.

Strange began to laugh. "Well, Henry, you can cease frowning at me. If I am a magician, I am a very indifferent one. Other adepts summon up fairy-spirits and long-dead kings. I appear to have conjured the spirit of a banker."

End of Volume I